BLUE FATE 4
SQUEEZE

CASS TELL

BLUE FATE 4
SQUEEZE

A novel from the Blue Fate series

destinée

PROLOGUE

Llanca, Spain
November

Justin was flipping through *The Economist* on his veranda when the doorbell rang. He had been paying more attention to the boats in the harbor than housing prices in the UK, and he sighed as he left the sails to their swerving journeys out to sea.

He made his way through several rooms toward the front door and opened it. In front of him stood a tall, thin man in a wrinkled tan summer suit. The man removed his hat and wiped perspiration from his forehead with the sleeve of his jacket. His marine-style, close-cropped hairline was receding up his scalp.

Justin assumed he had walked up to the house from the village.

The man looked him in the eye and said, "Hi, are you Justin Collins?"

He had a strong, American accent, with a touch of Texas.

"Yes, I am. Can I help you?"

"Yeah. My name is Grady, Curley Grady. Mind if we talk?"

"Sure, come on in." Justin led the man through the house to the veranda and motioned for him to sit in a comfortable chair under the umbrella.

"It's pretty hot today, Mr. Grady. Can I offer you a drink?"

"A beer would do me real good if you got one."

Justin went into the house and returned a minute later with a beer for Mr. Grady and a Vichy Catalan—carbonated water—for himself. He was curious to know what this man wanted, or what he wanted to sell. No one had ever come looking for him here, especially not an American with a southern accent.

Curley Grady spoke, slowly drawing out his words. "Mr. Collins, it sure ain't been easy to find you. It seemed like you almost disappeared from humanity."

"Well, Mr. Grady, that was exactly my purpose. I wanted some time to get away from the work-world for a while to rethink things."

"Sure seems like it's in the middle of nowhere."

"Why do you need to talk to me?"

"Well, finding information and finding people is my business, but I must admit that in your case it took some doing. It took me around forty telephone calls and a month of investigations, but I did it. My employers cover all my expenses and they usually keep me on the trail until the end, that is, if they believe in their case strong enough. They have a kind of aversion toward anyone stealing money from them and they're real curious 'bout this one." He stopped to wipe the sweat from his head, decided to put the hat back on and then pulled off his cotton jacket to reveal a severely wrinkled floral shirt.

"I'm not sure I understand, Mr. Grady." Justin didn't like the word 'stealing'.

"Most of the time I work for one or two large companies, sometimes for individual people. Once I had an alimony case that took six months. This lady didn't care about money. Revenge was her thing. She was a wealthy ex-wife who wanted her slime-ball of a husband put away for not contributing the court-prescribed child support, although she had more than enough to pay for a dozen lives without needing the guy for one cent ever. After I found the guy she attacked him with some pretty powerful lawyers who made him look like a serial killer."

He paused to swig from the beer, then continued. "The courts didn't like the guy so they locked him up for a while. You know how unjust the justice system is in the United States of America? Personally, I didn't think the guy was all that bad and his ex-wife was something else, a real bitch. Women are like that, you know. I was married once, but never again. Don't need them around making my life miserable. By the way, the company I work for uses the same lawyers that this lady used. They're a bunch of cold-hearted S.O.B.'s."

Grady took two more long swigs of beer, almost emptying the bottle, and then spoke slowly while carefully watching Justin's eyes.

Justin had his chin in his hand, fascinated by the man's apparent lack of a point.

But Grady went on, "You see, Mr. Collins, I'm an investigator. Right now, I'm working for Baltimore Life, one of the largest insurance companies in America. They always call me in when they get the weird cases."

At that point he reached into his shirt pocket, pulled out a business card, and handed it to Justin. The card read, 'Curley Grady, Consultant and Private Investigator, Baltimore Life.' There were two addresses on the card, one in Maryland and the other in Sandpoint, Idaho. Justin knew the insurance company was based in Maryland, but he was not sure why an Idaho address should be on the card.

He stared at Grady out of curiosity, wondering where he was going with the conversation.

"You see Mr. Collins, my company is curious to know about some payments they made as a result of an air crash that took place in the Mediterranean about fifteen months ago—August fourteenth, to be exact."

★ ★ ★

An historic Spanish tall ship was parting water toward the port. Justin watched its magnificent white sails full of wind strong enough to propel a vessel. He marveled that he only felt a faint breeze on his cheeks from here. He could feel that his face had drained of color.

What did this man want? Was he some kind of crook, or con artist, or what?

Grady sat watching Justin with narrow eyes. He made it a business of reading people's reactions.

After some moments of silence, Grady went on, "You see Mr. Collins, some rather large insurance payments were made after that crash, and the company who has engaged me, Baltimore Life, was the one that had to make these payouts. There was a large payout to the Pete and Dora Vine Foundation: ten million dollars. And another large payment that went to a certain Mr. Justin Collins, granted not as much. I'm not so concerned about the Vines since they aren't around to enjoy their share. You are. But that's not the problem. You see, there are some anomalies that have occurred which need a little investigating."

Justin tried to think. Vine Industries had a group life insurance for its employees as part of the company's benefits and compensation package. All employees in the company and their spouses were covered by a one-million-dollar life insurance policy in the case of death through accident, whether traveling for business or not. Likewise, the children of employees were covered by a half-million-dollar policy.

After the crash Justin had received one-and-a-half million dollars.

Justin gripped the handle of his lounge chair, his voice low. "Listen Mr. Grady. I don't know who you are, or what your scam is. You flippantly mention the loss of my family and friends. It just happened that they were covered by a standard company insurance policy. For me, the insurance money was nothing. Their lives were everything. I resent the fact that you have walked into my home and suggested that I profited from the loss of my wife and daughter. I'm going to ask you to leave."

Justin started to get up from his chair, but Grady sat back and folded his arms. His objective was to find small threads, piece them together into a rope, and then use that rope to hang somebody. It just took a little patience.

"Look Mr. Collins. Perhaps I'm a little too blunt at times. Maybe you would understand better if I provided a little more background. I think you'd be interested."

He paused and waited for Justin's answer, glancing at a sea gull winging its way after a small fishing boat that was passing in front of the house. The gull was squawking at the men on board who were up to their ankles in fish.

The gull would insist until he got what he wanted, exactly what Grady had learned over the years.

Justin remained standing. "And what further information is that?"

"Well Mr. Collins, it's like this. As I said, a lot of money was paid out, which is what insurance companies are all about. I was told to look into a few things. One was to see how you were using the Baltimore Life payment. Can't say that I've noticed anything other than that you're down here enjoying life in Spain. The other was to look into the plane itself. And here's the strange part." He downed the last inch of his beer and smacked his lips.

"Perhaps it was just a technical detail. A jet engine for a Leerjet 60—a mid-sized business craft—was returned to the Central Repair Facility in Louisiana. Now I agreed to go down there personally to see it with my own eyes. I also like fishing and did some fishing on that trip, caught me a big one. Anyhow, you know every jet engine has a serial number, and all those complicated serial numbers are different from any others. It just so happens that this jet engine had the exact same serial number as the one that was on that plane that went down in the Mediterranean on the fourteenth of August.

Justin sat down without planning to. "What are you saying?"

"Well this here jet engine came from a regional repair facility in Bahrain, you know that's down there in them Gulf States." He shook himself as if such geography disgusted him. "Now I found this very interesting, just like the people I'm working for, and I did some checking around. Turns out that plane was still quite new—all the parts under warranty.

"And I might add that it underwent a systematic and detailed check-up two days before its last flight. So we know for a fact that the engine on that airplane, the plane that's supposedly at the bottom of the

Mediterranean near Malta, is the same one that was checked by the technician in Paris."

Grady paused and watched Justin for some sign of guilt or admission. Seeing nothing he continued, "Now from my point of view and that of Baltimore Life, this is real strange. But we do have ourselves several possibilities. Such as, either the guy was a lousy technician and didn't know how to properly write down numbers, or they made two engines with the same serial number, or someone switched the engine during the two days after the check-up, or some fisherman fished that engine out of the water and then sold it." He leaned forward now, looking Justin square in the eyes.

"The last plausible supposition is that the airplane is not really sitting at the bottom of the sea. Instead, it's up in the sky flying around somewhere. Which would mean some kind of conspiracy. To be honest, Baltimore Life doesn't like conspiracies, especially when it costs them money." He sat back again, taking off his hat and fanning himself. "Now some of those ideas I mentioned are only speculations, and we could concoct more if we sat around shootin' the shit. But I expect you've got enough to chew on for the moment."

Justin sat in a trance. He vaguely remembered the way he'd been after hearing of the crash, the long empty minutes and hours of staring at nothing, of receding into some past place in his soul. He shook his head, almost sure he had not missed anything in this sitting. He noticed the gull had moved on, had the fishermen given it one of their catch?

He watched Grady pull out a photocopied page titled 'Verification Technique.' Under the model number of the plane and its registration number, a checklist of verified items had been signed by a technician. Grady pointed to the hand-written serial number.

"See that little old number there? That number was plugged into the computer back in Louisiana, and it checked out to be the exact same number that was on the engine that came with the original airplane. And *that* is the same engine that showed up at a repair facility in Bahrain. Now, I spoke with that technician in Paris and he knew his stuff. We were talking about the same engine. Now either that engine swam by itself from Malta to Bahrain, or we got ourselves a damn conspiracy."

CHAPTER 1

Justin made his way back to the veranda in a daze. He sat down on the edge of the table. It tipped slightly. He moved to the lounge chair, changing its position to follow the shade.

He had slammed the door on Grady when he left. The insurance man had managed to squeeze in that he would be at the Hotel Del Sol tonight and was leaving on the noon train tomorrow. If Justin were smart, he'd be willing to exchange information for information.

What information did the man think he had? Bigger question: was it even possible that the plane still existed, that it was still flying around in the air somewhere? This thought took up too much of his head. On a more practical level, Justin tried to think what it was Grady really wanted.

Justin went inside and dialed a number.

After one ring a familiar voice answered, "Hello."

"Hello, Stefan. It's Justin."

"Justin, so good to hear from you. How are you doing?"

"Good, but not so good."

"What do you mean?"

"I just had a visit from someone, and I am very confused. I don't know if the whole thing is a scam."

"Tell me about it."

Justin recounted the conversation in detail, his head throbbing. "Stefan, do you have any advice?"

Von Portzer was silent for a moment and then said, "We thought we had found the reason for the crash, but now this new information appears. It could be true or false. Which means that this Mr. Grady may be legitimate, or he may be dangerous. I suggest that I get someone down there to assist you. This Mr. Grady will be in Llanca until tomorrow? I will get somebody there who is quite successful at getting information, someone who can help you."

"Doby?"

"No, not Doby. This is another employee. You have never met him, but he is familiar with the case. He is the one who went to Romania. I will ask him to get on the next flight to Barcelona. He should be in Llanca by late afternoon or early evening. Don't do anything until he is there. Discuss it with him and then give me a call."

"Who is he?"

"He will introduce himself. You will know he is working for me."

"Thank you, Stefan."

"I just want to help. By the way, give me the telephone number of the insurance company. I would like to call them and find out if this Curley Grady is legitimate."

★ ★ ★

The doorbell rang. *Oh not again*, Justin thought.

He went to answer it. Gloria stood there with her arms full of groceries. "Thank you darling. I couldn't reach my key."

She pecked him on the cheek and hummed a Spanish ballad in the direction of the kitchen where she set her bags down. Justin realized he had just stood there, not assisting her. He mentally shook himself and followed her into the kitchen, helping her pull bright vegetables and bottles from the bags. He tried to get Grady out of his mind.

He smiled and held up a bottle of Mumm champagne. "What's this? Are we drinking for some celebration?"

Gloria leaned her hands on the table, a strange smile dimpling her cheek. "Well, you are drinking it. But I will certainly celebrate with you."

He must have looked as confused as he felt, because she came over to him and slid her arms around his shoulders, locking her green eyes on his.

"Justin, I have some news for you."

News. He didn't really want more news, but by the way her skin was flushed with happiness, he supposed it would be of the 'good' variety. "Yes?"

"The doctor said you are going to be a father."

Justin froze. This was too much to absorb in one morning. "What do you mean?" he asked.

"We are going to have a child." She ran her fingers up and down the nape of his neck.

"But we just got married."

She moved her head to the side as if to lecture a third-grade child. "Yes, and we've certainly been doing enough of what it takes to become parents."

Justin turned red. Or was it green? Gloria took his hand and led him to the living room. They sat on the sofa and she leaned forward to better see his profile.

"I know we said we wanted children," he began, "but I guess we both thought it would take some time."

"Yes. That's what I told the doctor," she laughed. "I knew you would be surprised."

Justin's mind was caught in limbo, somewhere between the conversations with Curley Grady, Stefan Von Portzer, and that fact that he was going to be a father. He wanted to start a family with Gloria. But with all the information that had flown at him this morning…he braced himself and smiled at a slightly worried Gloria. She had placed her hand on his knee, and he took it now, smiling. "This is all so sudden. I don't know what to say. Let's do it."

She broke out in relieved laughter. "At this point I think we have no choice."

With half of his mind, Justin laughed with her, with the other he saw a jet engine sitting in a Louisiana repair facility. No, it was sitting at the bottom of the Bayou being circled by the huge catfish he imagined Grady had caught.

He thought his head would split.

"What's wrong?" Gloria looked worried again.

No sense in keeping it from her. They had promised no secrets. "I need to tell you about something that happened this morning. But before I do, I want to say again how much I love you, Gloria. I am thrilled that you are pregnant. We said we wanted children, so we might as well get to work and have them."

Now he saw the same engine in Bahrain, its numbers immutable, indelible.

He sighed. "But there is something I have to tell you."

★ ★ ★

It was Gloria's turn to stare off into space. "Do you think this is possible?" she asked.

"I don't know. My guess is that this Grady is a scam artist. He probably goes around to people who have had insurance payouts and then makes up some story to extort them. For a small fee he'll disappear."

"So, what do we do?" she asked.

"The first thing is to find out who this Curley Grady is. Stefan is going to call the insurance company, Baltimore Life, to see if he can find the department that hired him, just to see if he is legitimate."

"And if he is?"

"Then I will discuss this with Stefan to see what he advises. He said he is sending someone down here to help, which is accommodating of him. We'll come up with a plan of action."

"What if it is true about the engine from the airplane? What would that mean?"

"I don't know. Maybe it's tied in some way to the terrorist gang that used the airplane to ship the explosives. I just don't know."

"And what about us?" she asked. The trace of uncertainty in her voice pained him.

"Let's not let this get in the way," he said. "The top priority in my life is my relationship with you. We will face each challenge as it comes. You and me—us. *We* matter to me most."

Gloria again searched his eyes, this time for reassurance. She found tenderness, and the lines in her brow diminished.

"Hey," said Justin, reaching for her hand. "I think we need to celebrate our good news like you planned." He tried hard to be cheery under a burdensome weight. "Why don't we go to Restaurante Herrera. We haven't been there in a long time. We'll have that Mumm Champagne tonight for the new 'Mum-to-be.'"

Without releasing her hand, he stood and pulled her up toward him. He held her close and kissed her forehead. "What do you say, Mrs. Collins, shall we congratulate ourselves?"

"I'll grab my purse," she smiled, the warm glow she'd worn earlier returning.

* * *

Restaurante Herrera was not yet packed. Señora Herrera must have seen them from the back, because she came forward to greet them at the door, surprised and pleased.

"Where have you been, my lost lambs?" she welcomed, spreading her arms wide with enthusiasm. She wiped her hands on her apron and smoothed her black hair, kept in a bun as always. Her smile was broad and her teeth perfect. "I began to wonder if you had moved back to Barcelona!"

Gloria laughed and reached for her hostess' hands. She squeezed them tightly. "Even if I had, you wouldn't be able to keep me away. It's lovely to see you again."

Señora Herrera seated them at a newly cleared table for two near the window, brought out two menus, and disappeared into the back.

"Justin," began Gloria, "what do you want more, a boy or a girl?" Her eyes lit up. Before he had time to answer, she continued, "How should we decorate our baby's room?" She stopped short. "Our baby, Justin. I don't think it has sunk in yet. Our baby!"

The waiter arrived and took their orders. No sooner had he gone than Gloria began again, ebullient. "I am carrying the child of the man I love. Maybe he will look just like you. Oh, then we'll have to think of names, too. What names do you like, *mi amor*?"

Justin had been silent without Gloria really noticing. She was lost in her new world of motherhood, and he delighted to see her revel in it. She wondered how they would raise their child, imagined her parents' response to the news, and debated between cloth diapers and disposable ones.

As much as Justin wanted to share fully in her excitement, he could not free his mind of the conversation with Curley Grady. It sat firmly fixed in the tape recorder of his mind. He wished he could turn it off, or at least hit the pause button indefinitely.

Justin, his mind in two worlds, forced a smile. "Maybe our baby will look like her gorgeous green-eyed mother,"

"Maybe," she agreed, nodding her head then laughing.

He laughed too. Curley Grady would have to wait. At least through lunch.

The waiter returned with their plates. "*Cuidado*, they're hot."

CHAPTER 2

After lunch, they went for a walk as they often did. When they reached Eusebi's barbershop, Justin stopped.

"Gloria, would you mind if I went in for a minute? I'll be right back."

"No, sure, go ahead," she replied. "I'll wait outside."

Justin pulled the yellow cloth aside to see Eusebi trimming a customer's beard. "Eusebi, *Como estas*?"

"Justin, *Como le ha ido*?"

"Is Jordi around?" Justin inquired.

Eusebi nodded and Justin went through the door in the back of the barbershop into the large courtyard on the other side. Jordi was there with his two friends, Sanchez and Pascual. They were poring over a pile of architect's plans spread out on a table in front of them.

When Jordi saw Justin he said, "*Hombre.* How are you and how is Señora Collins?"

Jordi began to clear off the table. Underneath one set of drawings was a barber's razor, folded, with a striking pearl handle engraved with the words 'POR HONOR' in bold capital letters. Jordi quickly removed the razor from the table and pocketed it.

"Gloria is doing well. She is waiting for me outside. I was wondering if I could ask your advice?"

"Sure, *hombre*, but first invite her in."

Justin went back through the barbershop and asked Gloria to come in, but she hesitated. Women did not pass through the old yellow curtain, but Justin assured her she had been invited, and they entered the barbershop together.

Eusebi nodded as they walked through and Gloria glanced quickly around. Upon entering the courtyard she said to Justin with a wry smile, "Nice calendars."

Justin smiled and shrugged. "What can I say? Tastes differ." He placed his hand on her waist and squeezed, emphasizing his personal preferences.

Inside the courtyard Jordi greeted Gloria, and the three of them sat around the table that had been cleared of its plans. Sanchez brought three cups of coffee and went over to the opposite corner of the courtyard to relax in a chair. Pascual was sound asleep in the lounge chair next to him.

"So, tell me," Jordi said.

For the third time that day Justin told the story of Grady and also added that his friend from Geneva, Stefan Von Portzer, was sending someone down to help.

Jordi spoke. "It sounds like this Mr. Curley Grady is a crook. Is that the right word? Crook?" He turned to Gloria to see if he was using the word properly.

She nodded.

"As you know, we don't like crooks in Llanca. I think I will ask Sanchez and Pascual to keep an eye on him until he leaves tomorrow at noon."

"Thank you, Jordi."

"And one other thing. When the man sent by your friend from Geneva arrives, could you give me a call? Perhaps I could be there when you talk with him. I might have some ideas."

"With pleasure. The more help I can get to solve this thing, the better. If this Grady were a crook, I wouldn't know what to do with him. Maybe we could turn him over to the local police."

"We will wait and see," said Jordi, sagely.

They left Jordi's place, walked back through Eusebi's and out onto the street. Justin turned to Gloria. "'Por Honor'—that means 'for honor.' Right?"

"Exactly, but in Spanish it has a deeper meaning than in English," she replied. "You do not have the same sense in the Anglo-Saxon world. Only someone from the Iberian Peninsula would understand it. It is something very entrenched in the soul—a feeling, a pride, a justice. It is difficult to describe. Why do you ask?"

"I saw it somewhere. I just wondered. I'm trying to improve my Spanish."

★ ★ ★

Six hundred kilometers northeast of Llanca, in Lyon, France, Sam Oliver looked out of his hotel room and watched the cars zip by on the street below. The hotel was close to the Rhone River, and he had a good view of it and some of Lyon's magnificent old buildings.

The past three weeks had been swallowed in a whirlwind tour. He was starting to get homesick for his own house, his own bed, and prime rib with twice-baked potatoes. At least Margaret was here with him. She made traveling a pleasure instead of a pain.

Most of the time, however, he had spent his days visiting the factories, divisions, marketing centers, and sales offices of EuroVinco, which was now a fully-owned subsidiary of Unipac. Many of those operations had been a part of Vine Industries before EuroVinco took them over, so they felt familiar. It was up to him to make a first introductory visit to each of the EuroVinco operations, to meet people, welcome the employees to Unipac, and give speeches.

But today he would not give a speech. He planned to relax in the hotel room while Margaret shopped to her heart's content. Maybe he'd order up room service or take a nap. He had needed a good long nap since week one.

That first week, he and Paul had visited the headquarter offices in London and Frankfurt, making observations, assessing the financial climate, talking to people and getting a feel for EuroVinco.

Although he was exhausted from his travels, what he had seen of EuroVinco had impressed him. The people within the company were first class, and the products top quality—one step ahead of the competition. People seemed to care about their jobs. At the same time, there was a general sense of insecurity among many of them. Takeover by 'an American Company' made European employees nervous.

During the numerous question-and-answer sessions he handled, he discovered that many people perceived American corporations to be cost cutters, not hesitating to lay off people who had mortgages to pay and children to feed. The main question in most people's minds was 'What is going to happen to me?'—especially when they knew that EuroVinco as a whole was not doing well. They expected that their new owners would not put up with low performance, and Sam sensed an element of fear among employees, fear for their futures.

Yes, Unipac was a rich and well-run company, but Americans were also known to be ruthless. In talking to people, Sam had sensed this impression of his country. In each of the places he visited he made a point of talking with people, spending hours on the assembly lines, asking questions to employees at all levels, from people working in administrative positions to secretaries, analysts, project leaders, engineers, sales people, and managers. He tried to communicate that the values of Unipac were based on people. When people felt secure in their positions, believing in their objectives, they became motivated. When people knew they had an opportunity to improve things around them, they took initiative and enjoyed their jobs. That kind of environment was what Sam Oliver desired to maintain. It made it good for the people and good for the company.

He had shaken scores of hands during his time here. "It's truly an honor to meet you," one gentleman had said to Sam. Several employees had likewise expressed sincere pleasure in Unipac's interest.

"What a privilege for me to meet the 'great Sam Oliver, a legend in his industry,'" another had said.

"Oh, I don't know about being a legend," Sam had joked. "I'm not in the grave quite yet."

Sam now laughed to himself. A legend. He studied pedestrians below, strolling the streets, poking their heads in and out of shops or enjoying a treat from the *Pâtisserie*. If he were going to be a legend, let it be for treating people right. This, at least, he knew how to do.

He watched a laden barge crawl up the Rhone, its purpose reminding him of his. As he had been visiting with employees, a set of questions had begun to form in his mind. He saw that the people he met were doing their best to perform well, that the products were good, and that the company seemed to have efficient, cost-effective processes in place. Yet, oddly enough, EuroVinco overall was not doing well. The European market was growing, but not as rapidly as some of the other areas of the world, particularly the Far East, and even North America. Was this the possible root of the problem?

Perhaps it was the governments who spoke of open markets and free trade but at the end of the day locked other countries out, always finding ways to protect their home industries. Perhaps it was the competition, but even that did not seem to be right. EuroVinco was well positioned with the competition. Something was financially wrong, but he could not put his finger on it. It seemed that the operations he visited did not seem to have the resources to get on and do their jobs; they were missing capital, or was it something else? EuroVinco was selling products, and plenty of them, but where was the money going?

Paul had sensed the same thing, asking Sam to dig deeper. And now, after two additional weeks on his own, the feeling was even stronger. Something was wrong in EuroVinco. Since he was no longer actively involved in Unipac's operational management, others would have to fix the problem. But as the company's senior statesman, he wanted to find whatever that problem was.

Tomorrow Margaret would be heading back to California and he wished he was going with her. But without her it would give more time to focus on his questions. He also considered visiting the Unipac factory in Barcelona. Hank Morgan, the young manager he had put in place to manage the factory was doing a great job. There just wasn't enough time to do everything and right now EuroVinco was more important.

CHAPTER 3

At seven o'clock in the evening Justin's doorbell rang. A broad-shouldered man, slightly taller than himself, stood before him. His piercing blue eyes, hard and penetrating, met Justin's. Justin guessed the man to be his age, somewhere between thirty to thirty-five.

"Hello, Mr. Collins. My name is Laszlo Vartek. Our friend from

Geneva sent me. I'm here to offer my help." The man spoke with what sounded like an Eastern European accent, although which country was beyond Justin.

"Please come in," said Justin.

Justin led him into the living room, introduced him to Gloria, and offered him a comfortable chair. Gloria went to the telephone to call Jordi.

"Excuse me. If you don't mind," said Laszlo, and proceeded to cautiously move about the room. He went from window to window and glanced around the room and finally sat down. Gloria returned and exchanged a look with Justin. What had just felt like the safe confines of their living room now felt strangely vulnerable.

"Mr. Collins, I don't think you know me, but I'm familiar with your situation. I have been employed by our friend for a number of years and often travel for him—do business for him. Stefan Von Portzer thought it urgent that I come here."

As the man talked, Justin had the impression that he had seen him before, but he could not place him. Perhaps he had seen him in Stefan's office on one of his trips to Geneva in the past. Usually Justin was very good with faces, although sometimes he was not good with names. Something was familiar about this face.

"You said you knew my situation. What have you discussed with Stefan?"

"Stefan and I have discussed your case, and he updated me on your telephone call this morning. He diagnosed the situation as sensitive, that is, he determined that I might be of help in working with this Mr. Curley Grady."

"Over the telephone Stefan said that you were the one who went to Romania to look up that factory. Did you find anything?"

"No, not really. Little more than you already knew. It seems that they were shipping weapons and explosives to terrorist groups and a shipment was put on the plane that killed your wife and daughter, but Stefan has discussed this with you. Stefan asked that you call him once I arrive."

Justin nodded, went over to the telephone, and dialed the Geneva number.

The phone rang a few times and Von Portzer answered.

"Hello, Stefan, this is Justin."

"Justin, I was expecting your call. Did Mr. Vartek arrive?"

"Yes, he is here. But honestly, now I am wondering why."

"Justin, what you told me this morning troubled me considerably. I have had ample experience in dealing with dangerous situations and have learned to be proactive before they become too dangerous to be handled, if you know what I mean. My friend Laszlo Vartek has helped me through many of these…," he paused, "…circumstances and is an expert in the retrieval of information and the protection of assets. I have a strong impression that you will need him."

"So, what do we do from here?"

"I think you need to talk with Mr. Grady, but first you should try to find out more about him. See if you can get access to his papers. It's normal that he would be holding back information from you, and it's always useful to get as much information as possible, even before you talk with him."

"And that's what Laszlo is here for, I assume?"

"Exactly. He is extremely good at this kind of thing. By the way, I called Baltimore Life and got through to the Insurance Claims Department and another department. It looks like this Mr. Grady is indeed working for them, although they would give no additional information as to the nature of his assignment. Laszlo will help you find out his motives. You can trust him."

Justin thanked Stefan then hung up the telephone. The doorbell rang and Gloria went to let Jordi in, leading him into the living room. Justin was relieved to see him and said, "Mr. Vartek, may I introduce you to Mr. Pujols?"

Laszlo and Jordi shook hands. They seemed immediately comfortable with one another. This was an unexpected bonus.

"It's nice to meet you, Mr. Pujols," Laszlo said.

"And you, too," Jordi replied.

Justin said, "I thought it would be helpful to have Mr. Pujols here. He knows Llanca very well. I spoke with him about this Grady today, and he asked two of his associates to keep an eye on him." Everyone found a chair. "Now, Mr. Vartek, how would you suggest that we progress from here?"

"First, please call me Laszlo."

★ ★ ★

Justin watched the western sky bloom white with dawn. He had slept poorly, dreaming terrifically grandiose and complex dreams he could not remember, other than that they had left him more exhausted than when he had turned out the light before sleeping. He pulled the blanket over his head and tried again.

The alarm jarred him awake some minutes later. He turned to Gloria.

She had barely budged at the beeping and lay sound asleep next to him. He followed the strands of her long reddish hair until they disappeared under the blanket. He studied the soft curve of her nose and the outline of those full lips that gave him both splendid words and kisses.

Justin crawled carefully out of bed. He went into the living room and picked up the telephone. He made a long distance call and left a message in a voice mailbox. He knew that Stefan would still be asleep, his usual waking time closer to noon. Stefan and his active nightlife. Justin hoped he'd have half the man's energy at his age. Or even now. In any case, Justin needed to contact him. He needed Stefan's advice.

As he shaved and showered, Justin began to think out the plan of action regarding Curley Grady, the plan discussed with Laszlo and Jordi the night before. He left the house with Gloria still sleeping and walked toward the port to meet Laszlo and Jordi in the Pacu-Pacu bar.

They were already there when he arrived.

"*Hombre. ¿Como esta?*" Jordi asked.

"Didn't sleep well," Justin said.

"You need a coffee," Jordi stated and waved at the waiter. "*Un café con leche por favor,*" he called. In a moment the coffee was served. Justin drank it and felt like his head reattached itself.

"Are we ready?" Laszlo Vartek asked.

Justin still had a difficult time understanding how this man fit in, but he was thankful that he was there. His massive size alone provided reassurance.

"Yes," Jordi answered. "As we decided, my two friends Sanchez and Pascual are already outside the Hotel del Sol, and they are waiting for us to signal them. The people who run the hotel are also going to help. They are my amigos. I helped them in the past, so they are willing to help us now. By the way, Mr. Grady asked for a wake-up call at eight o'clock, so we can guess when he will be going to breakfast."

Llanca had numerous hotels, pensions and guesthouses kept quite full during July and August but virtually empty during the rest of the year. In fact, most of them closed from October to March. The Hotel del Sol was one of the nicer hotels in the town. Even so it was very basic—clean rooms with clean sheets and perhaps a bathroom in the room. That was about it.

After Justin finished his coffee, the three of them moved out of the Pacu-Pacu bar and walked about one hundred meters along the promenade next to the port until they came to the hotel. Justin surveyed the scene around the building. The entrance faced the sea across the promenade. Two doors opened to the side streets. Breakfast was served on a veranda enclosed by glass, which meant that breakfast could be enjoyed outside during most months of the year. This area was protected from wind, and the view of the port made it a pleasant place for dining.

In a few weeks the weather would turn cold. The October sun would give way to the *Tramontana* wind blowing from the north. The rain clouds would start to gather over the Pyrenees, and the people of Llanca would begin to move their lives indoors until March. But today it was certain that Curley Grady would have his breakfast on the veranda, and this would give them time to make their move.

Jordi and Laszlo made their way to a side street where they could have a view of Grady without being seen. A smattering of tourists occupied several tables but many remained empty. They sat down and ordered coffee. Justin stayed out of sight down the street waiting for a signal.

Not ten minutes after their arrival, Grady appeared on the veranda wearing a pair of checkered Bermuda shorts, dark socks, dark shoes and a green golf shirt. He sat down and looked out at the sea. A waiter came to take his order.

He had a newspaper, probably a day or two old. He turned to the sports section. As the waiter started to pour the coffee, Laszlo signaled Justin. Time to make his move.

Justin made his way along the outside of the hotel and into an alleyway that ran parallel to it. The side door was open, and it provided a discreet way for him to enter the hotel.

When he got inside, the manager handed him a key with the number fourteen on it and pointed him in the right direction. He didn't hear any sounds or voices and so made his way down the dark hall until he got to room fourteen. He inserted the key and slipped inside.

Grady's worn briefcase lay open on the desk, his thin brown wallet in plain view beside it. Papers lay scattered across the rest of the surface. Justin gathered up all the papers and the wallet and shoved them in the briefcase. He then took all of Grady's clothing, his razor, toothbrush and deodorant and put these in the suitcase near the bed. Taking both the briefcase and the suitcase, Justin walked to the door, looked both ways down the hall, and walked out of the hotel.

Laszlo and Jordi saw Justin emerge from the hotel and walked further down the side street. Justin took the briefcase and suitcase and walked home, while Laszlo and Jordi continued surveillance of Curley Grady.

When Justin got back to his house, he immediately phoned the Hotel del Sol. The telephone rang a number of times before anyone picked up.

"Bon dia, Hotel del Sol."

"Bonjour, est-ce que je peux parler avec Monsieur Grady s'il vous plait'.

"Si, si Monsieur, attendez un moment. Il mange son petit déjeuner."

Grady was still eating breakfast.

Justin waited a couple of minutes and he finally heard Grady's voice. "Hello?" Grady said, curious to know who would phone so early in the morning.

"Hello, Mr. Grady. This is Justin Collins." The voice was polite and friendly. "Mr. Grady, I have been thinking about our conversation yesterday and would like to apologize for the way that I reacted. You see, this news came as quite a shock to me and I guess I over-reacted. I want you to know that I'm interested in continuing our conversation from yesterday."

"I was certain you would come to this conclusion," said Grady, proud of his persuasive abilities.

Justin continued, "Yes, Mr. Grady. Unfortunately I'm not available during the day today, but would like to invite you to dinner at my home this evening where we could spend some time talking and perhaps shed more light on the subject."

"This evening? I want to get out of this place today. Can't we meet sooner?"

"No, I am afraid not Mr. Grady. Due to another important engagement that has been planned for some time, I can only meet with you this evening." The important engagement was with Grady's papers, which he would go through in detail. He then planned to make a few telephone calls and prepare himself for the meeting. In any negotiation, it was better to dictate the time frames according to one's own needs rather than have them dictated by the deadlines of the opponent.

"Well…" A few seconds of silence catalyzed Grady's decision. "OK, I'll meet you this evening."

"That's fine, Mr. Grady. See you at seven thirty. Good bye."

"Bye," Grady said.

A whole day to waste, Grady thought. He hung up the telephone and pushed it back toward the clerk.

"Excuse me, sir," began Grady.

"*Si, Señor.*"

"Is there anywhere around here I can rent a car?" He pretended to hold a steering wheel, turning it left and right in the universal sign language.

"Sorry, Señor. No car rental."

"How about a motorcycle?" he continued. He held his fists out in front of him, pretending to rev an imaginary engine by jerking his knuckles backward a few times.

"Ah, no Señor. No motorcycle."

"A bicycle, then?" Grady asked. "Bi-see-cull?" he repeated, emphasizing syllables loud and slow.

"Sorry, Señor. No rent 'bi-see-cull.' Try *ca-mi-nar*," the clerk suggested, walking his index and third finger across the counter. He too knew the sign language.

"Ah, forget it," Grady resigned. "I should have figured as much."

He turned and walked down the hall to his room. He threw the newspaper on his bed and reached for his briefcase.

It was not on the desk. In fact, none of his belongings were anywhere in sight.

Grady opened the old wooden cupboard—empty. The dresser too. Was this his room? The bed was undone like he had left it.

Angered, Grady stormed back to the front desk.

"*Bon dia,*" smiled the clerk.

"Did you take my things?" Grady asked, flustered.

"I no understand," replied the clerk.

"My stuff. All my clothing, money, wallet, papers, train ticket, plane ticket, tooth brush, just little stuff like that."

"Señor Grady, things are taken all the time from hotel. You no read the words on back of door in room?"

"Oh, damn you," Grady said, stamping his foot.

CHAPTER 4

With Gloria watching in anticipation, Justin opened Curley Grady's briefcase, laid it on the living room couch and looked at each piece of paper, passing everything on to Gloria in case he missed something.

The passport read Curley Lawrence Grady. Resident of Sandpoint, Idaho. It had an entry stamp for Barcelona on 11 October, three days prior. There was also a French stamp that read 8 October. Grady had also been in Paris for three days before going to Spain, and that seemed to be the extent of his European travels. Still, one could move across borders quite easily within Europe, and the customs agents did not make a habit of stamping passports.

The only other stamp was for Mexico City dated three years before. Not exactly a world traveler, this Mr. Curley Lawrence Grady. If this man was an investigator, then he likely handled most of his cases within the four walls of the United States and was definitely out of his element when it came to international travel.

Justin found the man's air tickets and looked at the itinerary. Spokane, Seattle, Baltimore, Paris, Barcelona, Bahrain, Paris, Baltimore, Seattle, Spokane. Obviously he was on his way to Bahrain, probably to check out the flight facility. There must be some degree of truth to Grady's story.

Grady's wallet contained a photograph of two ugly kids holding a poodle. The children looked a little like him. He turned the photo. The back read, 'Happy birthday uncle Curley.' He showed it to Gloria.

In the wallet were stuffed a multitude of paper scraps with telephone numbers, coupons for free meals at popular diners, and five one-hundred euro notes. None of the items in the briefcase or wallet warranted suspicion.

Justin lifted the suitcase and emptied all the contents onto the couch. Out fell a stack of papers that dealt with the case of the aircraft engine. Some of them were papers he had seen the day before. Other papers outlined additional information about the aircraft and its passengers. Names of the people onboard, their addresses and other personal details were included. Not much new information.

None of Grady's clothing was ironed, and he owned enough floral shirts to comprise a garden. No special insights here either, unfortunately.

Justin wanted to share this with Stefan Von Portzer, but his watch said it was only quarter past ten. He'd have to wait a couple of hours.

★ ★ ★

Curley Grady was pissed, to put it mildly. First of all, this fleabag of a hotel refused to help him recover his valuables. Second of all, his passport and air tickets were gone. Stolen.

He hated to travel outside America. He did not like foreigners and this place was full of them.

And today he'd reached one of the lowest points he could imagine. Hardly any of the people around here even spoke English. To make things worse, all he now owned was a pair of bright, checkered Bermuda shorts and a green golf shirt. He needed to get some cash and work his way back to civilization, at least to Barcelona or Madrid where he could find a U.S. embassy to get a new passport.

He started by trying to make a long distance call to the U.S. to ask for a money transfer. The hotel refused to make the call. They wanted cash before they would put it through. Too many clients had made calls and then left the hotel without paying, they said. It was now their policy to get the cash beforehand, 'dinero before telefono,' they said. No matter how many threats he made, he could not persuade them to make the call.

The hotel manager advised him to try the telephone office. Possibly they would accept a collect call. Grady walked down the street feeling a bit ridiculous to be dressed as he was on a cooling October day. The people around him sported long pants, long sleeved shirts and light jackets. They were looking at him like he'd stepped out of a freak show. He was certain he was manifesting the ignorant-tourist stereotype. It didn't matter. He didn't give a shit what these taco benders thought of him.

Grady made his way over two blocks to a small, prefabricated building. He entered to find a wizened old man behind the desk and six telephone booths with a line of waiting people curving out behind them.

During summer time the line went out of the building and down the street, but today there were only five local people waiting to make calls. They chatted back and forth between one another as they waited, occasionally looking at Grady and then laughing to each other.

Grady went up to the man behind the desk. "I wanna make a long distance collect call to Baltimore."

"*No comprendo Señor. Espanol.*"

Grady had had one year of Spanish in high school and had been last in his class. Since then he had maintained an aversion to any foreign language.

"Look, I want to call America, Estados Unidos."

"*Oh si, si, Estados Unidos. California.*"

"No, not California. Baltimore."

"*Si Señor. Cabine uno.*"

Grady made his way to the small telephone booth and lifted the receiver off the wall. Talking to that bozo out there would get him nowhere. He needed to get through to the U.S. of A. After dialing two numbers, he heard a steady beeping on the line. He tried again, but to no avail.

Thirty-five minutes of trying and still no success. He thought of calling the U.S. embassy, but it was Saturday. For sure, those bureaucrats would not be open. The American taxpayers pay billions for those ambassadors to parade around in chauffeur-driven cars, he thought, but when an honest, paying taxpayer needed help, they weren't there.

One hour later he was still trying to get through. He made numerous attempts to get information from the man behind the desk, to no avail. After trying several more times he slammed the receiver down and went again to the man behind the counter. It was already noon.

"Internationale telefono no work this day. Two days try again," the Catalan man said matter-of-factly.

★ ★ ★

Grady tried the bank next. He noticed one, La Caixa, just down the street. A sign in six different languages posted Saturday closing time as 13:00.

He walked in, and within seconds all eyes turned toward him. "I wanna talk to your bank manager," he demanded, approaching the first available teller.

"*No comprendo Señor. No comprendo Ingles,*" replied the teller.

"Manager, the boss, the chief," Grady stated, in the most international words he could find.

"*Ah, le chief.* No here. *Attendez Señor.*"

The teller pointed to a small couch over in the corner of the bank and he motioned for Grady to take a seat.

Grady eventually understood and went over to sit and wait. After twenty minutes of watching clients come and go, he got up and went back to the teller.

"When is your chief coming back?" he asked, jabbing at his watch.

"*Diez minutes Señor.*" He motioned back to the couch and said, "*Attendez.*" Wait.

Fifteen minutes later the manager was still not back. Grady got up again and went to the teller.

"Look here, turkey. I'm getting tired of waiting for your boss, er, chief. When is he coming?"

"*Diez minutes Señor. Patience. Attendez.*" He motioned again for Grady to go toward the couch.

At two minutes to one the teller pointed to his watch and called to Grady, "Bank is *cerrado, fermer,* close."

"Closed?" Grady shouted. "I need money and I need to see the bank manager. Now, where is the guy?"

"*Lunes Señor,* Monday. Come Monday. *Le chief* here."

"What d'ya mean Monday," Grady protested. "I need money now!" He was livid.

"Attention Señor. I telephone police."

Grady thought for a moment. He had no money, no identification, and spoke no Spanish. He quickly determined this was no time to get arrested for vagrancy or even worse, bank robbery. The Guardia Civil were nothing to mess with in Spain. Grady calmed himself, pulled up his dark socks, and walked out of the bank with his chin in the air.

CHAPTER 5

The only thing Grady could think to do was to hitchhike out of this no man's land. If he could get to Barcelona, he could find a five-star hotel that would speak English. They would know what kind of service to give to an American. They would know how to provide assistance and get him money and clothing.

It did not matter that he had unfinished business with this Justin Collins. He could deal with that later. The first thing to do was to get out of this place in any way possible.

His stomach growled. His watch showed close to one thirty in the afternoon. No wonder he was starting to feel hungry. How good a plump Texas steak would taste right now with pan-fried potatoes on the side. It wasn't like him to go without a meal. He was in a fix, all right.

The worse thing about losing his clothing, money, passport and credit cards was that he had lost all the papers related to this case. It had taken time to piece together information. Lost, all of it lost, during breakfast. Damn.

Grady walked to the edge of town and found the main road running south to Figueras. This Llanca place was jinxed. He stuck out his thumb. How ridiculous, he thought. A skinny forty-year-old man standing in his shorts with his thumb stuck out in the wind.

Within seconds, a small battered brown car came slowly down the road and stopped next to Grady. Magic, he thought. "I haven't hitchhiked for over twenty years. I stick out my thumb looking like an idiot in a foreign country, and the first car that comes along stops for me. It must be my good looks," he mumbled to himself.

Grady got into the tattered back seat. One of the springs poking through scratched his bare leg. A line of blood rose up red on his pale skin.

Grady addressed the two men in the front seat. "I sure appreciate you fellahs stopping to pick me up. I ran into a bit of bad luck back there and I need to get out of this pit of a town." The car started to move down the road, shuddering loudly and shaking as though it were missing one cylinder and the muffler was half blown.

"Listen, I can make this very worthwhile for you two. It can mean big money, ten, maybe twenty dollars. Just take me to a place where I can get a call through to the U.S.—to Estados Unidos."

Neither man turned around. About two kilometers out of town the car turned off on a small dusty road that wound back into the hills.

Grady protested, "Hey, where you guys going? This ain't toward no big town."

To Grady's surprise, the man in the front passenger seat turned around with a gun in his hand, pointed it at Grady and said, "I like your shoes."

The driver added, "I like your shirt."

* * *

At four o'clock in the afternoon Curley Lawrence Grady found himself walking down a dusty road toward Llanca in his boxer shorts.

A gift from his two ugly nephews in Texas, the boxers flaunted little green frogs and the words "croak, croak" written everywhere.

Walking into town he kept to the back streets, but he was spotted by children who promptly doubled over in giggles. No shirt, wiry body, white chest and legs, no shoes and only a pair of shorts. Even adults in Llanca would laugh... if they saw him.

Upon reaching the hotel, Grady noticed the same clerk sleeping soundly with his feet propped up on another chair and his mouth wide open, snoring away. No wonder things got stolen.

Grady started toward his room slightly hunched over as if to tiptoe or go unnoticed. Neither worked.

The clerk woke up with a smile and wiped the sleep from his face. "Ah Señor, did you get your call to Los Estados Unidos? And I see you get to the beach in your shorts. The water not too cold?"

At this point, Grady could take no more. His anger and threats had gotten him nowhere. That left humility.

"Today has not been a good day. Would it be possible for you to do me a favor? Could you call Mr. Collins and let him know that I would be happy to join him for dinner this evening? And I would sure appreciate it if you could find me some clothing. This is all I have."

"Oh, Señor. Mr. Collins call here today. When he hear they rob you, he say he help you in any way, if and when you come back. He say he pay for your clothing and your hotel room. A local taxi pick you up at seven fifteen. Take you to his home. He say he send clothing to your room. Shirt, pants, jacket, shoes, everything."

He handed Grady a key to room fourteen. Grady thanked him and made his way to the room. He lay on the bed in exhaustion.

★ ★ ★

"What information did you get?" Stefan asked.

"I managed to get a hold of all his papers with the help of a friend in the village here. From what I can tell, Grady assumes I was responsible for the plane crash, or rather, the faked crash. His theory is that the airplane was sold to a rich prince in Bahrain, and the airplane was taken there for maintenance work. One of the engines was changed and then shipped back to the factory in the U.S. for repairs. Since I received money for the insurance claim, he thinks I had something to do with it. That I murdered everyone for the money." Justin took a deep breath. "The whole thing just doesn't make sense. That plane crashed. There was an oil slick, and they found Sophie's doll floating in the water."

"Justin, be careful. Whatever happened, Curley Grady's presence in Llanca indicates how dedicated the insurance company is to this investigation. Most troublesome is that the plane appears to exist. *That* needs to be investigated. Perhaps it's a paper error, but you need to track it down. That is where you can use Laszlo Vartek. Question this Mr. Grady again, and then Laszlo Vartek can work out a course of action with you."

Justin hung up the telephone. He needed a distraction so he turned to Gloria. "Let me help you with dinner tonight," he offered. "We have guests."

"Justin, you can't even boil potatoes."

"Come on, Gloria. I can at least peel them."

★ ★ ★

It turned out Curley Grady was who he said he was—an investigator from Baltimore Life.

Jordi and Laszlo had spent the day tracking Grady's movements. Jordi's friend at the hotel had been helpful in this, as had the man who ran the telephone office, and Antonio at the bank. Sanchez and Pascual had been particularly useful in taking Grady to the edge of town and leaving him in his frog shorts.

The Pacu-Pacu Bar had years' worth of story material from this day alone. Prime-time entertainment did not get much better than when that skinny man had to walk four kilometers in his underwear.

In actuality, international telephone communications were excellent from Llanca, and everyone in town spoke at least three or four languages. It was a tourist town. Yet that day, oddly enough (and there would be anticipatory laughter at this) not one single person spoke a word of English.

At least they had kept Grady occupied for the day.

CHAPTER 6

A taxi picked up Grady at quarter past seven and drove him to Justin's house.

The doorbell rang at seven thirty and Justin went to the door. Curley Grady stood before him in a jacket, ironed shirt, pants, and shoes. Everything was straight from the store. Justin smiled and invited him in. He introduced Grady to Gloria. Grady's demeanor had changed, and a fresh sunburn reddened his forehead.

Gloria brought Grady a beer. As he thanked her, the doorbell rang again. Jordi and Laszlo stood at the door, and Justin invited them in. They moved into the living room.

"Mr. Grady, I would like to introduce you to Mr. Laszlo Vartek and Mr. Jordi Pujols."

Grady said "Hello" without shaking hands.

"Mr. Grady, I have asked Mr. Vartek and Mr. Pujols to join us for dinner. They have both taken an interest in the information you shared with me yesterday, and I believe they can add to our conversation."

"Well, I don't know what they can add, but if you say so," Grady shrugged a shoulder.

Armed with beers all around, the four men sat down and Gloria disappeared into the kitchen to finish preparing dinner.

Justin began, addressing Grady, "Yesterday you said that the engine of the airplane that crashed near Malta has now appeared in a repair facility in the U.S., thereby creating a suspicion that the aircraft did not crash. You outlined several theories. Now, let's follow the one about this being the original airplane engine. Assuming this to be correct, where does that leave us?"

Grady answered, "We need to substantiate the evidence and see what further information we can gather, especially if there was an ulterior motive in the event, precipitated by the fact that there was quite a lot of insurance money that was paid out."

Laszlo and Jordi blinked.

Justin, annoyed by the unnecessary insurance jargon, cut to the chase. "Short and sweet that means I am a suspect."

"For now, everyone is a suspect, but especially those who profited, at least in the eyes of Baltimore Life," Grady said.

"What is your plan from here?"

"To be honest Mr. Collins, I don't think I am getting very far with you. If you are a suspect, you will never admit it. The evidence's gotta come from other sources."

"And what sources are those?"

"We believe the airplane exists, either as an entire airplane or in parts. Parts are expensive. Perhaps the airplane was broken into parts and then sold. Someone would stand to make a good sum of money. I want to find out where that engine came from before Bahrain. There must be an audit trail."

Laszlo spoke. "Mr. Grady, perhaps there is another 'audit trail' as you put it."

"What's your idea?"

"To start from Paris and work forward to Bahrain," Laszlo said.

"Sure, that's another way to do it, but I would rather work backward. I tried Paris and I didn't get very far."

"Then we would like to make a deal with you," Laszlo proposed.

"I am always willing to deal. What is it?"

"You go to Bahrain and we go to Paris. Then we meet back together to see what information has been found."

"How can I trust you guys?" Grady asked.

"How can we trust you?" Laszlo responded.

Grady said, "No, seriously. If Collins here is a perpetrator, then why should he be willing to cooperate? He made a lot of money from Baltimore Life."

Justin added, "Mr. Grady, if I am not the perpetrator, don't you think I would be interested in discovering the truth? If what you say is true about the engine, then something happened to my wife and daughter. Having closure on that is more important to me than Baltimore Life."

Laszlo nodded. "We are willing to help him and to help you."

"I don't want him going to Paris," Grady said. "You two guys can go, but not him."

"Why not?" Laszlo asked.

"Tampering with evidence. You don't want a suspect anywhere near the scene of the crime."

Jordi looked at Justin and shrugged his shoulders. "Justin, why don't you stay here? Laszlo and I can go."

Justin felt like he was being swept along in someone else's life. "I'm going to go to Paris. It was my family that got killed. I need to know."

"And distort the evidence," Grady said. "Stay out of it for now. If you are innocent, then the facts will prove it."

Justin looked at Jordi and Jordi nodded.

"I don't like it," Justin said, "but I'll stay, just this time."

"Fine," said Grady. "So since you all have this figured out, what's next?"

Laszlo took over. "I propose that tomorrow morning we all take a taxi to Barcelona. You," he jerked his chin at Grady, "fly to Bahrain and do your investigations and we," he flipped his hand between Jordi and himself, "fly to Paris. Justin will stay here, as agreed. We meet back in Llanca on Saturday."

"I agree to that," Grady said, "only there are two problems. The first is that I need to find an American embassy to get a passport, and I need to call Baltimore Life to have them send me some money."

"Mr. Grady," Jordi said. "You won't have to worry about that. Before I came here I was talking with one of the local policemen in Llanca. He said they found your briefcase and suitcase, although they did not find the people who took them. Everything seemed to be accounted for including your passport, air ticket and credit cards. It's now locked up at the hotel desk."

A look of profound relief spread across Grady's face. Then he regained his composure and said, "The problem is that this town lets these crooks run around. I hope they find them, throw them in jail, and toss the key."

"Mr. Grady, you mentioned two problems. What is the second?" Justin asked.

"I just mentioned it," Grady said. "It's this town. I hate this town. I ain't never coming back here again in my life. If we meet up on Saturday, I want to meet up in Barcelona. At least they must have hotels down there where people speak proper English. Barcelona or no deal."

"We can meet you there," Justin said. "Why not at the airport when you fly in from Bahrain?"

"OK, deal," Grady said, thumping his fist on his thigh. "Now, about Paris, what information do you need from me?"

Laszlo asked, "What did you do in Paris?"

"I started with the aviation company that rented the corporate jet to Vine Industries."

"Did you find anything unusual?" asked Justin.

"No, not really. Vine Industries was a regular client, renting a corporate jet a couple of times a month."

"That's true," said Justin. "Sometimes we would have three or four managers traveling together, often flying to two cities in one day. The corporate jet gave us flexibility. It was more expensive than the regular airlines, but we gained time."

"That's what I found out," said Grady. "The August fourteenth flight was just like any other. The only anomaly I found was that the regular pilot was switched just before the flight. The regular pilot's name was Pierre Bouquet. I remembered the name—bouquet like flowers. Anyway, I tried to track Pierre Bouquet down, but he was flying around Scandinavia for a few days. I couldn't afford to wait for him and wanted to get down here to Spain to talk with Collins. And now I plan to go to Bahrain. I would have looked up Pierre Bouquet on my way back."

"I remember Pierre Bouquet. He was our regular pilot, but not always. Do you have his address?" Justin asked.

"Yeah, it's with my papers in my briefcase."

Justin knew he had missed something in going through Grady's papers.

Laszlo spoke. "Did you get any other information from the aviation company?"

"Nah. Nothing unusual."

"So, I think we should start there," Laszlo suggested.

"Dinner's ready," Gloria announced, entering the room.

★ ★ ★

The table was set with roast lamb, sliced baked potatoes, vegetables, and salad. In Grady's mind, a man's meal. It was his first meal of the day since breakfast, and he ate and drank without reserve. The large bottles of regional red wine loosened the four men up. Grady described his miserable day in Llanca, his forehead turning an even brighter red from the excess wine.

At one point Jordi asked, "Curley, where are you from in the U.S.?"

"Call me Grady. Most people call me by my last name. I grew up on a ranch in Texas and then went off to Texas A&M where I did a degree in Police Science. From there I went to Los Angeles and worked for ten years as a detective, but I didn't like it. I liked the detective work, was real good at it, and nailed more crooks than you could imagine, but there were too many politically correct Californians running around. If you want my point of view, there ain't much justice in America. It all depends on how much you can pay for a lawyer. I had to deal with Hollywood weirdos everyday—wetbacks, Asian gangs as loony as can be, and rappers and all that black stuff. As far as I am concerned, California shouldn't be part of the U.S.A. I don't much care for the people there."

Justin had almost choked on the tomato he was chewing. Gloria was biting her lip and gave him a cursory pat on the back to help him swallow.

Jordi was trying to decide exactly what he had just been told. "Some of your English is complicated. What does 'wetbacks' mean?"

Grady answered, "Well, you know, everyone who is not real American like those that speak foreign languages."

Jordi raised an eyebrow high and so did Laszlo.

Grady continued, "During my time as a detective, there was this woman femi-Nazi that took a high-up position in the police department and she went on a crusade. If she had had her way, all the policemen would be wearing skirts. I had a run-in with her and she won. Just as well. I was goin' through a divorce then, so I just moved to the north of Idaho where decent law abiding people live. Now, up there I don't have anything to do with those Aryan Nation folks and the militia men, but at least I can live without some drive-by gang member shooting a gun at me whenever I drive down the street.

"I bought a house about five miles down-river from Sandpoint, Idaho right on the waterfront. I can just throw my fishing line right over the rail on the deck and catch lunch. It's a beautiful spot and there's no one to bother me. As I said, I'm good at detective work and I've got several insurance companies that call me in for the complicated cases. They pay real good, much better than police work. I enjoy it, but I don't like having to go outside the U.S. of A. Foreigners." He stabbed his lamb hard with a fork.

The foreigners—three of the five-person dinner party—sat in charged silence. Justin had given up all pretense of etiquette and had propped his elbows on the table. He held the sides of his head with the squares of his palms and stared at the oblivious Grady as if the man had sprouted the lettuce he was now eating.

Justin wondered how they would work with this bigot. And he seriously doubted Grady's detective capabilities, considering the fact that Grady's hotel 'thief' was now his dinner host.

CHAPTER 7

Laszlo and Jordi didn't have much to go on other than the address of Pierre Bouquet. Pierre Bouquet lived in Evry, a city of high-rise apartment buildings just south of Paris. It was one of those new cities built in the last thirty or forty years, built to handle the population overflow of the nearby metropolis. Evry was close to the Orly airport where many of its inhabitants earned their living.

It was well after six and already twilight. The days were getting shorter. With Laszlo driving and Jordi acting as navigator, the two men scoured the streets in their rental car, searching through the dusk for the home of Pierre Bouquet. Jordi had phoned the man's home earlier in the day and had been told that Bouquet would be home around now.

Finally, they found the correct street and apartment building. Laszlo parked the car. They entered the building and went up to the eighth floor. A small dark haired woman with brown eyes answered the door.

Jordi asked her in French if it was possible to have a word with Mr. Bouquet. She took in their broad frames and unsmiling faces.

"*Attendez*," she said and disappeared down the hallway.

Laszlo and Jordi heard voices in the background, and a few minutes later a slender man of medium height appeared. "*Bonjour messieurs.* May I help you?" His eyes were wary but his manner courteous.

Again, Jordi spoke. "We apologize for the inconvenience and for contacting you without notice, but we are friends of Justin Collins and wonder if you might provide information that would be helpful for our friend."

Upon hearing Justin's name, Pierre Bouquet's face relaxed and he replied, "Ah, yes. Justin." He invited them in. Passing through the hallway, they entered into a living room so full of plants it felt like a small forest.

"Please sit down and tell me about Justin." Bouquet motioned toward the chintz couches.

They seated themselves and Laszlo looked around the room while Jordi spoke. "Mr. Bouquet, may we speak English for the sake of my colleague here?"

"Yes, go ahead."

"We are working for our friend Justin Collins who is seeking to piece together information concerning the crash of the airplane that his wife and child were on."

Bouquet looked at the floor. "Yes, that was a terrible event. What can one say?"

Jordi waited and then asked, "May we ask how you came to know Justin?"

"Occasionally, about once or twice a month, Vine Industries would lease a plane. Whenever Mr. Vine came to Europe, which was around four times a year, he would visit up to eight cities in a week. For an older man, he was full of energy and hated to waste his time in airports. He usually stayed for one week and then would return to the U.S. Justin often flew with Mr. Vine, and occasionally Mrs. Vine and Mrs. Collins came along with them."

Laszlo spoke. "We understand that you should have been the pilot on August fourteenth. But another pilot took your place. Why was that?"

Pierre Bouquet took a few moments to reflect, trying to remember events long- forgotten. He started to speak slowly. "This was a terrible tragedy. Yes, I should have been the pilot that day but fate saved me. You see, I had food poisoning the night before the flight and ended up in the hospital. The doctors told me it was the mushrooms I had eaten. You know you take your chances when you eat at those North African restaurants."

Laszlo and Jordi looked at each other.

"Which North African restaurant?" Jordi asked.

"I won a promotional offer granting me a free meal at Le Magreb, which was only valid the night of August thirteenth, and that is where I got sick. The funny thing is that although we both ate couscous, my wife did not suffer from anything. Perhaps it was just stomach flu, but the doctors said my symptoms were those of food poisoning."

Pierre went to a wooden table and rummaged through the drawer. "Yes, I still have it," he said. "Here's the business card from the restaurant. I keep all business cards. You can have it. I don't recommend that you eat there, though."

Jordi took the card and read, 'Compliments of Le Magreb.' It was signed, 'Shafi Khanoum, Manager.' Jordi recalled the name. He showed the card to Laszlo who looked at it and nodded. Both recognized the name of the man who had been shot and killed some months ago.

Jordi put the card in his pocket and said, "Thank you for the card. So, you were supposed to fly on August fourteenth, but you got sick?"

"Yes, it was the flight for Vine Industries. The plan was to take Mr.

Vine to Malta."

"Was that the final destination of the plane?"

"No, it was scheduled to go on to Rome, to pick up an Italian banker and then back to Paris. But as we know, the flight never made it to Malta."

"What about the pilot? Who flew the plane?"

"All our regular pilots were either flying or on holiday. We work with several companies, and it was not difficult to find a qualified replacement pilot. In this case, they found a North African pilot who was in Paris and needed to get back to a small charter company he worked for in Tunisia. It was convenient for him to take the plane as far as Rome where there would have been a change of pilot.

"What was the pilot's name?"

"Let me think…Habib something. He was often around the circuit and was well qualified. I think he was primarily based in Algeria, but he would fly for different companies based in Algeria, Morocco, Egypt, Tunisia and Libya. There are a number of pilots like him, free-lancers contracting themselves to many different companies, often flying planes they know nothing about. Yes, you'd be surprised to find out what really goes on in this business. This was not the case with this pilot, however. Habib had flown the Learjet many other times. I believe it was a mechanical problem that took the plane down. It's not something a pilot likes to think about. You know, despite the security checks and the maintenance, things happen. We do not live in a perfect world."

Jordi nodded. "We apologize, Monsieur Bouquet, for taking up your time, but before we go, do you think you could provide us with a description of Habib? What does he look like?"

"What do you mean, what does he look like? He looked North African, dark hair, moustache, and brown skin. But, wait a minute."

Bouquet left the room for a minute and returned with a folder of photos. He pulled out three and handed them to Jordi as he spoke. "There, that's him, the dark one in the corner. This photo was taken over a year ago at a staff party. The others were taken just a few days before the crash." Pierre paused and then continued, "After the accident, I wanted to contact Justin to see how he was doing, but you know how it is. Days turn into weeks, which turn into months, and when you remember to call, it's too late. Life moves on. I hope Justin has moved on. How is he doing?"

"He is recovering," Jordi said. "Would you mind if we kept the photo? We will have a duplicate made and then return it to you."

Bouquet replied, "*Pas de question*. You can have the photos. I have digital copies in case I need them, but I don't think I will. And here, you can also have this. It's Habib's business card. I found it stacked together with the photos."

Jordi and Laszlo thanked Bouquet again, shook hands with him, and headed back down the elevator.

"Any ideas where we should go?" asked Jordi.

"I'm getting hungry. I could go for a nice couscous." Laszlo smiled without humor.

CHAPTER 8

The streets of Paris near the Gare de Lyon were dark. Few Parisians ventured into these streets where rumors of illegal transactions, vagrant criminals, tramps and derelicts were at least half true.

In this neighborhood, there was no good or evil. Only loyalty. What mattered was whose side you were on.

"What does Le Magreb mean, exactly?" Laszlo asked as they neared their destination.

"It's the common name of the desert area of North Africa," explained the Catalan man.

A rocky area north of the Sahara that stretched from Morocco to Egypt, Le Magreb was known as the land of the Bedouins and Tuaregs and other nomadic tribes. Many of the region's people had moved to France, bringing their culture with them—a culture forged by winds, sand storms and a fierce sense of freedom. Their integration within the peaceful, sedentary French culture had not always been very smooth, and they often preferred to keep to themselves, living in neighborhoods around Paris called '*cités*'.

These were places where the police seldom went, places where misery mingled with communities struggling to keep their honor and identity.

Le Magreb was a restaurant typical of such environments. When you stepped inside, you stepped out of France. Outside, the paint on the walls was cracked and peeling but the interior décor resembled that of a Moroccan household, with arches and inlaid stones.

The tables were low on the ground with large bright cushions around them. The waiters wore the traditional North African attire, with fez hats on their heads and pointed slippers on their feet.

Laszlo and Jordi sat in the corner and watched while the place filled up. They ordered succulent roast lamb with eggplant and sat back to devise a plan. A plan with a proposition. They finished with Loukoum, a sweet pastry filled with nuts, dripping with honey. Turkish coffee was tempting, but they opted to finish off the meal with a mint tea.

As they speculated on potential obstacles, the volume of the music increased and a plump belly dancer veiled in silk and chiffon began weaving through the dining tables. Coin-shaped gold pieces dangled from the fringe on her jewel-belted hips, her undulating abdomen captivating the male eyes of her audience. She curved her arms and fleshy hands in serpentine patterns through the air. Men held out euro notes which she gracefully slipped into her glittering brassiere. Once she made her rounds past all the men, she danced toward a door and disappeared from the room.

Jordi requested the bill, and as the waiter returned with it, he expressed his gratitude. "This was such an excellent meal," he commended, "and we have very much appreciated your service. Would you be so kind as to let me know the name of the manager here?"

The waiter was pleased for the compliment and Jordi's graciousness. "Yes, his name is Mr. Khanoum," he replied.

Jordi and Laszlo briefly caught each others' eyes, acknowledging the name. Jordi assumed it might be a relative of Shafi Khanoum. North African families tended to be quite large and businesses were often a family matter.

"I would like to write him a note of thanks. What is his first name, if I may ask? So that I know how to address my letter?"

The waiter looked puzzled. He said, "It is Shafi."

"I wonder if it would be possible to have a few words with Mr. Khanoum."

"He is in his office. I am not sure he wants to be disturbed."

"That is fine if we meet with him in his office. We have some things we would like to discuss with him in private—regarding lucrative business affairs. I think Mr. Khanoum would be interested, and he would be very happy with you, as you will be the one to bring him many riches."

The waiter sensed that he had little choice so he led them to a door next to the cloakroom. He knocked and waited. He spoke some words in Arabic and motioned them to enter the room.

It was small and crowded with various statues and crystal objects in a display of Arabic luxury. Antique hand woven carpets clashed with splashy modern paintings. At the end of the room behind a dark heavy desk sat a round man in his forties wearing a gold chain around his neck.

"We apologize for bothering you, Mr. Khanoum, but we have a proposition we are sure will interest you. Could we speak to you in private?" asked Jordi. Khanoum barked at his waiter in Arabic to exit the room and making a surreptitious sign to him with his hand. He carefully examined the two visitors and waited for one of them to speak.

Laszlo spoke. "Mr. Khanoum, we are seeking information and have been told that you might be able to help. A little over a year ago an airplane crashed in the Mediterranean near Malta, on August fourteenth. The pilot scheduled to fly that plane ate in this restaurant the night before that flight and got sick. We discovered you were involved in this affair."

A look of anger spread across Khanoum's wide face. "How dare you." He lunged at Laszlo with his fist. "Get out of my...."

Laszlo grabbed Khanoum's fist and spun the man's arm behind him, locking it there before Khanoum had finished his sentence. Laszlo's breathing remained slow and consistent. On the contrary, Khanoum was wheezing. Laszlo forced him into his seat and maintained his position behind him, the arm still firmly in his grip.

"This is our business proposition. You give us the information we are looking for and no harm will come to you. Is that acceptable?" Jordi did not wait for a response. "Now, we are trying to understand what happened about a year ago. A customer, Mr. Bouquet, ate at your restaurant and became ill. The doctors said it was food poisoning, but the strange thing is that it happened only to him, and not his wife, who ordered the same dish. What can you tell us about this?"

Khanoum's face stiffened. He knew if he tried to break loose from Laszlo's grip, the blond man would break his arm. Great drops of sweat were rolling down his face. Laszlo tightened his grip enough to encourage Khanoum to speak.

"Food poisoning. That is not true. No one has ever become sick eating at my restaurant. It has always cleared every inspection from the French Ministry of Health."

"Not true," Jordi interrupted him. "We know Mr. Bouquet got sick from your meal. I find it strange that he received a free meal for that night only, and strange that he got sick right before the flight. Very convenient. What do you say to that?"

Khanoum was silent, eyes pleading for a way out of the situation. Laszlo whispered in his ear while putting more force on Khanoum's arm, "Be cooperative. We will not involve you in any other way. Otherwise." He put more force on the arm.

Khanoum winced in pain. "What can I do?"

Jordi sensed a note of desperation in his voice.

"Either way," Khanoum continued, "someone is going to kill me. If not you, then them."

"Who is 'them'?" asked Jordi.

"They told me to put the poison in the food. You see, if I did not do it, they would stop paying my mortgage for me, and then I would have to close the restaurant," Khanoum persisted.

Laszlo twisted Khanoum's arm a little tighter.

Jordi asked again, "Who told you to put poison in the food?"

At that, Khanoum explained how he had come to France as an illegal immigrant, how the stricter laws on immigration had made his life a living hell, instilling fear that kept him always on the lookout for a police check. They could stop anyone in the street and ask for papers.

"If you had no papers on you," his eyes widened, "they would bring you to the police station and expel you out of the country. No exceptions."

Khanoum had obtained papers from an organization that facilitated the integration of illegal immigrants into French society. They had provided false papers for him, authentic as gold. With these papers he had been able to bring the rest of his family to France. When he needed money to start his restaurant, they had granted him a loan. Of course, these favors were not free of charge, and he was indebted to remain at their service. Many immigrants had become slaves to such *Mafiosi* organizations, knowing full well that if they refused to cooperate, the organization would denounce them to the police and that would be the end of everything they had worked for. Khanoum said he had not wanted to poison Mr. Bouquet but was given no other choice.

Laszlo doubted that Khanoum was not so much of a victim as a low-level thug attempting to work his way up through the system.

"Thankfully, after that," Khanoum explained, "they didn't ask anything of me again. But I live in fear, waiting for the next time they will come by and ask the unpleasant." At this point, Khanoum broke down and sobbed, his whole body trembling uncontrollably.

Laszlo, not convinced of Khanoum's sincerity, gave Khanoum a minute to compose himself and demanded in a low steady voice, pausing between each word to give them weight, "Who. Are. They?"

"I am not really sure. Albanian Mafia. All I know is that there is a man in Europe who is at the top of all of this. I've never seen him and I don't even know his name. His hired assassins usually give me instructions by telephone, and I know better than to question those instructions. I just do whatever they tell me. Once a friend of mine tried to find out their identity and he is now with Allah. This is all I know. I just obey."

Laszlo was about to ask Khanoum one last question when the door flew open and a man dressed in a dark suit rushed in firing a gun. Laszlo, still behind Khanoum, could feel him jerk backward as the bullets hit. Jordi sprung forward, metal flashing open in his fingers as he grabbed the gunman's arm with his left hand and with his right hand sliced the man's neck. As he pulled it out, the edge of the barber's razor shone with blood. Laszlo felt Khanoum's body fall in front of him.

Jordi quickly reached down, wiped the blade clean on the gunman's shirt, picked up the gun from the floor, threw it to Laszlo and said, "Let's go."

They hurried out the office and through the restaurant, Laszlo mere steps behind Jordi. Out of the corner of his eye, Laszlo caught sight of a gun pointed in Jordi's direction. He raised his own and fired, hitting the man in the shoulder. Jordi pushed open the door and they raced into the street, turning down several dark blocks, not stopping for breath until they reached the car.

They drove out of Paris in the direction of Lyon, neither of them uttering a word for twenty kilometers. Out of the rearview mirror, Laszlo watched for cars. Jordi continually glanced behind them.

Jordi broke the silence. "It looks like we are in the clear, and I don't think they saw the car—dark streets and fast driving. And I doubt these men are the type to go to the police. Seems we got what we came for. And just in time."

"You were very quick with that barber's razor. May I ask where you learned that?"

"The razor has been one of my tools for some time. There is a barber in Llanca who is like a father to me. He taught me a few things." He took a deep breath. "Death sickens me, and I will not sleep well tonight. Still, it was him or us."

"A few people seem to like death," Laszlo said. He changed lanes and slowed his speed. "There is one thing Khanoum said that is bothering me. He mentioned the organization that gave him orders. If they do exist and he was telling the truth, I am assuming it's the same organization that went after Justin in Llanca. I think we need to get back to Justin before anyone else does. The waiters saw us and could identify us. It's a long shot that we are associated with Justin, but you never know.

"Do you think the police will get involved?" asked Jordi.

"It's doubtful," said Laszlo. "The kinds of gangs that operate around people like Khanoum have a way of covering things up. They don't like the police sticking their noses in things and the police know it."

"But don't you think someone may have informed the police? After all, we were in a public restaurant."

"Possibly, but no one knows who we are. If we're lucky, the police will find no suspects. In any case, we need to get to Justin as soon as possible."

"There is one other thing," Jordi said.

"What's that?"

"Louis Abdouelle. He is a liar. He knew Khanoum was still alive."

"I know. Abdouelle knows more than we think. Hopefully, we will have a chance to meet him again on a future visit to Paris."

"Perhaps we can turn him into an honest man."

CHAPTER 9

Ziginiglou was nervous about making the call. He spent the morning visiting the five people in the accounting group, checking in with the two computer hackers, and 'managing' his team when he knew he should be calling *Le Patron*. Speaking with *Le Patron* was the one thing he really didn't like to do.

Louis Abdouelle had phoned that morning and had given him information about a shooting at Le Magreb Restaurant. Ziginiglou knew he needed to inform *Le Patron*, but the man was busy and did not like to be called all the time. On the other hand, he had instructed Ziginiglou to contact him regarding all important matters. What to do?

Ziginiglou jumped at a knock on his door. He spun his chair around to face one of his two computer engineers standing in his doorway.

"We are making some progress on finding the outside hacker," he informed him, then turned around and left. Recently they had found out that someone had accessed their computer system. Ziginiglou had thought that an adequate firewall was in place. He was wrong.

What the person was doing in their system and how much information they had found, he did not know.

His computer engineers had built a unique 'reverse worm,' meaning that if data were stolen, that data contained a worm that would work its way back to Nice while keeping a record of the path it had taken. Therefore they would know who had their data. And their data was on the sensitive side, to say the least.

He did not like the idea of discussing this with *Le Patron*.

Finally, just before noon, he steeled himself to call the designated number. If *Le Patron* was not at that number then the call would transfer through to his cell phone. Always traveling to different places, *Le Patron* was not an easy person to keep up with. At least his cell phone would ring. Unless, of course, it was off.

After two rings he heard *Le Patron*'s voice. "Hello Ziginiglou."

Ziginiglou hesitated a few seconds then said, "I have important news."

"Go ahead."

"This morning I received a call from an associate, Louis Abdouelle, who runs a… real estate agency in Paris."

"Yes, I know who the idiot is. Go ahead."

"Abdouelle informed me of an event that took place at a restaurant last night in Paris. Le Magreb. It is—was—run by a Shafi Khanoum. Abdouelle told me that Khanoum has done special projects for the organization in the past."

"Yes, go on."

"It turns out there were two visitors at the restaurant who ate dinner and then asked one of the waiters to see Khanoum. When they were in Khanoum's office the waiter was listening at the door. The two men were asking Khanoum questions about the crash of an airplane on August fourteenth last year. At that point the waiter signaled to the security man who is always at the restaurant. The restaurant serves as a front for other activities, so there is always a hired gun around."

"Yes, yes, continue." *Le Patron* grew impatient.

"Well, the security man went to Khanoum's office, there was gunfire, and Khanoum was killed. The two men killed the security guard and then left the restaurant. On the way out they shot and wounded one of the waiters."

There was silence for a moment and then *Le Patron* said, "Get Yass and Turk up there right away to question people working in the restaurant. I want to know who those two men were."

"Yes sir. And there is one other thing."

"What is it?"

"Do you remember I mentioned someone trying to access our databases?"

"Yes."

"Our computer engineers think they are getting close to finding him."

"When you do, find out who he is and let me know. And then we will take care of him."

★ ★ ★

"Hello, my name is Sam Oliver and I have a reservation for two nights," Sam said to the hotel receptionist. While she checked her computer, he flipped through brochures on the offerings of Grenoble and its surroundings.

Shortly, the young woman handed him a set of keys and signaled to a porter who was standing nearby. "Mr. Oliver, you are in room 630. The bellboy will take your bags and show you the way." She handed him the keys.

"Do you want me to sign anything?" he asked.

"No sir," she said. "Everything has been taken care of. Oh, there is an envelope here for you."

Sam took the envelope and followed the porter to the elevator. They went up to the sixth floor and through a thickly carpeted hallway. Gold lamps lined the walls and gave the red carpet a ruby glow. The porter opened the door. Sam stepped into one of the most magnificent rooms he had ever seen.

The porter followed and set down his bags. "When the president of France comes to Grenoble," he said, "he stays at this hotel, in this room. Usually his personal staff and bodyguards take all remaining rooms on this floor."

Sam thanked and tipped the porter who pulled the door softly shut behind him.

The sizeable Presidential Suite consisted of a sitting room with two large couches, an oval wooden table with a large bouquet of fresh flowers, a thin, wide-screen television in one corner and a grand piano in another. His bedroom, carpeted in soft turquoise, was adjacent to a bath featuring a triangular whirlpool tub, a separate shower, and a double sink, all fashioned out of smooth glossy marble and trimmed with gold.

He whistled low and reached down to pat the queen-sized bed. He realized he was still holding the envelope the receptionist had given him. He opened it.

Dear Mr. Oliver,

On behalf of the staff of EuroVinco Grenoble, let me express a big welcome. We look forward to have you visit the factory tomorrow and hope you will find the visit to be rewarding. It is our request, but not an obligation, that you might address the employees tomorrow morning when you visit the factory. This address would be scheduled at eight o'clock in the morning. It is a wonderful opportunity for them to hear from you. I would propose to pick you up at the hotel at seven thirty.

If I may also take this opportunity, may I invite you to dinner this evening? I will give you a call regarding your availability, and also to confirm tomorrow's speech and logistics.

Yours sincerely,

Jean-Claude Dubois
General Manager, EuroVinco Grenoble

★ ★ ★

"We found some information that may be of interest," Laszlo reported. They sat in a quiet corner of the hotel bar in Barcelona where Jordi and Laszlo were staying. Justin and Gloria were staying with her parents.

Laszlo described to the couple the meetings with Pierre Bouquet and Shafi Khanoum, mentioning nothing of a gun battle. No need to alarm them. Plus, the fewer people who knew about it the better.

Justin nodded. "The meeting with Bouquet was helpful, then.

Good. He was competent and got on well with Pete Vine and the rest of us." Justin reflected for a moment, registering the new information. He turned to face them. "So this gang was exchanging our regular pilot for their own."

"According to Abdouelle, using private jets like this was a simple way to move their illegal goods around Europe, North Africa and the Middle East. They preferred to have their own pilots on board the airplane. That is why they drugged Bouquet's food."

Jordi pulled out a photo, the one given them by Pierre Bouquet. "Have a look at this," said Jordi. Justin crossed over to Jordi and took the photo.

"Do you know this man?" Jordi asked, pointing to Habib Benhabib.

"No, I've never seen him before."

"He is the one who replaced Pierre Bouquet. He was the pilot of the airplane on August fourteenth."

Justin's heart jumped. There was now a face to the person who had flown the airplane. He felt his temples tighten. Had this been a suicide mission of some kind? People flew commercial airplanes into buildings, and suicide bombers walked into restaurants and blew everybody through the roof. Anything was possible, but did such an explanation really make sense?

Perhaps Curley Grady had been right. Someone had dredged the aircraft engine from the sea, sold it and it eventually made its way to Bahrain. But that explanation was equally absurd.

He returned to the sofa, sat next to Gloria and said nothing. Aircraft fuel and oil had been found on the water, as had floating objects from the airplane. Sophie's oil-stained doll was now in a shoebox in storage in Paris.

The airplane did crash. Yet, if this Mr. Benhabib was still alive, something was inexplicably wrong.

Jordi waited for Justin to speak.

Gloria had not said a word through the entire explanation. She placed her hand on Justin's clenched fist but spoke to Jordi. "You said that Mr. Khanoum told you about an organization using planes to smuggle illegal contraband around the Mediterranean. How was Mr. Benhabib connected with the organization? Do you know anything more about the man?"

"No. Not really," said Jordi. "We did get a business card with his name on it."

"May I see it?" Gloria said.

Jordi handed the card to Gloria. She studied it carefully and then said, "It's an address in Tunisia. Perhaps you should consider going to investigate this 'Sahara Charters.'"

Laszlo said, "You're right. We should at least consider that option. But we said we would meet Curley Grady at the airport tomorrow. I don't think there is anything we can do for now but wait. Tomorrow morning we can all go and meet with Grady. Just in case, I think we should pack light travel bags in the event that we need to go somewhere."

Justin noticed Laszlo said 'we.' Was he suggesting that Gloria go with them? He certainly didn't want her in Tunisia. Quite honestly, he didn't want to involve her in this at all. He didn't want her to carry this burden in any way. This sort of stress was not good for anyone, let alone a woman expecting a child.

"I agree with Laszlo," Justin conceded. "Let's meet at the airport at ten-thirty tomorrow before Grady's flight arrives. Until then, I think we need some rest."

Everyone accepted this, and Justin and Gloria took a taxi back to her parents' house. En route, Justin turned to her. "I'm sorry to involve you," he said. "I know we said we would share everything, but this is my emotional burden, and I wish you did not have to carry it. You are carrying our child. That is plenty." He smiled, resting his hand on her still-flat belly.

Gloria turned his chin to her serious face and said, "When we got married we made a commitment to each other. I cannot love you without participating in your life. This is an important thing for you and I will share it with you. When I said I would be your wife, I knew I was marrying a man who had been married before, who had a wife and child. They were taken away from you. I know this wounded you and I accepted those wounds and accepted the pain with you. I knew what I was getting into."

"Yes, but you didn't know that this would continue. That the airplane crash came back to haunt me—us, I mean."

"Justin, this is difficult for me, I admit that. When we got married I thought this was finished, behind us. I thought we only had to deal with a memory. Then this intolerant Grady appears in our lives with some bizarre information, and next, Laszlo and Jordi confirm that a gang was behind the crash."

She took his hand that still rested on her womb. On it he wore his wedding band. She pressed her hand to his, letting their rings touch.

"I have no idea where this will lead. But wherever it is, I will be there with you."

CHAPTER 10

As Sam put the envelope down, the telephone rang.
"Hello, this is Sam Oliver."

"Hello, Mr. Oliver, this is Jean-Claude Dubois. May I be the first to welcome you to Grenoble. I apologize if I disturb you, but I just wanted to see if you received my note."

Obviously, the hotel called him the moment I left the lobby, Sam thought. The professionalism was working to perfection. "Yes, thank you very much. I would be pleased to meet with you for dinner. And thank you for arranging the hotel room. It's lovely. More than adequate." Sam wondered what this was going to cost, but then again, he was tired. A couple of nights in an elegant hotel room were very welcome.

"We wanted you to be well treated during your stay in Grenoble. I hope you enjoy it. If it's all right with you, I will be at your hotel at seven o'clock. We can walk a few blocks through Grenoble to a restaurant in the old town that is known for its fine regional cooking," Dubois said.

"I'll meet you in the lobby at seven," Sam said.

★ ★ ★

After a shower and a change of clothing, Sam took the elevator downstairs. At precisely the appointed time he entered the lobby. Waiting for him was a slender man of forty with reddish-blond hair, clad in a suit, light blue shirt and yellow and blue tie. The man introduced himself as Jean-Claude Dubois.

The cool of the evening refreshed Sam, tired as he was. The two men walked four blocks through narrow cobblestone streets to the restaurant. Jean-Claude Dubois talked about the economy of the Grenoble region and the many French and foreign high-tech companies with operations in the area. He mentioned that the local university and business school offered courses in business and technology. But through his easy speaking, Dubois sounded faintly nervous to Sam.

The small restaurant was quiet and elegant. Despite a selection of available tables in the main dining area, the waiter led them to a private table in the back. Dubois translated from the French on the menu, making a few recommendations. Sam decided on a starter of small pieces of *fois-gras* with *fromage de chèvre,* garnished with walnuts from the region. The main course was *filet de canard* served with an orange sauce. A Beaujolais wine chosen by Dubois rounded out the meal.

The *fois-gras* arrived as Sam talked of his time in Europe. The men discussed the future of Unipac and the merger with EuroVinco, but Sam could tell that there was something else on Dubois' mind. He turned the conversation.

"How long have you been with EuroVinco?" asked Sam.

"For a little less than one year, ever since EuroVinco bought the factory from Vine Industries. I was very thankful when their general manager for Europe assigned me to the factory here."

"Who was he?" asked Sam.

"Justin Collins."

That name rang a bell, but Sam could not place it, even though he had been a personal friend of Pete Vine and he knew several of the managers in Vine Industries. "Did Justin Collins transfer over from Vine when EuroVinco bought the operations in Europe?"

"No. It's a sad story. His wife and daughter were on the same airplane as Mr. and Mrs. Vine, the one that crashed in the Mediterranean. I think that Mr. Collins was offered a job in EuroVinco, but he was devastated by the loss of his wife and daughter. He left the company. No one seems to know what happened to him after he left. He just disappeared."

Then Sam realized that is why he knew Justin Collins' name. His wife and daughter were on the airplane.

★ ★ ★

The main course arrived and the waiter poured the wine.

Sam decided to get to the point. "Has becoming part of Unipac impacted your operations in any way?"

"Yes, in a number of ways. When we were part of Vine Industries, the factory here in Grenoble was doing quite well. But now we are having a difficult time making our profits."

"What do you mean?" asked Sam, knowing what was coming. He had heard the message in almost every other place he had visited.

Dubois stiffened slightly. "When we were part of Vine Industries, we were allowed to make a lot of our own business decisions. Now, much more approval is required from the top. We can live with that. The main problem is that the profits seem to be drained from our operations. Corporate overheads are too high. We do not have enough to reinvest back into the operations and recently had to go through a major cost cutting exercise and let people go."

Sam heard the magical words again, 'corporate overhead.' He decided to ask a harder question. "Jean-Claude, if you are cost cutting, may I ask one thing? I don't want to be rude, but why do you put me into an exclusive, expensive room, one that the President of France stays in? That doesn't look like cost cutting."

Jean-Claude Dubois blushed and said, "The room may seem expensive, but my brother is the manager of the hotel. He gave us a standard corporate rate for the room, the same we would pay at any other business class hotel in the area. I wanted you to have something nice."

Sam regretted his challenge. "I am sorry, but I did have to ask. And I appreciate the room. It's just what I need after a long trip around Europe. I apologize for questioning your intentions and kind hospitality." Sam wiped his mouth with his napkin. "Concerning the excessive corporate overhead costs, as you call them, how is the money being spent?"

"It goes into a corporate pool and is then distributed to departments in the different headquarters. It's a bit of a mystery and with so many management hierarchies and reporting lines in place, it's not easy to question the system without someone reprimanding you. In any case, it's demotivating to have to dismiss staff. The corporate overheads are three times higher than in Vine Industries." He reached for his wine.

"So, instead of gearing up the business, you are in fact having to wind it down," Sam observed.

"Yes, the future is uncertain because of that."

Sam thought for a moment and admitted, "This is not the first time I have heard this message over the past three weeks. I promise you I will look into it."

★ ★ ★

Louis Abdouelle sat in his office chair and felt sweat trickling down the side of his face. He had met the two men in front of him before, and they were not men to fool with. Yass and Turk were their names.

Yass, the one in charge with the southern French accent, spoke, and Abdouelle could feel his shoulders tensing. "Louis Abdouelle, our old friend. Thank you so much for calling the office in Nice. Now, please tell us what you know."

He did not think they would come to visit him. He had called Nice that morning and had spoken with a person whose accent sounded Mediterranean though the voice was unfamiliar. His name was 'Zig' something. He had recounted the full story of what had happened the previous night at Le Magreb Restaurant and had provided the details that would incriminate him the least. It was now late Friday afternoon. Had they arrived a few minutes later, he would have been closed up for the weekend.

"I told the story this morning," he said.

The man across from him smiled, a smile that expressed neither happiness nor contentment. Last time he had encountered these men, he had not liked the smile. Now they were back, and nothing had changed.

"We know you told it this morning, but we are asking you to tell it again, in case you missed anything."

"Well, I wasn't there. I got the information second hand, but I have pretty good contacts at Le Magreb Restaurant. There were two men who went into Shafi Khanoum's office to ask him questions about an airplane crash that took place on August fourteenth. The security guard went in to assist Shafi. Shots were fired and Shafi got hit. The security guard also died. They say there was blood all over the place. His neck was slit open. One of the waiters pulled a gun when they left and he was winged but will live."

"Sounds interesting. Who were the men?"

"No one knows. No one had ever seen them before." Abdouelle was attempting to turn his video machine on with his knee.

"Are you sure?" the man across from him asked.

"Yes, I am sure."

Yass remained motionless for several seconds, then abruptly signaled Turk who rose and moved toward Abdouelle.

Abdouelle had had so many of these kinds of visits lately. The thought of more pain was unbearable. As Turk neared him, Abdouelle blurted, "I don't know who they were, but I think I know."

"That's nice of you to think. Now, tell us your thoughts."

Turk did not move back to his original place but did cease moving forward. Abdouelle took a thankful breath. "There were two men, one about two meters tall, blond, with piercing blue eyes. The other was shorter but also tall, muscular, perhaps Mediterranean. I suspect it's the same two who were around here in July. Back then they asked me a bunch of questions about Shafi Khanoum."

"What did you tell them?"

"I told them that Shafi Khanoum had been killed. A few days before those two were here, a tall American also came asking about Shafi. His name was Justin Collins. I sent him to Shafi's old address. The American left, and then some days later these other two arrived and asked me about the visit of the American." Abdouelle was trembling, his nerves overwrought with fear.

"So, is there anything more you would like to tell us?"

"No, that is all." Abdouelle pulled a handkerchief from his jacket and wiped his face.

"Mr. Abdouelle, thank you for your information. If you can think of anything more, please call the special number in Nice."

Yass reached into his coat pocket. Abdouelle, anticipating a gun or a knife, crouched, on impulse, behind his desk. The man pulled out an envelope, threw it across the desk at Abdouelle, and said, "Here. Something for your help. Like I said, call us."

Abdouelle peered over the desktop in time to see the door close. He remembered that he had a videotape of the two men who had visited him before, the ones who put the knife hole in his desk. He thought it best to leave it in the drawer for now.

CHAPTER 11

At eight a.m., Dubois walked over to a microphone and said, "*Bonjour*," to the cafeteria full of Unipac employees. He switched into English. "Good morning."

The crowd, who had been drinking coffee and talking in a low hum, became silent. Dubois continued, "As you all know, EuroVinco and Unipac have now merged, and we are part of a much larger family that will open new markets for the products we manufacture here in Grenoble. And so it is my pleasure to introduce Sam Oliver, Chairman of the Board of Unipac."

At that he stepped away from the microphone and Sam approached it, looking out at faces that seemed to be asking what this merger would mean for their jobs. "Thank you Jean-Claude," Sam began. "It's a great pleasure for me to be here in Grenoble and to personally visit this operation. I've known about this division for some time, because I was a personal friend of Pete Vine. He was proud of this place and loved to come here to visit." Sam paused for a moment. "What I'd like to do today is give you a very brief history of Unipac, say something about the management team and then about how the merger will be implemented. Let me start with the history..."

A quarter of an hour later, Sam concluded, asking, "Perhaps we can take a few questions."

A hand went up. "Mr. Oliver, you mentioned that you believe that the Grenoble operation has excellent potential for the future. We have seen recently that there has been downsizing here in the factory. How do we explain that?"

It was a good question and a tough one. Sam knew that. He also thought he understood the reason for the downsizing, yet he could not say it in front of this crowd, so he took a different tack instead.

"One of the benefits, we believe, resulting from the merger of EuroVinco and Unipac is market synergy. The factory here makes excellent products and these products are in great demand in North America. Unipac has a deep network of relationships with most large corporations in the United States, and this represents a huge market for our products manufactured here in Grenoble." Sam was careful to use the word 'our.' "It's because of this synergy that I believe reductions are not required."

Sam looked out over the crowd as several other hands went up all at once. He pointed at a woman he guessed to be in her forties.

She asked a similar question. "We have seen in most cases that there are major reductions in staff when American companies merge with other companies. Will you make major cuts now that Unipac and EuroVinco are merged?"

"Your observation is frequently accurate. Often the justification for the merger is that there are synergies and economies of scale that can be gained by bringing the two companies together, which results in reduction of staff. In Unipac we think somewhat differently. If you can't get synergy from all the competent people who are already there, and if you have to cut people, then a merger is just a top manager's excuse for downsizing. If people have to be cut as a result of a merger, then the merger is just a lie to the shareholders. A successful merger comes about when you leverage all the good people who are there and don't get rid of any of them."

The questions continued for another half an hour, much longer than planned, but Dubois recognized the importance of warranted interaction. As the session drew to a close, people moved off to their work places. Dubois approached Sam, extending his hand. "Thank you. Thank you so much," he said. "I have been struggling with motivation of the staff lately. Your answers have helped."

* * *

"Who is it?"

"Your best friend."

"That's wrong. You are supposed to follow protocol." Ziginiglou could tell it was Yass. He also did not like to follow the procedures dictating that each person calling in was to give a special code before using their name. But if *Le Patron* called, he wanted to make sure he was doing exactly what he had been told to do.

"What did you find out?" Ziginiglou asked.

"Khanoum was killed. He is now in paradise."

"I know that," Ziginiglou said. At least he knew about Khanoum being killed. He seriously doubted that he was in paradise. "Did you learn anything more?"

"We talked with Abdouelle. He was helpful and we gave him the payment. We also talked with one of the waiters at Le Magreb, the one that was listening behind the door to the two men who were questioning Khanoum."

"Do you know who they were?"

"No, but I have an idea. I think they are associated with this Collins. It's the same description that the watcher in Llanca gave us of two men that went to visit Collins at his home there."

Ziginiglou was concerned when he heard this. *Le Patron* had told him to call if it ever seemed that Collins was doing anything suspicious.

"Please call me back in ten minutes," he instructed Yass. "I need to call *Le Patron*."

* * *

After the question-and-answer session had ended, a number of people stayed behind, crowding around Sam in hopes of speaking to him personally. But the day's agenda necessitated Dubois' diplomacy in leading Sam away to the conference room. Here, Sam sat through a long morning of presentations from different managers on technologies, production, and the market. The quality of the people impressed him.

After lunch in the company cafeteria, Sam wandered around by himself in the factory, meeting people, posing questions regarding their individual job descriptions, and asking personal questions when possible.

At one point he saw the woman who had asked the second question of the morning. She was sitting in front of a box of electronic parts, inspecting each one. While looking through a microscope, she made necessary adjustments with a specific tool. Sam walked over to her and said, "Thank you for your question this morning. How long have you worked here?"

"Ever since it was built by Vine Industries," she replied. "Before that I worked at another factory in the area."

"How do you like working here, truly? Don't tailor your answer for the Chairman of the Board." He smiled.

"Honestly?"

"Yes."

"It used to be better when we were part of Vine Industries. We became afraid for our jobs when EuroVinco took over. And now the merger with Unipac makes things even more uncertain."

"That's not good," Sam replied.

"In my case, Mr. Oliver, I cannot afford to be without work. I have four children and my husband died of cancer. Without this job I don't know what I would do. I am good at what I do and work hard. The company gets its money's worth out of me, but I am worried."

"Tell me your name."

"Adelle Leclerc."

"Adelle, please call me Sam. You know, companies are strange places full of odd politics and mysterious decisions. At the same time, people's lives depend on companies. I understand that and Paul Kent understands that. We will do our best."

"Thank you Mr. Oliver—Sam."

He smiled, she smiled, and they shook hands, negotiating a tacit agreement. Sam knew he had some work in front of him.

* * *

Ten minutes later Yass called back.

"Yass, is that you?" So much for the protocol.

"Yes."

"*Le Patron* says you and Turk should fly down to Barcelona on the first available flight. You missed the last one today, so you are booked on one leaving tomorrow morning. Once there, rent a car and go up to Figueras. You will meet Serge and Pierre. They are being given instructions. *Le Patron* wants this Collins taken care of."

"Good. We will be on the first flight."

They disconnected and Yass curled his lips in his own version of a smile. He had wasted enough time going back and forth to Spain, and now he was ready for action. He didn't like the fact that Serge and Pierre were going to be there. He didn't like the two Frenchmen, but they were the preferred workers of *Le Patron*.

Someday he wouldn't mind eliminating them. Then he and Turk would be next in line.

But the only thing he and Turk had to kill now was the evening. He decided to visit an *Imam* friend of his uncle in a suburb in the north of Paris—one who shared his uncle's religious ideology.

They had already missed evening prayers, but on Friday evenings his uncle's friend always met with a select group of believers. Fighters for the faith.

This was also an opportunity to convince Turk to strengthen his religious beliefs. Several times Yass had taken him to see his uncle in Marseille. After the first time Turk had been reluctant to go back again.

Yass actually had his own plans for the evening. He intended to leave Turk for a long session of religious teaching while he paid a visit to the Albanians, the ones he and Turk had worked for in the past.

Of the two types of merchandise the Albanians handled, Yass was not interested in drugs. He was interested in their concubines—chosen young women from the Balkan countries who had been promised respectable jobs in factories.

But once smuggled into Western Europe, they had no chance to send merchandise down a conveyor belt. *They* became the merchandise.

He was going into battle tomorrow. He needed a concubine tonight.

CHAPTER 12

Curley Grady came through customs wearing his wrinkled suit. The sunburn on his forehead had faded somewhat.

Jordi greeted him, hand extended. "Welcome back to Spain."

Grady replied, "Spain OK, but you'll never get me back to that crazy town north of here. I don't know how you can live there. Where is everyone?"

"Waiting at the end of the reception hall."

Jordi led Grady to a small coffee bar where Justin, Gloria and Laszlo were seated around a small round table. Grady shook hands with everyone, and Grady and Jordi each took a chair.

"How was Bahrain?" asked Laszlo.

"Never saw so many rag-heads in my life," answered Grady. "At least most of them spoke English. More than I can say for that primitive village of yours."

"Did you visit the repair facility in Bahrain?" asked Justin, trying to ignore the Grady-isms.

"Yeah, they tried to be helpful, but they didn't have that much information. Americans ran the place, with Pakistani and Indian technicians. Their clients are mainly camel jockeys, rich as can be."

"What about the aircraft engine, what did you find?" asked Justin.

"The aircraft engine was the same one that was registered by the technician in Paris, the same one that was on the August fourteenth airplane."

"Where did the engine come from?" Laszlo asked.

"From Tunisia," Grady answered. "The engine was sold by a company called Sahara Charter. Evidently they deal in all sorts of airplane parts."

Justin looked at Laszlo and Jordi, and Jordi took out a business card from his pocket and handed it to Grady. The business card of Habib Benhabib.

Grady took it, looked at it for a moment, and then finally said, "Looks like all roads lead to Tunisia."

Gloria spoke. "Justin and I talked about the next step, whatever it was. We think that you should go to Tunisia to investigate. I will stay with my parents here in Barcelona."

Justin looked at Gloria, knowing the situation was hard for her. He said to the group, "I want to track this down, at least to find out what is going on with this Sahara Charter. Are you willing to go with me?"

"I have to go," Grady said. "It's my job. I'm getting paid for it."

"I'm curious," said Laszlo.

"It's a dishonor not to go," said Jordi. "Anyway, it has been some time since I have been to Tunisia. I have Legionnaire friends down there, and maybe I will have a chance to see them."

They managed to get on a flight that was leaving in one hour. As they walked to the baggage and customs check, Gloria and Justin lingered behind.

Justin turned to her and asked, "How are you holding up?"

"Well enough. I know we need to see this through. If we just let it pass, it would always be there in the background. Both of us need to resolve this, as hard as it is."

"Thank you Gloria." He ran his fingers a short way down the placket of her blouse, feeling the small pearled buttons. "I love you."

"I love you too. Take care."

They kissed, conscious of the tiny life between them. Further reason to take care. "I'll call you from Tunisia to let you know what we find," said Justin.

★ ★ ★

Their plane arrived in the afternoon, and they shared a taxi. Jordi sat in front and the other three in the back, Grady squeezed in the middle. Jordi knew Tunisia and had contacts there, and they asked him to handle logistics. He chose a hotel in the center of Tunis. They tried to act as though they were tourists. Grady did not have to try in his fuschia Hawaiian shirt.

The hotel wasn't exactly the Holiday Inn and Grady stared at the run-down façade in disbelief. "You mean people actually pay money to stay in this dump? They should pay *me* to stay here."

The cracked and peeling exterior was not much different than the interior, where bare walls flaked their former layers of paint onto the floor. The rooms boasted metal-frame beds with surprisingly clean sheets.

"How did you find this place?" Grady asked.

"The Legion has a network around the world. Once a Legionnaire, always a Legionnaire. I called a contact in Tunisia and he made the arrangement. This is exactly what I asked for. We need to stay away from any hotel that has a computer where our names will be registered, and once we leave this hotel, the manager will make sure that no records remain. We have never been here. It's the safest place to lay low while in Tunisia."

They settled in two separate rooms, Justin and Grady in the room facing a noisy street and Laszlo and Jordi on the opposite side of the hall. They met in the street-side room. Grady sprawled on his bed, Justin sat on his, Jordi stood in the corner, and Laszlo took the sole chair.

Justin spoke. "I would just like to thank all of you. I would be quite lost without your help."

"Hey," replied Grady, "I'm just on Baltimore Life's payroll. No skin off my back." He scratched that part of his anatomy as he said this, sitting up and poking at the blanket he had been lying on. He hated foreign bugs.

"Well even so, thanks for helping me get to the bottom of this," Justin said.

Laszlo said, "We have to accept the fact that we may not find anything. All we know is that this North African pilot uses Sahara Charter as his base. We will be lucky if we find him, if he is still alive. He should know the person who hired him to fly the plane, and perhaps it's the same person who ordered the restaurant manager to poison Pierre. But he probably won't want to tell us. Hopefully he will take a bribe."

"Don't worry about that," Justin said. "Whatever it takes."

Laszlo said, "We must learn if the airplane went to Tunisia. It's not a coincidence that Grady came up with the same address. Why did this Sahara Charter sell the engine to the facility in Bahrain?"

"Do you have any idea where this Sahara Charter is located?" Justin asked Jordi.

"No, not exactly, but there are some Legionnaires here who will know. I suggest Laszlo and I pay them a visit this evening. Why don't you and Grady take that time to go walk around, get a feel for the place? Grady, you need to change that Hawaiian shirt. It attracts attention."

Grady replied from his bed, "I like my shirt and there is no way I'm gonna go walkin' around in this place."

"Why not?" asked Jordi.

"It's full of A-rabs. Rag-heads. Just driving here gave me the creeps. Men running around in robes just like them terrorists I've seen on the news. It's not as bad as Bahrain, though. You should see the place, so many robes, and all they want to do is burn our flag and see us dead.

You know the worst thing is that in countries like these, you can't even look at a woman without some guy sticking you with a knife. And who wants to look at their women anyway. They're draped in damn black tents. No, I'm just gonna stay here and get some sleep. You guys get a feel for the place."

There was a collective sigh from the other three men.

"OK, it's up to you," Jordi said, then nodded to Laszlo who stood up. Jordi continued, "I'm not sure when we will be back. And we can all use a good night's rest. Let's have breakfast tomorrow at eight and take it from there."

The two men left the room, and by the time Justin put his small travel case in the closet, Grady was fast asleep and snoring.

CHAPTER 13

Justin went downstairs past two women who giggled and winked at him, saying something in Arabic.

He went onto the street. The noise, the colors and the smells were loud, bright and strong. He walked away from the hotel down a side street where he came upon a *souk*—a large market selling pyramids of fruits and vegetables, bottles of spices, rolls of blankets and rugs, clothing, lamps and more.

Not many tourists came to this area of town, and Justin immediately became the central attraction. Sellers and beggars saw a walking wallet coming their way. They rushed to the American, tugging on his shirt, trying to shove objects in his hands to buy or sticking their hands out for alms. Justin shook his head and with some effort managed to wave them away.

He wandered a little further through the streets, feeling quite alone in the robed masses around him. A man shoved past him, and Justin stepped sideways on the black hem of a woman's garment. Apologizing profusely, he took a deep breath and turned away. He closed his eyes and saw the empty, barren hills rolling toward Llanca's stretch of sea. He wanted to be running along them.

★ ★ ★

Grady was the first one up and in the restaurant the next morning, already on his third helping of white cheese and tomatoes, dried meat, and dates, all of which he washed down with strong black coffee.

Justin was the second one to emerge.

"Man, I slept like a baby," Grady said. "Just can't seem to get over this jet lag. By the way, the food here is pretty good. I'll go home and tell my folks the terrorists aren't starving. Sure, I'd sell my soul for a good serving of bacon, eggs, and grits, but the coffee here is strong enough to wake up the dead. Ours is kids' stuff compared to this."

Justin had a headache. And it seemed to get worse every time Grady opened his mouth, so he said nothing in response. But Grady could carry on a conversation with a rock.

When Laszlo and Jordi entered, Grady asked, "How are the two scavenger hunters? Find anything, or did the blond hulk here scare everyone away?"

Jordi turned to Laszlo and asked what a 'scavenger' was. The blonde man shrugged and Justin did not have the humor to elaborate.

"We know where to find Sahara Charter," said Jordi. "My friends suggested we have additional equipment so we did a little shopping. At ten a car will wait for us behind a gas station five kilometers north of Tunis. Laszlo made a list and an old friend of mine arranged to obtain everything for a small price. It will cost four thousand euros, but we will have an adequate arsenal."

"Thank you," Justin said. "I'll pay."

Hearing this, Grady said, "You know Justin, you don't fit the prototype of insurance scammers after all. Scammers do everything possible to hide information, yet you're willing to pay whatever it takes. Nah, maybe I read you wrong."

* * *

An hour later a taxi dropped them off at a gas station. Justin paid the taxi driver and noticed a man standing near several parked cars.

Jordi smiled at Justin and jerked his head in the stranger's direction. "My friend."

The four of them walked toward the man, and Jordi extended his hand, addressing him in French. The man was wearing a short-sleeved shirt that left his tattooed arms highly visible. Four blue letters marked his knuckles: R.A.C.A.

"*Salut, Jordi, tout est en ordre,*" he said. "*Vos choses sont dans la voiture blanche.*" They shook hands again. Justin handed forty hundred-euro notes to the man who stuck them into his pocket without counting.

The Legionnaire turned to Jordi and said, "There are only four of you. You are entering a dangerous area of Tunisia where there are many bands of violent men. Are you sure you don't need any help?" he offered.

Jordi smiled, saying, "I think we have enough resources. We want to stay discreet. The less people to know about our mission the better. But if we see that things get rough, we will call on you."

The man nodded and reached an arm covered in swirling dragons to grasp Jordi's shoulder. "Just be careful." He dropped the arm and folded it in his other. "I'm not sure you fully realize what you are stepping into. I know your capabilities." He glanced at Laszlo. "It looks like your friend can handle a lot too."

"That's your car." The man motioned to the left with his head. "It doesn't look like much, but it drives. Your goods are in a bag in the back." Jordi looked over the man's shoulder at an old rusted Peugeot station wagon with bald tires and cracked windows. It looked like most every other car they had seen on these roads. Jordi uttered something in French. Both he and the Legionnaire laughed and Jordi slapped him on the back. The man turned around, mounted his motorcycle, and revved off in a cloud of dust.

Laszlo took the driver's seat in the station wagon. Jordi told Laszlo to drive north onto the highway and pulled out a beer coaster covered with notes scribbled on it.

Grady spoke. "I can't believe it. You didn't even check what's in the sack in the back. They could be filled with gummy bears for all we know. I have one basic principle and that is to never trust an A-rab."

"How many Arabs have you ever known?" asked Justin.

"Maybe two. At least, they had names that sounded like A-rabs. One of them married my sister and they got two of the ugliest kids in the world."

Justin remembered the photograph he had seen in Grady's wallet and chuckled.

"Why don't you open the bags?" asked Jordi.

Grady whistled as he pulled a shiny .38 out of a canvas bag. "Hey, this is really nice," he said. "Maybe them A-rabs ain't so bad after all."

★ ★ ★

"There is no one there," Yass said into the telephone.

"Where are they?" asked Ziginiglou.

"Not there, I told you. We have been waiting all day and the place is quiet," Yass reported. Yass had been sitting in a small Llanca pub with Turk, Serge and Pierre, taking turns checking Collins's house for activity. There had been no movement. Serge and Pierre had downed Sangria after Sangria and were now starting to giggle.

Yass was growing impatient.

"Then go to Barcelona. We know that Collins and his wife sometimes stay there on weekends to visit her parents. You have the address, don't you?"

"Yes," said Yass. The agency in Barcelona had given him a report on Collins which included the address of the woman's parents. Yass had seen the woman leaving the hospital in Figueras. He had not forgotten her.

"*Le Patron* wants Collins eliminated," said Ziginiglou. Ziginiglou didn't like to give these kinds of instructions. He was an accountant by trade and now he found himself having to give orders to kill. This particular duty nauseated him, but he would put himself in a difficult position if he did not give the orders. Better nauseated than dead.

"We know that," said Yass. "As soon as we find him we will take care of him."

If we eliminate Collins, Yass thought, I know exactly what I will do with his woman.

CHAPTER 14

"This is it," Jordi said, parking the car near the entrance of the building. They had found the airport in Benzart where Sahara Charter was located. A large blue and red sign said as much. Nine buildings scattered across an otherwise barren plot of land. There were five large hangers, and Grady counted twenty-some small planes on the tarmac as well as several corporate jets.

"What do you suggest?" Justin asked Laszlo.

"It's very simple," he replied. "We are tourists and want to charter a private plane."

"Do you think we look like tourists?" asked Justin.

"Yes, if Grady comes," said Jordi.

Grady did not catch the sarcasm and said, "Sure, I'll come."

They climbed out of the car and entered an office overlooking a large room in which several men sat, smoked, and drank coffee. Two dismantled airplanes lay in the large space, their parts spread across the floor.

A man seated behind the desk in the office asked if he could help them. Grady told the man that he needed to hire a private jet. "My buddy Frank McKenzie told me you guys were decent, so I want your best pilot to fly me to Saudi ASAP."

The man sighed. The problem with Americans is that you could never tell how rich they were. They always dressed so casually. This Texan was probably an oil prince. He replied, "We don't lease airplanes here. This is the parts facility of Sahara Charter. Go up to the second floor and someone can help you with a charter."

They walked up a flight of stairs to the second floor door that had 'Sahara Charter, Flight Leasing' stenciled on its window. Justin knocked and went inside. The small room contained a pile of canvas bags in a corner, a couple of old desks and an old couch. The stuffing was coming out of the couch in numerous places and was covered with cigarette burns in others.

Justin called out, "*Est-ce qu'il y a quelqu'un ici*? Is there anyone here?"

A moment later, they heard sounds in an adjacent room. The door opened and a man walked in.

The man from the photograph.

Justin's heart started pounding. *This man was the last person who had seen his wife and daughter alive.*

Grady took over and said, "We need a flight to Saudi, urgently. Can you fly us there?"

"Yes, two airplane available," he said in broken English. "I have Cessna and small private Jet. Which plane you like to hire?"

Grady replied, "Whatever's fastest."

Anger, fear, confusion, and incredulity battled inside Justin's skull. Impatience won. "I would rather hire the plane that crashed in the Mediterranean on the fourteenth of August one year ago—the one you supposedly died in, Mr. Habib Benhabib."

Habib's face paled. "I think you make mistake," he said. "My name is Faziz Benhabib."

Jordi pulled the picture Pierre Bouquet had given them from his pocket and held it in front of Habib's face. The pilot glanced from the photo to the four men. "This is photograph of my brother. Many say we look very much alike. He is the one to die in crash last year."

"You're lying," Justin said through clenched teeth. Immediately, Jordi and Laszlo seized Benhabib and pulled him into the other room. It was filled with cans and boxes. Grady slapped a piece of tape across Habib's mouth and tied his hands together with such ease it was apparent he had done it before.

"Now listen, Habib," the Texan said, "my boss here is an impatient man. He doesn't like to waste his time. So, when we will pull this thingy off, you will talk, and when we put it back on, you will shut up. The rules are simple: off, you talk; on, you shut up. You understand?"

Habib mumbled and Grady slapped him hard across the face. "I said, tape on, you shut up. Is the tape off? No, it's on. So you shut up."

Backwater bigot or no, the man knew his business.

Grady continued, "OK, Habib, we only want the truth. Perhaps you have a short-term memory, but we know you were the one flying the plane, and not your brother. What happened?" At this point, he ripped the piece of tape off Habib's mouth. "OK, tape off. Talk."

Habib's voice started to break. "No, it's no me. Is big mistake." Grady tore off another piece of tape and stuck it on Habib's mouth again. He turned to Laszlo and asked, "Sir, would you be so kind as to start breaking Mr. Habib's fingers one by one until the stinking A-rab tells the truth."

Laszlo stepped forward, face blank. He reached down, took hold of Habib's tight fist, and pried his little finger loose. He started to bend it backwards while Habib's face turned red. Habib kept silent because of Grady's instructions, but the pain got to him. He started to yell, muffled sounds coming through in whines, sweat rolling down his forehead, while the large strong man held his finger back at a 45-degree angle. A little more pressure would snap the finger like a pencil.

Grady reached down and touched Laszlo's hand. He said, "I think Habib wants to say something. Right? And it better be the truth, or next time we will not play. My friend here was just warming up, but once he starts for real, he gets carried away and there's no stopping him. This could be quite harmful to your health."

Habib looked at the four men in front of him and nodded his head. The tape was ripped off once more, pulling hairs from his thick moustache.

"Before I begin, I need bargain," Habib said.

Justin cut in. "What do you mean, bargain? You are in no position to bargain."

"You understand when I am finish. I am man caught between violent men. As they say in English, between rock and hard place. If I tell you my story, you must agree to protect me. If I tell you anything, they kill me and if no tell you, you kill me. So, what must I choose?"

"It's your choice," said Grady.

"If you want, kill me, but if I tell you anything, protect my mother and sister. I no know who you are, but you must be men with power, so you are able protect my family."

"Why would we do anything for you, Habib, if you're just as rotten as the rest of them?" Grady asked. "Why should we bother about your family when we can just get the information we need and kill you and maybe them too? It's obvious you're not very resistant to torture."

Justin knew Grady's threats were partly show, but he still did not enjoy all of this. "Let's hear what he has to say."

"OK," Grady said. He sat down on a wooden crate and pulled out the 38-caliber revolver from under his coat. He cocked the trigger and aimed it at the pilot. "Let the guy talk, but I'm gonna blow off his knee at any point if I think he's not telling the truth."

Justin and Jordi stood on either side of Habib as he started his story. "Few years ago," he said, " I leave the Moroccan Air Force to join Air-Morocco as pilot. That was lasted only one year. When Air-Morocco experience money problem and have to leave people go, I start to fly as free-lance pilot, taking work where I can, but there are few jobs only. I have mother to support and sister who is not marry. Do you understand?"

"I don't understand nothing," Grady said, "but go ahead."

"There is a man everyone know in Tunisia. He help people out when they in trouble. He come to me and ask if I need some work, to work for organization. I know that I must repay favor from this man sooner or later. But my family and I are in great need of money and I never expect the price I have to pay later."

"What price?" Grady asked.

"He get me job as replacement pilot for French company. Somehow, he always know when they need pilot, and I find myself 'by chance' in Paris every time they need me. I fly for them, this organization, a few times and they know I am good pilot. On those flights they making special shipments to Tunisia and other places around the Mediterranean. I make these special flights from the Mediterranean to places in Europe and even to South America."

"Why do you call them special flights? What was on those flights?" asked Justin.

"Drug, weapon, explosive, sometimes girls—is easy way to get through customs, but they prefer to keep pilots that work for them when they make special shipments. I no want to do it, but what do I choose? I only do my job and keep mouth shut. I never touch box. Their shipping people handle many boxes. Fourteenth August flight different. Very different."

"Why?" asked Justin.

"Objective I no understand. One day, they tell me they have 'special job' for me. They tell me I fly special shipment, some weapons, from France to Tunisia. It's nothing difficult. I do it before. Big traffic of weapons go on, you see. The poor country fights, so they demand weapons. The wealthy country discuss and they supply. It's very convenient for every one."

"Fine, but why was the August fourteenth flight so special?" Justin asked again.

"At August, I no worry with it. What we carry is very little compare to the tons of guns sent by Europe companies and United States. Except our shipment go to different customers. I need extra money, so one week after I receive instruction, I fly to Paris. A man meet me and tell me the details what I should do. I follow instructions."

"My insurance company is interested in this one," said Grady. "What happened?"

"I suppose to fly direction of Malta. I reduce altitude as low as possible over the water and avoid radar detection. This is no difficult. I fly first for Morocco Air Force so I know defense systems of different country around Mediterranean. It's no difficult for to be invisible."

"So the airplane didn't crash?" Grady asked. "Obviously not, because you are here."

"Everything work. On the day we arrange, the air charter company call me and I replace sick pilot. I go to airport and plane is ready to go, all passenger on board. We also have copilot and steward on board to serve food and drink and look after passenger. There is one thing differ from original plan. There is more people than they tell me. I think if no harm come to the passenger, OK. But there is woman and small girl that board the plane. Is beautiful woman and little girl look like doll." He hung his head. "I no can tell."

"Yes you can," Grady said, poking Habib's knee with his gun.

Habib raised his head to half mast, letting it loll to the side. "We take off and I fly towards Malta. I remember it's windy day and sky is stormy, not like usually in August. During flight, high over Mediterranean, strange thing happen that they no tell me. The steward come into the cockpit and inject syringe into neck of copilot. He die instantly. I am shock, but I know I must fly plane. The steward then hand me gas mask and tell me put it on. He too put on gas mask. He throw something back into cabin. Then I hear many small scream in back. A man is fall to floor. He shout, 'Help, we can no breathe.' That only last few second and it stop.

"This make me more terrify than ever. The man tell me fly to this private airport here in Tunisia and we land. There is no control tower and no one know what airplanes coming and going. We keep mask on whole way to Tunisia. I begin to wonder what kind of gas. Perhaps it is no sleeping gas but something worse. I feel terrible for passenger, but I know the steward can kill me, and I have family for worry about. The end of the flight seem almost to never come, but it come and we land."

"They died," Justin said to the wall.

"What happened then?" Grady asked.

"Five men wait for me. They look like gang, or terrorist group from Mediterranean. What branch of terrorist? I no want to ask, I just want for survive, and so I keep quiet. The men quickly board plane and everything out, people and weapons, the boxes."

"What about the people?" Justin refocused. "Tell us about the people."

"The people are still asleep, at least, that is what they tell me, but I find out different later. The men put everything in two cars and then they drive away. I am relief because the man who kill copilot drive away with them."

"Back up, back up," said Justin. "What did you find out about the people? They were not asleep—the people who were on the plane?"

"The gas is poison gas. All people die. They take them away and bury in hills south of airport. When I hear that news, I cry, and I many time have nightmare thinking of small child. It's not right that they kill her, and kill other passenger. Why is child on plane that day? But Allah wills."

Justin could only breathe. He thought of Chantal and Sophie unable to do just that in their last moments.

"What happened to the airplane?" asked Grady.

"Plane stay here and they take apart. Many part worth several million dollar when you sell. This is very good money-making business. The large room downstair is use for tear airplanes apart. They make good business at that and combine with smuggling of drug and weapon, they make plenty money. But for what I tell you, you must promise me protection or I am dead man."

"What about the oil slick and airplane parts…and the doll?" Justin asked.

"Same day, Piper cub flies to Malta. Different pilot. Flies over water, drops parts, oil, doll. Makes officials look in wrong place."

"So you have worked here for one year?" asked Grady.

"On that day I ask them when they pay me and they tell me there is change of plan. They tell me I am now legally died and give me new identity, as Faziz Benhabib. I continue fly, but under new papers. I no argue. I tell you, I am happy for to be alive. They tell me they keep me alive because their boss like to have qualify pilot available, in case emergency."

"What was it all for?" asked Jordi.

"I not know much about these men. Two I see several times since then, but no all the men. There is one I see only once, on August fourteenth. His name is Yass and he appear to be leader that day. I know this because I hear another one mention his name. He has scar on his left cheek that make him look evil."

"Explain," Grady said, now tapping the opposite knee with the gun.

"He is one giving instruction on what to do with many weapon package in airplane and what to do with all passenger body. It seem he enjoy people die. I only see him once, but it's enough. For some time, I think he must be leader of gang that operate from here, but now I no think so. He is only here once, on day of pretend crash, so I think he is only lead that one event. About two week later I fly him back to France. I never see him again, Allah be praised."

"Did you fly him back to Paris?" asked Jordi.

"No. I fly him to Nice. I am happy when he leave my plane. One kind of man is harder than other kind. I tell you truth, I am no sure how they all connect and I am no sure about all they doing, but I know that they smuggle much guns to different terrorist group around Mediterranean. But I never talk. I just fly."

"Where do you fly them to?" asked Jordi.

"Many place—Lebanon, Syria, Sudan, Yemen. It's this kind of place where terrorist is look for weapons. Sometimes fly from Kosovo to Europe. Drugs. Girls. I don't like. No choice."

"And what are they doing here?"

"I think this group has place along coast from here. Once, after I fly several men in from Beirut on corporate jet, after they leave with car, I am very much curious. I take Piper Cub that belong to Sahara Charter and I follow their car, make sure I follow from very high altitude. Keep many kilometer away. They go to a house along coast about thirty kilometer from here. I think it is center for these activities, or place for storage, or even training camp. I no sure."

"How do you really know the passengers on that August flight were killed?" Justin asked, finally able to breathe and speak.

"When I fly Yass back to Nice I hear him talk with other man. The gas in can is poison. The steward no want to shoot so no damage the plane. Plane is worth money and they no want to damage any part. Airplane part sell for plenty money in many country in Middle East and especially in country has trade restriction by the United State or European Union."

At that point Habib hung his head and said, "You know, I am so much in regret I am part of this. I bring the guilt of this to my grave. I am always live in fear, and I no want to go to authority. I know these men must take very much revenge against my family. What way they harm me is no matter at this point. I think at that time I make some money by fly airplanes, but I never think it lead to murder. I am man with blood on my head. How Allah can forgive me?"

Laszlo, quiet all this time, looked directly at Habib, his cold blue eyes as sober as his voice. "You will take us to the house where the men are."

Habib looked up in fear. "No, you can no do this. These men are violent. They kill me."

Grady, sitting in front of Habib, broke in at that point and said, "Habib, you have a choice. I am anxious to use this new gun that was given to me by one of my good friends here. You can take your bullets right now, or you can delay things and take your chances with the rest of us."

CHAPTER 15

Justin sat in the car like a stone, seeing Sophie's gap-toothed smile changing to gasping, to being locked in a hasty grave. He wanted revenge, but more than that he wanted to know where Chantal and

Sophie were buried so that he could give them a proper burial. His soul needed at least that much closure after all this opening of old wounds.

Laszlo had driven off a dirt road and around a bend into a small waddi where the car could be parked unnoticed. They left it and walked several kilometers through the hot, arid morning. They had stayed off the dirt road and had instead taken small trails that wound through the stony brush-covered terrain.

It was now late afternoon and the four of them were crouched down behind large rocks and bushes atop a hill, looking out to sea. They had left Habib with his hands and feet tied on the other side of the hill, where they would rejoin him after completing surveillance. Laszlo looked through his binoculars, focusing on the scene below.

In front of them, the hill sloped down toward the sea. Calm waters met a curved segment of the shoreline at the foot of the hill, forming a large inlet. At the far edge of the inlet was a cove surrounded by a leveled area on which several buildings, including a large house, had been constructed. It was ideal for seclusion. Their observation point was situated only half a kilometer away from the buildings. They had a good vantage point, and at this time of the day, they judged it best not to move any closer. Instead, they used the time to formulate a workable plan and familiarize themselves with the lay of the land.

Justin examined the scene below. The most prominent building, a large French Colonial house, sat about one hundred meters back from the sea. Three other buildings formed a horseshoe, surrounded by a stone fence about three meters high. The house looked like it had been built when Tunisia was under French rule, probably as a vacation house for a French diplomat. It had seen better days.

As Justin looked out over the compound, he heard an engine start and watched a car move from around the far side of the main house to the primary gate where a man in the passenger seat got out. He unlocked the gate and the car drove through. Securing the gate behind him, he got back into the car, sped up the dirt road and disappeared. That meant that at least two men were in the car—the driver and the one who opened the gate. If they did not come back, the number of combatants they would have to face would be decreased. After some minutes, Laszlo handed the binoculars to Justin.

Just as Justin noticed that the top of the fence was cemented with broken shards of glass, he saw a man and a large dog emerge from the main building, cross the yard, and enter a neighboring building.

He passed the binoculars to Jordi, and when Jordi had surveyed the scene, he passed them to Grady.

Laszlo signaled that they should retreat over the crest of the hill. Until this moment they had said nothing to one another, careful not to risk making any noise. Although they were some distance away from the house, they knew that voices could carry if conditions were right.

Their entry would require the weapon of surprise.

Reaching the other side of the hill, Laszlo spoke quietly. "We need to wait until it's dark, and then I suggest that we move to the large outcropping of rocks not far from the house. We can approach it through the dry streambed. Jordi, did you see those rocks?"

Jordi nodded.

Laszlo went on, "We should move into the property and take prisoners for interrogation. If we are fired upon, we will return with force. We must work as a team and remain aware of where the other three are at any point in time."

For the next few hours they waited and watched, checking their weapons and breaking for food shortly before sundown. Justin carefully held the handgun in front of him. He had never fired a pistol. When he was a teenager he had gone camping several times with his grandparents in the California desert and they had shot tin cans with an old single shot .22 rifle. But a handgun was something different altogether. The situation they were in demanded a caution and quickness that tin cans did not.

Justin watched Grady eat several sandwiches and then put another sandwich in a small plastic bag that he stuffed into his coat pocket.

"What's that for, Grady?" Jordi asked. "Do you think you will starve before dawn?"

"It's a midnight snack for a friend of mine," Grady replied. He then stretched out on the sand, put his head back against a rock and went to sleep. Jordi shrugged and returned his concentration to the compound.

There were no clouds, and the sunset turned a deep pink that lightened the western sky as the eastern sky darkened. Jordi had lived in the desert during his years in the Foreign Legion and he knew that the only light they would have tonight would be the millions of stars filling the heavens.

★ ★ ★

Throughout their wait, they took turns posting themselves behind rocks and bushes and kept watch over the movements within the complex. They hoped to gain a fair estimate of how many men they might find themselves up against.

They often checked the ropes on Habib but had long since removed the gag. Laszlo warned him to keep from talking and to only reply quietly if given instructions or asked any questions. At this point they treated him as a captive bystander. The look Laszlo had given him was enough to keep Habib silent for a month.

At midnight Grady returned from over the hill and they began to finalize their plans for infiltrating the property and main house. They followed Laszlo's earlier suggestion to move down through the dried-out streambed. It originated beyond the adjoining hill and wound its way down, meeting the sea beyond the house. They kept low along its bed, invisible until they reached the house.

They had spotted three different men during their evening watch, and each appeared to be carrying weapons, two with side arms and another with a rifle or machine gun. They guessed there were more men inside. They also caught sight of the large dog from time to time and could occasionally hear it barking.

According to Habib, some organization used this place, but what organization, he did not know. There were so many of them across North Africa, in Tunisia, Algeria, Morocco, Libya. There was no telling. Whereas some of these groups were considerably small and self-contained, others were connected to large networks that worked formally or informally with each other, depending on the objectives of the moment.

As they got closer, Justin managed a better look at the compound. It was easy to see why terrorists had chosen this place. The wall was higher than he had previously estimated and the broken bottles at the top imposed an impressive deterrent. The place was isolated, and the small bay with its sandy beach served as an ideal site for loading and unloading incoming supplies or contraband.

In addition to the stone wall, a chain-link fence ran parallel to the sea. There appeared to be only two ways into the compound: through a gate in the stone wall where the main approach road ran, or through a small gate in the chain link fence going out to the cove.

Grady stumbled over some brushes and ripped his jacket. "Damn this camping."

Justin thought he saw the corner of Laszlo's mouth turn up.

Jordi moved about thirty meters in front of the others, who waited for the signal to join him. In spite of the blackness of the night their eyes adjusted enough for them to maneuver their way down the dry riverbed. A shooting star streaked across the sky above their heads, leaving a luminescent trail that ended as soon as it had began. They were left with the Milky Way and its cousin constellations.

Grady mumbled to himself, "Just like dark nights in Texas, but down there you got mosquitoes to worry about. Texas mosquitoes are so big they sometimes eat Texas Longhorns. Heck, Texas mosquitoes are more dangerous than the men in that house down there."

"Quiet, Grady," whispered Laszlo.

Jordi continued to take the lead, occasionally stopping and signaling for the group to join him. In this manner, they made their way down the gully to their destination point. All the external lights were out by now, and only one or two remained on inside the main house. Justin considered the probability of an in-house guard.

Laszlo whispered, "We should see if there is a way over the wall."

Grady spoke up. "I don't plan on going over any wall. Afraid of heights. Give me a few minutes to scout around."

"No way," Laszlo objected. "You are like…what do your Americans say? A bull in a china shop. You will make so much noise that they will find you in two seconds."

Grady protested, "I ain't gonna let you guys tell me what to do. Either you let me go sniffing around, or I stomp out of here right now."

Before they had a chance to answer, Grady scrambled up over the top of the ravine and disappeared toward the house. As they peered up over the top of the ravine, they saw Grady moving forward, crouched low to the ground in a half-squat, his silhouette resembling that of an animated monster stomping through the black of night.

"Is he crazy, or what?" asked Laszlo. "We should have tied him up and left him with Habib."

"Don't worry, he will kill them with fright if they see him," said Jordi. He leaned back against the side of the gully shaking his head.

Grady disappeared around a corner of the wall and in a few minutes the dog started to bark. Laszlo, Jordi and Justin stood alert.

"The dog probably smelled him," said Jordi.

The dog stopped barking. Several minutes later, Grady reappeared, breathing heavily. "I've given you guys a private entrance into the compound. Going through the front gate or climbing over that jagged glass was not my idea of fun," he said in a stage whisper.

"What do you mean?" replied Laszlo.

"Today when I was watching things down here, I saw the dog walking around inside the compound, and then I saw him walking around outside the wall, going to do his thing, if you know what I mean. I kept watching him. I was missing my dogs back home. Well before you know it, I see him disappear around the wall and then he's inside the compound again. He has his own entrance. He's a big dog, so I thought to myself, if he can get through it, I can get through it. I suppose even Laszlo can get through it."

"We'll have to be careful of the dog," said Justin.

"Nah, not for a few hours anyway. He liked my sandwich. And the little pharmaceutical I put in the sandwich. The dog is out cold."

CHAPTER 16

Justin stopped short. Two men lay sprawled in grotesque positions, pools of dark red blossoming around them on the crème tiled floor. His stomach spasmed and he leaned forward, bracing his hands on his kneecaps, waiting for the nausea to pass. Another man lay felled in the dirt outside, the lookout man. Justin had not fired his gun but had stayed close to Laszlo. Grady and Jordi had done the shooting. Kill or be killed.

Laszlo and Jordi stood at the room's entrance, anticipating attack. Justin tried to copy their stance of readiness, but he felt like an actor in a play who did not know the lines. Grady stood to one side of the front door, scanning the darkness of the compound.

Justin stayed quiet, not knowing what would follow. He raised his upper body and stood tall, his breathing even once again.

"So much for interrogating the prisoners," Justin said in a low voice.

Grady added, "I'm generally not fond of shooting first and asking questions later either. But hell." He shrugged.

Laszlo translated the gesture. "There was no choice. Come, let's search the house. Maybe we will find something."

Grady stayed to guard the entrance. Laszlo and Jordi proceeded to make their way from room to room, opening closed doors, covering each other as though they had functioned as a close team for years. No signs of movement on the ground floor.

Justin made his way to the kitchen, found a chair and sat down. No longer in the presence of dead men, he sought to regain composure.

Laszlo and Jordi headed up the stairs to the second floor. A nightlight at the far end of an extensive hallway revealed six closed doors, three on either side. They systematically opened each door, searching for signs of life and aware that one careless move could bring instant death. Whose death remained to be seen.

They passed a bolt lock, and Laszlo broke it with a single shot, kicking open the door. Nobody moved.

Jordi, still outside the room, inched toward the doorway, his back against the wall. He listened but heard nothing. In the dimness he saw faces, indistinct forms. He sprang across to the opposing side of the entrance in time to see Laszlo lower his gun.

"Justin, come up here."

It was Laszlo's voice, but the tone was unfamiliar.

Justin rose awkwardly from his chair, his body heavy and tense. As he rounded the top of the stairs, he saw Jordi at the end of a hall, standing in a doorway. Jordi motioned him forward and Justin entered the room.

On the floor in front of him, leaning against the wall with her legs stretched out in front, sat an older woman he recognized. She had aged significantly since he had seen her last. Her hair was matted, and her clothing wrinkled. But it was Dora. It was Dora Vine. She leaned forward, whispering, "Justin? Justin, is that you?"

His eyes fell on the young child beside her. A girl. Loose blond locks fell disheveled about her face. He stood transfixed.

"Papa? Are you Papa?" Sophie asked him.

* * *

All night Doby had been seeking information. He had not been active on the Collins case for a couple of weeks, and the previous morning at seven o'clock he had dedicated himself to this project, making quite an advance in interpreting the data he had accessed from the computer in the Nice location. Much of the data contained lists of banking and accounting transactions. It would take time to make sense of all of this. He had also developed a relationship map using his network association methodology. The data included records of telephone calls made from a particular number in Nice. The map revealed main relationship nodes in California, Paris, and Tunisia.

The Nice number was called quite frequently, but it was difficult to associate a specific name and address with the number. This was strange in that most telephone databases normally included auxiliary information associated with a particular telephone number.

He decided to let Justin know how he was progressing, so he shot off a quick e-mail to the account he had set up for him.

From: Doby
To: Justin

Justin,
Found some info. The telephone number you gave me of Schmidt in Nice, France. Associated with office address at Rue Jacoby, 32, Nice. Used as central communications center. Several key numbers regularly called in California, Paris, Nice, Tunisia. Am currently writing report and will send it to you asap by e-mail.

Regards,
Doby

★ ★ ★

"Yes, Sophie, it's Papa," Justin said, reaching down for his daughter. She had grown so much since the morning he had kissed her goodbye. Grown. *Alive.*

With one arm he held Sophie, and with the other reached out, pulled Dora to himself, and hugged her. Dora began to cry.

Sophie looked directly at Justin, her eyes wide.

"Papa. I want Mama."

Justin looked to Dora and back at Sophie.

"I want Mama," she repeated, swatting his shoulder with her hand.

He glanced at Laszlo and then Jordi, who stood equally silent.

"What does she mean?" asked Justin, addressing Dora. Dora continued to weep, shaking her head. She buried it in Justin's shoulder and her body convulsed in deep sobs.

When she stopped shaking, Justin gently pulled away and handed Sophie to Laszlo. Then, with a hand on Dora's shoulder, he waited.

"Justin," she began, wiping her nose, "today three of the men here took Chantal away. They put her in a car and drove off. I tried to stop them, but I couldn't."

"Chantal is alive?" breathed Justin, glad he had given Sophie to Laszlo. His limbs had turned to water, and a distant roaring filled his head. When it passed, he had an image of Chantal in their Paris bed, opening the sheets to him in invitation. In Habib's office, he had imagined her in an ignoble, rough grave. The contrast sent his senses spinning.

"Yes, we are alive, although we know that they made it look like we were killed in a plane crash. They showed us the newspaper articles. After they brought us here they gave us copies of English-language newspapers. We saw the articles reporting the plane crash and our... deaths." She said the last word as if she had experienced it.

Justin's thoughts were still with Chantal and the fact that he had missed her by mere hours. But someone was missing. "Pete, where is he?"

Dora Vine's face went vacant. "He died a month after they brought us here. Heart attack. But it was really caused by the strain of being captive in this place. His daily mental battles with his captors," she paused and lowered her eyes, her voice sounding almost faint, "and... another incident."

"But why? Why have they done any of this? They were smuggling weapons. Why keep innocent people hostage without demanding ransom?"

"We still don't know the full truth," Dora sighed. "But it's obvious it had to do with more than weapons. Pete was able to gather a little information related to Vine Industries, although we never found out for sure. Pete's theory was that they were going to use us for a ransom, but we had no way of knowing. We have been here fifteen months, never knowing why. Or whether we would wake up in the morning."

Sophie squirmed in Laszlo's arms and Laszlo put her down. He held onto her hand, but Sophie remained restless, pulling and tugging.

"Did they treat you harshly?" Justin asked carefully.

"No, not really, except for," she paused, "except that they were... violent, physically, in the beginning. That's what upset Pete so much. But afterwards, they only yelled and threatened. Only." She laughed bitterly. "They kept us locked up within the walls of this compound, always guarding us when they let us outside for a few hours every day. The rest of the time we had to stay inside. In the evenings we were locked here in this room. It has been mental torture, and losing Pete..." That more distant grief shifted to a present one. "And now, now I am so worried about Chantal."

Sophie pulled away from Laszlo and ran for Justin.

He lifted her to his shoulder as he had done a thousand times. Clinging to Justin, she lay her head against his chest, thumb in mouth and at least half of her world reconciled. She muttered "Mama," as if it were an unanswered question.

Laszlo finally said, "We need to move. We don't know when that car will be coming back."

"What should we do?" Justin asked.

"I don't know," Laszlo said. "We just need to get out of here before more people show up."

They went downstairs through the living room. When Dora saw the bodies, she exhaled in deep relief. "Thank God."

Justin reached for her shoulder and lightly steered her toward the front door. She glanced over her shoulder one last time as if to make sure the captors were truly dead. Moving forward she repeated, "Thank you, thank you."

In the pitch black of the night, a dim light shone in one of the peripheral buildings. Grady stood at the door to it. "Come here," he whispered, motioning with his arm.

Inside were stacks upon stacks of wooden boxes, some open, full of rifles, ammunition, grenades—weapons of destruction in mass quantities.

"They had some kind of a business operating here," said Dora. Boats would come up and unload or load these boxes. I think they were selling these weapons to terrorist groups."

"Let's blow it up," Grady said.

"No," said Jordi, walking over to a box and pulling off the lid. "I have another idea."

CHAPTER 17

At five o'clock in the morning, the airport in Benzart was still dark and empty. There were no lights on the runway. They would have to wait until the sky was light enough to take off in one of the Sahara Charter corporate jets.

They parked the Peugeot and went up to Habib's office. Justin carried Sophie, now asleep, on his shoulder, and Dora Vine walked beside him holding his arm.

Grady was still shaking his head and repeating himself. "One of the weirdest… How do I explain this to Baltimore Life?…A plane crash that didn't crash…Captive for over a year…."

Justin wasn't paying attention. He was conscious of the new weapons in the Peugeot trunk and the fact that several Legionnaires were going to be able to do something about their intense dislike of terrorists. He supposed Jordi knew what he was doing. And Justin certainly wanted nothing to do with a warehouse whose contents were for killing. He'd seen enough death already.

In the office, Justin noticed a telephone on Habib's desk. It was early, but he needed to hear Gloria's voice. He turned to Dora. "Could you hold her for a few minutes? I need to make a call."

Dora took Sophie and walked toward the old couch. As soon as she sat down, exhaustion spread through her and she closed her eyes. Sophie had the right idea.

Justin dialed the Butlers' home number in Barcelona.

It rang once, and then James came on the line.

"James, this is Justin. I'm sorry to call so early, but I've had a rough night down here in Tunisia, and I don't know when I'll find another telephone. I need to speak to Gloria. I'm sorry to wake her up, but…."

James interrupted, "Justin, I am so relieved that you called. We don't know where Gloria is. Yesterday evening she went for a walk down the street to get some things at the local grocery store. She never came back."

"She's not there?" Justin felt his scalp tingling.

"No. We called the police last night and they came by and are now investigating. We just don't know what happened."

"Did she leave a note?"

"No. No note."

Justin tried to think. "Was she upset about anything?"

"No, not really. She was worried about you being in Tunisia, but we all understand what you are doing. Did you find anything out?"

"Yes. We found out the circumstances about the August flight. I will tell you all about it soon." The news about Gloria kept him from concentrating. Where could she be?

"Where are you now?" asked James Butler.

"At an airport in Tunisia. We plan to fly out as soon as there is enough light." Justin answered, his mind fixed on Gloria.

"We are so worried about Gloria," James Butler said.

"So am I," Justin said, his mind racing. "Is there anything I can do?"

"I don't know," James Butler answered. "The police said they would make it a top priority. I am supposed to call them this morning at seven."

"Then I'll try and call you back today. I'm not in a safe place and we need to get out of here."

"Are you in danger?"

"Not for the moment."

"Then please go. Let me wait to hear from the police and try and call me back after seven thirty."

They said goodbye and Justin hung up the phone. It occurred to him that Gloria might have gone back to Llanca. It was a long shot and it didn't make sense, but he dialed their home number.

After four rings the call switched to his answering machine and he heard Gloria's voice on the prerecorded answer. "You have called the home of Justin and Gloria Collins. We are not here, but please leave a message after the beep and we will get back to you as quickly as possible." She switched to Catalan and said the same thing again. Justin pushed the special number to access any recordings and a message came up on the machine.

"Hello, Justin Collins," a male voice began to say. "Someone has become very annoyed with you. Go to the police and Gloria Collins will be dead. You will receive further notification when we feel it necessary." Beep. No more messages. Justin punched in the number seven to replay the message and listened to it again. The voice was French.

Justin's head whirled. He thought about calling James Butler again, but reconsidered. The recorded voice had warned him not to go to the police. With the police in Barcelona already involved, it was uncertain what kind of a position he would be putting James in. Not to mention Gloria. Justin sat down in silence in a chair next to the telephone and stared blankly.

"What happened?" asked Jordi.

"Gloria has been kidnapped."

"*¿Que?*" exclaimed Jordi.

Laszlo stepped closer, attentive. Grady remained near the door with Habib.

"She didn't return to her parents' home. Then there is a recording on my answering machine in Llanca," he said, a double-fisted fear rising in him. "His voice was French."

"French?" Jordi asked.

"Yes." Justin said, his voice strangled.

"We could go back to Barcelona," suggested Laszlo, "but I suspect that Gloria has been taken somewhere else. We have nothing to go on, except perhaps if Doby has found something. Is there any way we can contact him?"

"He said to contact him either through Stefan Von Portzer, or through an e-mail address he had given me. I have not checked my e-mail for over a week."

Grady turned to Habib who leaned against a wall, still bound. "How do you get e-mail in this office? You gotta have an Internet connection," he demanded.

Habib jerked his head in the direction of the computer. "There is computer with Internet."

Grady untied Habib's hands.

"Get me online," Justin said.

Habib went over to the computer, sat down, and then hesitated.

"What is it?" Justin asked.

"Reservation. For airplanes," Habib stated.

"What do you mean?"

"The group from the house. Yesterday they charter airplane."

"How do you know?" Justin demanded.

"Reservation system says. Three people. To Nice. My friend pilot fly them."

Justin looked at Laszlo and Jordi and said, "Do you think Chantal was on the airplane?"

"It is very likely," Laszlo said. "Nice fits into this somehow."

"Why?" Justin asked.

"See if you have any messages from Doby," Laszlo said.

Habib hit some buttons and shortly they heard sounds of the modem connecting. Habib retreated to his wall across the room with Grady at his elbow.

Justin logged onto his email system. Doby had sent a message at 03:00 a.m. today. Justin read it.

Rue Jacoby 32, Nice. "We have the next piece of the puzzle," Justin said, pointing to the message on the monitor. He typed a quick note of thanks and turned toward the others. "It looks like we should fly to Nice rather than to Barcelona."

Laszlo nodded, remembering that the car that hit Justin in Llanca had a Nice prefix on its license plate.

"Let's go check out that office," Justin said, logging off and shutting down the computer. "Hopefully Doby's report will be finished by the time we get there. We'll need to find a computer there with an Internet connection."

"Who's Doby?" asked Grady.

"Someone doing market research for us," Laszlo said. He left it at that.

The eastern horizon was beginning to grow pale and pink with dawn. The runway was now visible.

CHAPTER 18

It had taken the two computer engineers over a week to find the hacker who had accessed their databases, but they had succeeded and success tasted sweet. They were quite proud of their 'reverse worm' that had worked its way out of the copied database and back to their own site, picking up a record of each site it visited along the way. They now had a roadmap back to the hacker.

Once Ziginiglou had the hacker's address, two men from Lyon were sent to Switzerland to locate him. *Le Patron* had given clear instructions: "Find out what he was after and then get rid of him."

Ziginiglou disliked calling the two men from Lyon, but *Le Patron*'s instructions were law. And too, he vividly remembered the splatter of Spiros's blood across his face.

* * *

Jordi sat in the cockpit with Habib. Once well out of Tunisia and over the Mediterranean, Habib made contact with the air traffic controllers in Nice and requested a landing slot. Theirs would be just one of many private jets landing at the Nice airport each day. Habib had been through the airport often and would know how to deal with the officials. Clearing customs was a mere handshake with a bill passed in the middle.

The flight over the Mediterranean was smooth both outside the plane and in. Justin had been worried that Dora might have difficulty being on a plane again—especially one so similar to her last flight, similar down to the same pilot. But she merely sat still, her eyes closed.

Justin was unable to digest the recent chaos his life had become. Not just his life, that of the people he loved. Was he in a dream? If so, it was the worst nightmare he could imagine.

Here was his daughter Sophie flying with him over the sea she had supposedly been at the bottom of.

If this was how fate worked, he wanted none of it. But he hadn't chosen any of these events—what made him think he could choose to accept the responsible force itself? He looked out at the sea below him but saw only blue in every direction.

He had no control and could not understand the bigger picture. This is what bothered him. And it was contrary to his training. MBA schools taught that through reason, through rational thinking, one could control and master events. Yet here he was being swept along without rudder, reign, or compass.

It was a cloudless morning. The faint edge of the moon hung low and still visible in the western sky. Under that same moon, he had proposed to Gloria, had swum with her on their honeymoon. As the light of day became brighter, the moon would disappear. He hated to consider whether there was any symbolism in that.

He was thankful for Laszlo and Jordi's help. They had little to gain from this. Laszlo was working for Stefan, and Stefan was doing this out of friendship. And Jordi was doing this out of honor, out of a sense of nobility and principle. Justin was also strangely thankful that Grady had come along. An odd but useful character. Here was fate at work again, putting a bizarre collection of highly different individuals on a Tunisian chartered plane.

He looked again at Sophie and Dora, both of them sound asleep. Sophie rested her head on Dora's lap. They had been through so much. Dora looked years older. An older woman, but one of resolve. He understood living through the death of a spouse. He could only imagine the personal pain and suffering she had experienced compounded with captivity.

An hour and a half later, he felt the jet quaver. He must have fallen asleep. He opened his eyes and saw the runway speeding along outside beneath the airplane as Habib applied the brakes. He looked over and noticed Laszlo sitting wide-awake. He wondered if the man ever slept. Grady was out and looked as if he'd been knocked out. His arm dangled in the aisle. Dora and Sophie were starting to stir. Sophie looked up and him and smiled.

Justin asked her, "Did you sleep well?"

She nodded her head.

He smiled back at her and said, "We will need to leave the airplane in a few minutes."

Dora, more fully awake, asked, "What are we going to do now?"

Laszlo answered, "We need to be very careful. If we go to the authorities, there is a chance that we may lose Chantal, and Gloria is being held by the same people. Whoever we are dealing with is powerful enough and has enough motive to keep you as hostages for over a year. The best thing we can do at this point is get you and Sophie to a safe place. Then we can pursue our investigations."

Dora wanted to ask who Gloria was, but she decided to wait. She simply nodded in response to Laszlo's answer and turned to stare out the window.

Before the heart attack Pete had a theory that they were being held for a ransom and had tried numerous times to determine what sums of money they would be asking. But the captors had only always said, 'we do not have instructions', or 'you must wait.' They waited without ever knowing the reason and remained perpetually without information.

The control tower instructed Habib to taxi the airplane to an area full of what seemed to be hundreds of private airplanes. He parked the airplane, stopped the engines and in a few minutes opened the door.

As they were leaving the airplane, Dora came up to Justin. "As soon as possible, I need to have a few words with you, privately."

* * *

The constant noise from the trains near their hotel was starting to drive Yass crazy. It kept him awake, woke him up early, and got on his nerves during the day.

The previous evening they had been in Barcelona. The Spanish woman had been an easy snatch. Turk, Serge and Pierre had waited in a white van while Yass followed her on foot from her parents' house toward a grocery store down the street. Yass had come up behind her and grabbed her, covering her mouth. He liked the feel of her struggling lips behind his fingers. The van had pulled up alongside them and the moment the door slid open, he had thrown her inside.

He had kept his hand over her mouth until they were out of Barcelona, enjoying the smear of lipstick and saliva on his fingers. He had used his free hand to explore other parts of her body. Tying her hands behind her back, they had blindfolded her and headed north.

According to *Le Patron*, the agency in Barcelona was going to provide a representative to take up a direct physical presence in Llanca. He and Turk were to stay behind as well, ready to move in case Collins showed up there.

Evidently this Justin Collins was causing trouble. They had associated him with the two men in Le Magreb restaurant in Paris. Since *Le Patron* had decided that Collins needed to be eliminated, he had ordered Collins's wife to be taken hostage as bait to lure him. Yass was disappointed that *Le Patron* had not allowed him to take the woman to Nice.

While Serge and Pierre had taken her on to France, Yass had decided that he and Turk would spend the night in a hotel about twenty kilometers from Llanca where they had left a car. What a mistake.

Another train went by and Yass vowed to find new lodgings in the morning. He turned onto his side, readjusted his pillow, and pulled the thin covers high over his ears.

★ ★ ★

Doby leaned back in his chair and put his feet on a wobbly stack of papers at the edge of his desk. He had worked through the night and had just completed his report for Justin Collins. He had also managed to strip data from the Nice computer. Not an easy job. The firewall seemed airtight. But that was the challenge and he had enjoyed it.

He had made a copy of everything they had on their system.

It was extraordinary data to say the least. He wondered about many hidden codes, codes he had never seen before, and it was only by chance that he found them. Online, he saw that the data from the Nice office had attached a routine to his e-mail system. It had then sent a message to a Hotmail address. It was a very clever routine and had circumvented his virus scan software. That worried him. His next task, after sending the document to Justin and getting some sleep, would be to figure out how that routine worked.

He was ready to push the button to send the document to Collins when, out of the corner of his eye, he caught movement on an inside monitor, a monitor linked to his security cameras. He then heard the dogs barking. The barking ceased suddenly and he saw armed gunmen moving across the property.

Doby quickly pushed the send button and then went into flight mode. He shut the door of the large bomb shelter, knowing that from the outside, the door blended perfectly into a wood paneled wall and was virtually impossible to see. Even if the gunmen found the door, they would have to hammer through half a meter of concrete and steel to break through.

He watched the two men move around the property. Through one of the cameras he saw the lifeless forms of his two dogs. Damn.

The routine imbedded into the data had done its job. It had found its way back to the source, and the source had sent these men to get him, the guns in their hands clearer than code.

As much as Doby did not count on the Swiss army for protection, he had learned a few tricks from them. The country's philosophy was to sacrifice the plains and protect their mountains in case of an invasion. The army had built entire camps inside mountains, and Doby had seen planes fly out of them as he drove down the Rhone Valley. His own setup was a miniature reproduction of this system. He had hoped he would never have to put it to trial.

His heavy-duty electronic equipment was located one floor below the house, and a small decoy technology room was set in the barn attached to the dwelling. This room was full of old computers, test and measurement equipment and various other kinds of instruments and wires, mostly found in junkyards. The lights were on in some of the terminals, giving the impression this was a real geek's playground.

The real equipment was in the bomb shelter. Bomb shelters were standard in many Swiss houses and office buildings, but this one was especially large and built off to one side of the house, underground. Building it directly beneath the farmhouse would have meant tearing the house down and rebuilding it.

The practical solution had been to create a substantial amount of space underground next to the house, construct the bomb shelter, and cover it over with several meters of dirt. No one attempting to access his property would conceive of a two hundred year old farmhouse 'next-door' to a bomb shelter. Like most bomb shelters in Switzerland, it had two entrances—a main one which could be accessed from inside the house, and a second, smaller entrance designed to prevent entrapment within the shelter. A tunnel adjacent to this particular second entrance led into a forest behind the farm.

Doby watched from his surveillance cameras as the men searched the house. Even if they found the room downstairs and destroyed it, all his data was backed up on a computer offsite.

The intruders raced through the living area inside the house and into the barn where the decoy electronic equipment was positioned.

They proceeded to destroy it, picking up terminals, old computers and test and measurement equipment and crashing them to the ground. Destruction complete, they left the building and waited on the terrace lounge chairs for the occupant to return home.

Doby shut down several pieces of equipment, leaving only one computer running. Using the smaller entrance to the bomb shelter, he hurried through a hundred meters of underground tunnel into the forest beyond. He pulled on a helmet, straddled his motorcycle, and coasted two kilometers downhill before turning the key and starting the engine. He rode toward Nyon and on to Geneva.

On the road he took out a cell phone. Stefan Von Portzer answered on the second ring.

CHAPTER 19

Dora's words echoed in Justin's mind. *A few words alone, privately.* They would have to wait.

Dora again held onto his arm as Justin carried Sophie. They walked into France straight from the tarmac through a gate Habib showed them—all without seeing a single customs agent.

Grady stayed close to Habib, whose gait resembled that of a small submissive lap-dog walking next to its owner. Habib carried two of their overnight bags, and Laszlo and Jordi carried the rest, including two full bags of warehouse materials from the Tunisian compound.

Laszlo and Jordi had been conferring, and Laszlo came up to Justin. "We are not sure where we go from here. All the circumstantial evidence so far points to Nice. Perhaps Stefan has some advice, but you know him. It's rarely possible to contact him before noon."

Justin agreed and said, "Doby said he would send a report. How about we rent a couple of cars and look for a cyber-café?"

They left the rest of the group at a bench in a small park next to the airport and returned in twenty minutes with a minivan. Grady and Habib climbed into the back seat, Justin and Dora in the middle with Sophie between them, and Laszlo rode shotgun next to Jordi. It took a quarter of an hour before they spotted a shop with an 'Internet' sign.

"There," said Justin, "to your right up ahead."

Jordi parked and Justin entered alone. Ten minutes later he came out with several sheets of paper in his hand. "I think we are in the right place," he said, climbing into the van. Holding the report out before him, he leaned forward in his seat and read aloud:

From: Doby
To: Justin

Subject: Research of The Specialized Trading Department

Objective: To understand in greater detail Department communication relationships

Methodology: Over a two-month period, two primary methodologies have been employed.

First, an effort has been made to understand the 'network association' of the Department to determine strength of relationships, that is, who may be providing directives to them. The methodology involves analyzing the frequency of telephone calls and length of conversations over a recent historical six-month period, using billing records of various telephone companies. While many calls were made to and from the Department, it has been determined that the most important linkage is a telephone number of an office in Nice, France. A second analysis of the network associations was made of the office in Nice and a number of key relationships have been determined as per the following diagram:

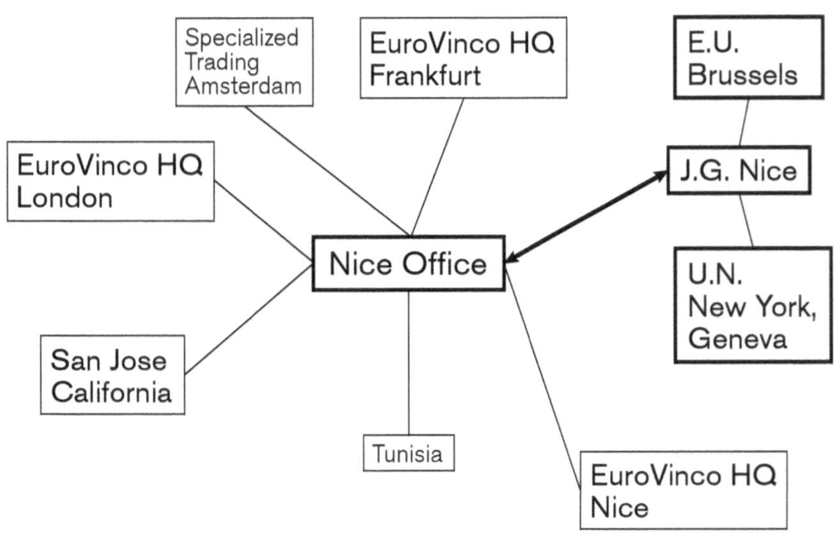

While the Department in Amsterdam has now been closed, the communications from the Nice office continue. Key relationships are in the form of frequent communications with:

1. *Individual persons within the three headquarter offices of the EuroVinco Corporation in London, Frankfurt and Nice. The individual persons work in the accounting departments of those respective offices and their names are now identified.*
2. *An office in San Jose, California. Two directors of the Unipac Corporation use that office.*
3. *A telephone number in Tunisia, although through additional research, it has been determined that telephone calls have been made to this number on a weekly basis over the past year. The nature of that office remains undetermined.*
4. *An unlisted number in Nice, France. Significant research was required, but this number has been first traced to GauLux Holding and more specifically to Jacques Gaubert. He makes frequent calls to numbers at the European Union in Brussels and to offices of the United Nations in Geneva and New York. I have not completed my research on these last two.*

The second methodology employed was to obtain the databases of the computers of the Nice Office. These contain records of accounting transactions and bank account numbers.

Telephone numbers, bank account numbers and amounts of holdings are listed in detail on the following page.

Justin turned to the following page to find these lists referred to in the diagram. Names of particular individuals' information had also been provided. Besides Jacques Gaubert, there were also the names of Randolph Sutter and Karl Schubach in the United States, Jean Roseau, the previous CEO of EuroVinco, a law firm in Monaco, and even the names of high ranking politicians in Brussels and officials in the United Nations. In addition he saw a list of bank account numbers in different countries with the amounts held in each account. The company or person who owned the accounts was also listed.

Most of the funds were held in a numbered account in Conquest Bank, a discrete private bank. It was not indicated who was behind this numbered account.

At the bottom of the page the accounts were totaled.

Jordi let out a whistle. "There is over five hundred million dollars in those accounts," he said.

"That's a lot of cash," said Laszlo. "Where do you think it came from?"

"According to the data in the diagram and the accounting entries," said Justin, "the money was being transferred from the three headquarters of EuroVinco, as well as the now non-existent Specialized Trading Department in Amsterdam. It looks to me like money was being taken from EuroVinco and moved into these accounts."

"How could they do it without anybody finding out?" asked Jordi.

"There are many ways," explained Justin. "The simplest way is to make false billings and then make payments based on those billings, but there are other methods. Sometimes money can be moved from one account to another and eventually moved into jointly owned entities. From there it's moved outside the company. That is what something like the Specialized Trading Department could be used for."

"But wouldn't auditors be able to recognize that this was going on?" Jordi asked.

"Not necessarily. If a valid purchase order exists, and if there have been proper approvals to pay the bill, then it's seen as a legitimate expense. Most companies have people who make approvals at different levels. The auditors are primarily looking to see that purchase orders exist and that bills are paid according to company approval policies. They are not there to determine if the business reasons for the payment are necessarily valid."

"So, someone was approving payments and then the money went into these accounts," Jordi stated.

"That's one hypothesis," Justin answered.

"Who were these people?" Jordi asked.

"Look at the diagram," Justin said. "There are linkages from this mysterious office in Nice to the three headquarters of EuroVinco in Nice, Frankfurt and London. Doby has listed the telephone numbers within each of those offices, as well as the names of the callers. He said that they are in the accounting departments in these headquarters. If my payment authorization theory is correct, and if they were getting instructions from this office in Nice, then we know who was doing it."

"Five hundred million dollars is a lot of money," said Laszlo.

"I don't know much about EuroVinco," said Justin, "but I do know that their profit position was always weak. It was often blamed on excessive taxes from European countries, but seeing this," he tapped the pages in front of him, "I think it's safe to say there were some hidden charges that the public didn't know about. True, European countries are excessive in their taxes, and that's one of the reasons that European companies have a difficult time to compete, but Doby may have come across something more."

Justin studied the papers he was holding, particularly the diagram. "This EuroVinco link with GauLux Holding and Jacques Gaubert is strange," he said.

"Isn't he a French politician?" Laszlo asked.

"Right," replied Justin, "and he has quite a reputation. He's constantly in the French news. He started out as a businessman, quite a successful one. He then bought one of the big football teams in France. While he is successful, he is also controversial. Often his business ventures, as well as the football team, face financial difficulties, even bankruptcy. Somehow he always seems to pull them out.

"About three years ago he sold many of his business investments and his money sort of disappeared, much to the displeasure of the French tax authorities. He was always under investigation by them. He is a very charismatic person and well liked by many people, despite allegations that he has strong connections with the French Mafia. Based on his popularity, he ran for office in the French government and won. He also holds a place in the European parliament."

"How about GauLux Holding?" asked Laszlo, glancing back over the diagram in Justin's hands. "Why does Doby mention it in the report?"

"Charles Graves mentioned them to me when we were discussing the audit in Amsterdam. GauLux Holding was one of the biggest shareholders in the EuroVinco Corporation. Jacques Gaubert founded GauLux and he continues to be the majority shareholder."

"Who are the other shareholders?" Dora asked.

"I'm not sure."

"Why would Gaubert be talking so much with this office in Nice?" asked Laszlo. "Can you think of any connections?"

"Only that Gaubert is a shareholder and they were using that office to handle some kind of communications with EuroVinco. It's the accounting transactions that make everything suspect."

Laszlo sat there quietly, reflecting on the information and then he said, "From an airplane crash to Tunisia to a holding company."

Jordi finished his thought, "A strange connection."

Justin said, "I was thinking the same thing." He looked out the window, also thinking of other things. Softly, he said. "Gloria and Chantal. We need to find them."

"And find out how they fit into this," said Laszlo.

"From the diagram and the information in that report," Jordi said, "it looks like there are two important sources of information right here in Nice. I think we should start here."

Next to Justin, Sophie began to squirm. She had done considerably well for having been awakened in the middle of the night, flown across the Mediterranean, and kept in a parked van while adults talked. Just as he turned to comfort her, Dora patted Sophie on the back. "It's alright honey. We'll find a place to stay pretty soon."

"We need to find a hotel so that Dora and Sophie can rest," Jordi said.

"I have another idea," offered Justin. "Wait here."

Justin walked across the street from where the minivan was parked and walked into an office of the *Agence Immobilaire, Maison de Vacances.*

A short time later he came out carrying a set of keys in one hand and a map in the other. As he pulled the van door shut behind him, he held out a set of keys. " I rented a large vacation house for a week. It will be less expensive than a hotel and will suit our needs much better." He handed Laszlo a simple brochure.

"A vacation house?" Laszlo questioned.

"Yes, Nice and the towns in the Cote d'Azur have thousands of apartments and houses that are rented to vacationers, mostly in July and August, just like Llanca. During the rest of the year most of them are empty, and they can be rented for off-season prices. I negotiated a good one that will give us a place to set up a base."

Laszlo looked down at the brochure. The house Justin had rented for them had eight bedrooms, came fully furnished, included sheets and towels, and featured an indoor jacuzzi.

A vacation house without the vacation.

CHAPTER 20

That afternoon, Jordi sat alone in the minivan, pretending to read a newspaper.

He had found a parking lot near a department store with an abundance of customer traffic. Here the van did not raise any suspicion. If anyone asked, he was waiting for his wife. But he kept eyes on the entrance of an office about half a block down the street. It was a two-story building, quite modern and resembling the structures surrounding it.

He guessed that there might be around ten rooms inside, judging from the size of the building and the number of windows that were visible from the outside.

His task was to watch the office and assess its level of activity based on the number of people coming or going. He had been sitting there for two hours. It was now three-thirty and so far only one person had entered the office. He missed the lunch break, which would have given a better idea of how many people worked there.

Justin and he had agreed that if Jordi was going to keep constant surveillance on this building, it would help to have backup. Sanchez and Pascual were already on their way. Jordi expected them around five o'clock. Jordi decided they should work in shifts so that the office would be under surveillance around the clock.

With the two women being held, they would need to work fast. Jordi hoped the women were here in Nice.

Justin had recommended that Grady stay at the house to guard Habib who now sat handcuffed to one of the beds. "After my experience in that stupid Spanish town," Grady had said, "I don't want to get out there on my own with all them Frenchies." He spoke no French and had already established a unique working relationship with Habib. He seemed the logical choice to stay.

Jordi had the feeling that Grady would soon drive Habib *loco*.

Laszlo was assigned to survey the home of Jacques Gaubert. If Gaubert was a wealthy businessman he likely had ample security surrounding his estate. Laszlo knew his way around security. He also had a little Tunisian backup in his coat pockets.

Justin chose to keep an eye on Dora and Sophie, but would coordinate between Jordi and Laszlo. Every few hours he would make the rounds to visit them at their lookout posts.

Jordi observed a man leaving the office. He was of small to medium height, had dark hair, wore a business suit, and had a noticeably large nose. Jordi had to make a decision. Either follow the man, or stay where he was until Sanchez and Pascual arrived.

⋆ ⋆ ⋆

Justin went back to the rented house after spending an hour with Laszlo. No movement at Gaubert's place. He entered the house, walked down the hall, and peeked into one of the bedrooms where he heard Grady talking. Grady was sitting on one of the beds, Habib handcuffed to the other bed frame.

"Habib, you have to be careful not to get yourself in with the wrong people. It'll get you into bad trouble every time. Now when I was a detective back in L.A., I saw plenty of young teenagers getting in with the wrong gangs. Few of them ever got out. That's what you're doing. Just like a teenager gone astray you have got yourself in with the wrong people, and look where it's gotten you."

Grady sighed. "We'll probably turn you over to the police here in France and you will get a long prison sentence. If we turn you over to the French police, you can count on it that they'll be way too soft on someone like you. Some centuries ago they would have cut off your head, and it would have rolled down the street. It's unfortunate that they don't do that anymore.

"Now-a-days, someone like you is put away in one of them dirty, rat infested prisons, where you'll rot away for the rest of your life, both hands chained to a stone wall. Think of the movie about the Count of Monte Cristo, how he spent his life there in the stink and the slime. He got out. You won't. Most of the French prisons were built around three hundred years ago. Now they stuff twenty people in a cell that was originally designed for one. Can you imagine what it will be like to be in there with a bunch of Frenchmen?" Grady shuddered at this. Habib just sat there, wide-eyed in fascination and horror—both more of Grady than of anything he was telling Habib.

Grady went on, "They don't take baths and they don't use deodorant. And remember, they hate rag-heads like you. You don't know what they'll do to you. I can only imagine. Habib, it's just too bad you made the wrong choices. Any respectable Texan knows you have to stand by your choices. You did a bad thing. Then again, maybe we won't turn you over to the police. Do you remember those guys back at that house in Tunisia late last night? That's what we might do with you. You deserve to get killed one shot at a time. First your toes, then your knees, then your you-know-what. If they let me, I'll do it real slow."

Habib swallowed.

Justin thought Laszlo and Jordi were right. Lea Habib with Grady was the worst punishment of all.

Justin continued down the hall and then went up to the bedroom where Dora and Sophie were staying. He saw Sophie sound asleep on a bed, her toddler face looking innocent in the bliss of sleep. How much she looked like Chantal. How much he had missed them both. Missed being with his little girl, reading books to her, watching her grow up. He had been wrong to spend so much time traveling for business, and he knew that he now had an opportunity to change all of that. He thought of Chantal and all that she had been through.

Then he thought of Gloria. His whole body ached to know if she too was alright. He had so recently held her in his arms. She had to still be alive. He clenched his fist so hard that a fingernail pierced his palm, despite its being cut close to the skin.

★ ★ ★

Downstairs in the kitchen, he found Dora making tea. He remembered what she had said coming off the airplane. He pulled up a chair at the table.

She took a long look at his haggard face. "You look exhausted. Did you get some rest?"

"Maybe an hour," he replied. "How about you?"

"Some," she paused, "enough." She pulled down another mug from the cabinet. "I've had such a hard time sleeping since the day we arrived at that compound. I actually dread going to sleep."

As Dora poured, her hand shook, and tea spilled onto the table. She put down the pot and wiped the spill. "I have nightmares," she began again, picking up the pot, "nightmares of terrorists, of shootings, of being tortured. I can't seem to shake them." As if on cue, her hand began to shake again, and Justin reached for the pot. She released it without resistance and seated herself across from him.

"They're haunting me," Dora continued, in a monotone. "For a whole year I woke up in a sweat. Completely drenched. Sometimes I would wake up so terrified, I would find myself looking left and right, in search of my tormentors. But waking up was also a nightmare because my dreams resembled reality. It has been dreadful—one continuous nightmare, day and night." She looked at Justin, her eyes wide with a fear she could not let go of.

Justin took a sip of his tea and pushed one of the mugs toward Dora. He sat in silence, waiting for her to continue.

She said, "Justin, there's something you need to know... about Gloria... but I don't know how to say it. Not now." She shook her head and walked out of the room.

CHAPTER 21

Three cars had driven up to the gate in the past ten minutes, and each time the security guard had gone out to see who was in the car. Only after checking passengers would he open the gate. When a car approached the house, a man came out and shook hands with the people, smiling. The man was Jacques Gaubert.

During the day Laszlo had done some research. He had found a cyber café and he looked up Jacques Gaubert, and he had printed out pictures. Laszlo was becoming convinced that he needed to get a smart phone or a Tablet that would access the internet. He knew that many of his methods were old-school. He would ask Doby to advise on the best solution.

A taxi arrived at the gate and was checked by the security guard. It then rounded the long driveway to the front of the house. A man got out and Laszlo got a good look at him. Late sixties, broad in the shoulders, gray on top, had an air of confidence about him. As Gaubert came out to greet the man, Laszlo got the impression they were meeting for the first time.

From his vantage point on a hillside in the midst of some pine trees, Laszlo had a view of both the gate as well as the front door of the house. Gaubert's mansion was situated on a hilltop, his estate overlooking the Mediterranean. The entrance, a metal gate attached to stone pillars, was lined with twenty meters of concrete and stone fence on either side. The rest of the property was surrounded by a metal fence about three meters high, with a strip of razor wire at the top. Surveillance cameras were mounted to several fence posts. The security guard worked from a small construct next to the gate, with several monitors in front of him.

Gaining direct access to the house would be difficult. He was not certain about the best plan of action. But he couldn't think in exhaustion. He headed back to the rented house.

★ ★ ★

For two minutes, Justin forgot everything. The jacuzzi proved more soothing than he had thought. His tense muscles relaxed, and his shoulders slowly released the weights they had carried for days. He tilted his head back and felt the bubbles teasing his neck. He vaguely wondered what it was that Dora had wanted to say to him in private.

He had wanted to ask when he sat down to tea, but was now glad he had chosen not to. He would wait for a better time.

"Is falling asleep in a hot tub a popular practice in America?"

Justin jerked awake at the sound of Laszlo's voice.

"What?" Justin asked, looking around. He stretched his arms out around the rim of the tub and blinked his eyes in an effort to wake himself. He noticed the tiny wrinkles on his fingertips and began to climb out of the tub. "You should give it a try," he said to Laszlo. "It's quite soothing."

"I can see that," Laszlo replied, "but I think I need to sleep first. I prefer a bed myself."

Laszlo disappeared into the hallway and up the stairs. Justin dried off, dressed, and headed for the kitchen.

He reached into the cupboard, took a glass and filled it with water from the tap. Standing at the sink, he drained one glass, then another. As he filled his third, Dora entered the kitchen, pulling the door shut behind her.

"Is Sophie still upstairs?" he asked.

"Yes," said Dora. "She is still asleep, poor child. It seems to be catching, though. I saw Laszlo heading into his room just as I was leaving mine. He looked utterly exhausted."

Justin placed the glass in the sink and, leaning against the counter, turned toward Dora, waiting. Eventually, he opened his mouth to speak, but she spoke first, her attention fixed on the horizon behind him through the window.

"The first two weeks of our captivity in Tunisia was a living hell. We had been gassed on the plane. Pete was the first one to come out of it, and he told me what happened. He had awakened shortly after the plane was on the ground, when they were escorting us off the airplane. They already had him tied and his mouth taped, but he saw some of what happened.

"The leader of the group that day was a man named Yass, an evil man, about as evil as they come."

Justin remembered the name. It was the same name mentioned by Habib.

Dora continued, her tone still calm. "Yass was the one who handled our transfer to the house and gave all the instructions to the men who were keeping us. Immediately upon our arrival in Tunisia, Pete saw that Yass was interested in Chantal. A utility van and a car were waiting near the tarmac. We were loaded inside. They didn't tie Sophie's hands. A two-year old doesn't pose much of a threat, I guess." Her voice had hardened.

"During the trip from the airport to the house, the rest of us woke up. It was an uncomfortable ride and we were terrified. We were on the metal floor of the van. It was dirty and dusty. We were all petrified, not knowing what they planned to do to us.

"The van eventually stopped. We were moved into the house—all into one bedroom where we stayed for two weeks. They fed us in the bedroom. We had to ask permission to go to the bathroom down the hall, where we were escorted individually.

"Yass was crazy. The other men were afraid of him. While he was there, he did all the setup, arranging guards, routines, making the rules that we had to live by. He spoke, most of the time, in Arabic and French, but often in English when he wanted us to understand what he was saying. Through the entire two weeks he kept ranting and raving about the right of believers to take the infidels, and he kept looking at Chantal the entire time."

Justin's mouth had gone dry, despite the three glasses of water.

"Often he would come into the bedroom and start lecturing to us about holy wars and death to infidels. He would leer at Chantal, telling her she should be his concubine. He had a divine right to take her, he believed. Pete tried to protect Chantal, yelling back at Yass when he came to threaten.

"We had been there about two weeks. One evening, Chantal was allowed to go to the bathroom, and we heard scuffling sounds. She started to scream. Pete banged on the door of our room, but of course it was locked."

Dora now turned to Justin, looking for the right words. But there were none. She could see in Justin's eyes that he knew.

"Justin, Yass took Chantal into one of the rooms and… and violated her. We could hear noises through several walls." She could not go on.

Justin turned to the sink, heaving for breath. He grabbed the glass and hurled it against the wall. It shattered on impact like his soul, bits of glass flying everywhere.

★ ★ ★

A long while later, they sat next to each other at the kitchen table, Justin's head in his arms. Dora squeezed his shoulder and persuaded him to sit up. He sprawled back in his chair, his entire being riddled with grief. She hated to add to it, but went on. "After twenty or thirty minutes Chantal was brought back to our room. She went to the bed, curled up in a ball, and cried. Pete and I tried to comfort her, but she cried all night. Her nerves were shattered. It was like she was broken, destroyed. It was one of the worst nights of my life. We all took it very hard, but especially Pete. He was enraged, and we didn't know if or when it would happen again. It did not happen again, thank God. Yass left the next day.

"We were all taken down to the living room where Yass gave final instructions before leaving. When Chantal saw him she started to cry, but he yelled at her, telling her to shut up, that it had been her duty. Pete became so angry that he attacked Yass. He grabbed him by the neck and started to choke him, but there were too many men and Pete was overpowered. Just after that fight Pete had his first heart attack. He was greatly weakened."

Justin's expression remained blank. He stared past her at the bare white wall. She took a deep breath and continued.

"That day Yass left and we never saw him again. But he left instructions with the other men to not touch Chantal. He said that she belonged to him, that she was his concubine. None of the other men ever came close to her. They were terrified of Yass, not knowing when he would come back again. He never did, but we always had the fear that he would show up one day and start again.

"After Yass left, Chantal went through weeks of torment. I was constantly with her. When she wasn't having nightmares, she was numb and withdrawn. At the same time Pete's heart was weakened. It was a terrible strain for him—first the physical fight with Yass and then the emotional torment. He experienced heart pain every few days. We kept asking for a doctor, but they did nothing. Pete died about three weeks later." Her voice decreased to a whisper. "It was the saddest day of my life.

"We wrapped him in a sheet and buried him outside the walls of the compound, up on the top of a hill overlooking the sea. It was the only time we were allowed to leave the compound, and armed guards were there the whole time. Chantal said a prayer. It was all we could do. I want someone to go back there and dig up his body. I want him to rest in California, to get him out of that evil place."

Justin looked at her, grief for so many lives wrapping his words. "Dora, I am so sorry."

She looked at him again and placed her hand on his. "There is one more thing."

Justin felt like he was the one drowning in that whale tank of his dreams. More water kept deluging him. He could barely take in air.

"After six or eight weeks Chantal began to feel dizzy, nauseated. She was pregnant."

Pregnant. His emotions shut down, but he managed to say, "Go on."

"At first she was disgusted and talked about killing the baby within her. But Sophie was there and Chantal knew she had to be careful. It was her love of you and her love of Sophie that kept her going through that time. After a couple of months I began to see a change in her. She prayed often and came to accept the life inside her.

"Just about this time, our guards figured out that she was pregnant. They didn't want the complication of having an infant around the place, so they brought in a doctor."

This seemed to be harder for Dora to tell than the rest. She started to cry. "She bled for several weeks after that, and her depression was worse than just after the rape."

In a dangerous monotone, Justin said, "If I ever meet this Yass, I will kill him." Something inside had snapped from emotion to rationale. He asked, "How was she when you last saw her yesterday in Tunisia?"

"She was very surprised that they said they were taking her away. Just like that. They received a telephone call, and suddenly they were in the room, tying her hands behind her. Three men got in the car with her and off they went. She was so scared. So very scared."

Justin remembered seeing the car driving away from the compound. If he had only known that Chantal was in that car…he had been so close to her and now she was gone.

"Justin, there is one other thing. As she was being taken away, she turned to me and said, 'If you ever see Justin, tell him I love him very much.' Justin, you need to know that the one thing that kept her going during all that time in Tunisia was the hope of being together with you again."

CHAPTER 22

The security guard at the gate waved Sam Oliver's taxi driver forward, and they entered the grounds of Jacques Gaubert's private residence. Sam was beginning to get peopled-out, and he wondered how long this dinner party would last. This was France, after all.

He had made it safely to Nice, had enjoyed a casual Sunday walking around the town, and on Monday had begun the day with a tour of the EuroVinco Nice Headquarters. Three hundred people worked inside that sizeable glass and metal structure.

Again, the same problem had come up. They were short of cash.

Having given yet another speech, sat through several further hours of presentations, and shaken the hands of hundreds, the last thing Sam wanted to do this evening was go out to dinner. He wished Paul Kent were here to do the honors, but Paul planned to fly in during the middle of the week for the meeting with EuroVinco's top managers on Thursday and Friday.

He had managed to call Margaret, who had made it safely back to California. Their granddaughter had called from Cambridge and was looking forward to seeing Sam next weekend. When Margaret asked about his past several days, Sam could not help but vent his frustrations regarding EuroVinco's financial situation. He told her he planned to discuss this with Paul. They had to consider ways to reduce corporate overheads.

Sam sighed. This evening he had been invited to dinner at the home of Jacques Gaubert to meet some previous shareholders of EuroVinco, who were now new shareholders in Unipac. GauLux Holding had been the major shareholder of EuroVinco, and now it held a small percent in Unipac, whose share price had gone up a few dollars since the merger was completed. The six percent of Unipac held by GauLux Holding was now worth much more than the forty percent of EuroVinco it previously held.

Sam paid the taxi, which had stopped on the circular drive in front of Gaubert's large, modern house. A man in his late forties bounded through the front door with energy and a big white smile, opening Sam's door.

Sam knew a bit about Jacques Gaubert, and one of the managers in the office that afternoon had taken the time to give him more details about the businessman and politician. Jacques Gaubert was one of the shareholders in GauLux Holding and seemed to be one of the key decision makers within that holding company. Sam felt it was important to get to know him. With Jacques Gaubert's political connections in Europe, he would undoubtedly be helpful for Unipac in the future.

Gaubert extended his hand. "Hello, Mr. Oliver. I am Jacques Gaubert. Welcome to my home. It's a great pleasure to have you here."

Sam returned the greeting and said, "Thank you Mr. Gaubert. It's an honor for me to be here."

They ascended the steps. At the door, Gaubert stood to the side to allow Sam first entry. Then he gave a small bow. *Don't get this treatment in the States,* Sam thought, straightening his tie.

Sam entered an immense entrance hall, with fine white marble floors and massive, modern paintings on the walls. He recognized a couple of Picassos and a Cézanne, and many more he could not identify. They came to another room, just as large and elegantly furnished. Here stood a table set to perfection with fine porcelain, crystal goblets and polished heirloom silver. Across in one corner were four men, comfortably seated on a matching set of pale yellow armchairs. Near them waited a wooden coffee table covered in glasses of sherry and Port. They all stood when Sam and Gaubert entered the room.

"Mr. Oliver, please let me introduce you to four gentlemen who are also joining us for dinner. This is Lionel Banneret, Jean-Marie de Pineau, Jean-Paul Féret and Claude Jaccoud."

"It's nice to meet you," said Sam.

"Our pleasure," said Lionel Banneret.

Jacques Gaubert asked, "Would you like something to drink?"

"Yes, thank you. I see you have some Port there."

Gaubert poured a glass of Port and handed it to Sam. "Please have a seat gentlemen," he said. "We will begin the meal in ten or fifteen minutes, if you don't mind."

Gaubert continued, "Mr. Oliver, I thought you might enjoy meeting some people who have been supporting EuroVinco and who can be of assistance to Unipac. Mr. De Pineau is a representative in the French parliament and also in the European Parliament. He has been most helpful in accelerating European Union approval of the merger between Unipac and EuroVinco. Mr. Féret and Mr. Jaccoud are lawyers who have a financial management company in Monaco. They handle the legal advice for GauLux Holding, particularly concerning legal structures, and they have done legal consulting for EuroVinco in the past. Their expertise might be drawn upon for any complex international legal and structural issues.

"Mr. Banneret is the Director of the United Nations Conference on Trade Assistance. It is an organization that helps developing countries to develop their export trade, and they also work closely with the World Trade Organization. Mr. Banneret is a long-time friend and associate of mine and he has been helpful through his excellent political connections."

Banneret smiled and shook Sam's hand.

A politician, two lawyers and a director in the UN. Sam thought he might be in for an interesting evening. "What do you gentlemen think about the merger of Unipac and EuroVinco?" he asked.

"As Jacques mentioned, I was very supportive of it at the EU," responded De Pineau. "I direct the committee that reviews these kinds of things and we managed to have it approved in record time. Who says that bureaucrats move slowly?" Several of the gentleman chuckled.

Sam smiled. "Thank you so much for doing that. We thought the entire thing would take about a year and were so surprised when both the United States Securities Exchange Commission and the European Union approved it so quickly. It was very helpful."

Jean-Paul Féret asked, "I understand you have been traveling around visiting the different offices of EuroVinco. How has that been?"

"It's been exciting," said Sam, "and it's difficult to excite an old hand like me. Everywhere I go the people seem competent and optimistic."

"Have you found any problems during your visit, anything that will need to be changed?"

Sam knew he must be diplomatic. These were not people working directly in EuroVinco, but Gaubert was connected with GauLux Holding, a good-sized shareholder.

Sam said, "In running businesses there are always things that need to be changed. But I'm not the guy who has to do the changing anymore. That's the responsibility of Paul Kent and the rest of the management team. They will be deciding what to do."

"But you have made this trip, and you must have some recommendations," said Claude Jaccoud.

"Well, I guess what surprises me, or concerns me, is EuroVinco's profit levels. They are below that of Unipac in the U.S. That is something we should look into."

"I hope it doesn't mean dismissing employees," said Lionel Banneret, swirling the dark garnet liquid in his glass. "Politicians in Europe don't like that."

"No, I don't think so. Unipac likes to keep its people. What I'm talking about is looking into some of the expenses. We should try and get a better handle on that."

"Maybe it has to do with tax structures," suggested Gaubert. "In Europe we have comple tax systems and there are many social costs added to the taxes. As politicians with a business orientation, Mr. Banneret, Mr. De Pineau and myself are very much aware that something needs to be done here. We are doing our best at both the French and European levels to change things."

"If that's the problem, then we just have to live with it," said Sam. "We should look for any legal way to minimize our tax burden." But after seeing so many EuroVinco operations around Europe he wondered if taxes were really the problem. The expenses were coming from somewhere else.

While the other guests launched into general lament for their tax system, Gaubert turned to Sam and asked if he had time to meet with him tomorrow.

Sam had planned on a day off before meeting Paul Kent on Wednesday. He said, "Why don't we meet at my hotel for their continental breakfast?"

"That would be fine…" Gaubert agreed, starting to say something else.

Just then a waiter appeared and informed the host that the dinner was ready. The men moved to the dining table and sat down to an eight-course meal with multiple bottles of Gaubert's own vintage.

Sam twisted the thick, fat, silver handle of his butter knife, wondering. The palace of a house, priceless art, gourmet food. Where did Gaubert get his wealth? And how did these other men—so anxious to approve the merger with speed—fit into GauLux Holding?

In Sam's experience, politicians never did anything without a personal motive.

CHAPTER 23

The telephone rang and *Le Patron* answered, "What is it?" He looked at his watch. It was eight o'clock in the morning.

"You told me to call you when we found the hacker," Ziginiglou answered.

"I told you to call me when you found out what he was after. Have you?"

"Well no, not exactly," Ziginiglou said.

"What did you find out?"

"They found where he lives and they destroyed all the computer equipment."

"They destroyed his equipment?"

"Yes."

"And now do they have him?"

"No."

"Idiots!" *Le Patron* blurted out.

Blood. Whenever *Le Patron* was pissed at him, Ziginiglou couldn't get Spiros's blood out of his mind.

Ziginiglou knew they had failed. "Well, they stopped his operation. Isn't that good?"

"How do you know he doesn't have a backup somewhere offsite?"

"We don't know."

"Ziginiglou. You had better get this one right. Instruct our two gentlemen from Lyon to extract information from this hacker. Make sure they get all the data, including backups. And more important, find out why he wanted that data. Then eliminate him. Do you understand me? Clearly, our two computer engineers are not doing their jobs. How did they let him through their firewall?" He paused as if considering. "Maybe we don't need them and maybe we don't need you."

"Yes, sir." Ziginiglou's knees were shaking.

"Then do it," *Le Patron* commanded.

"There is one other thing," Ziginiglou said. "You know the house where the phone is tapped in Santa Cruz, California? The man called his wife last night, and our people sent a recording today. It seems as though the man has some misgivings about the company here in Europe. He is going to ask his managers to make a thorough investigation of the different accounting departments of the company.

It seems he suspects something."

"Sam Oliver? Misgivings about EuroVinco?"

"Yes."

The line stayed quiet for a moment and then *Le Patron* said, "We have made considerable progress. It is time to remove him, according to plan."

"Do you know where he is?" asked Ziginiglou.

"Yes, he is in Nice."

"Do you want me to arrange anything?"

"No. Leave this one to me. I want to make sure it's done right."

★ ★ ★

The next morning, Gaubert got into a black car waiting in front of his house and drove toward the front security gate. As it started to open, Laszlo was already halfway down the backside of the hill where he had been watching from behind the pine tree.

His rented motorcycle was parked behind bushes. He slapped on the crash helmet, turned the key for the electrical starter and heard the engine sputter. Three attempts and precious seconds later, he sped around a curve and came to a stop as Gaubert curved out in front of him.

Laszlo waited, then began to follow from some distance behind. Gaubert drove fast into the center of Nice, but Laszlo could easily maneuver through the traffic with the motorcycle. Eventually Gaubert drove up to Le Meredien on the *Promenade des Anglais,* facing out to the sea. He parked his car in the middle of the hotel driveway and went inside. A few moments later one of the hotel staff came out and drove the car away.

Laszlo's objective today was to track Gaubert and identify people he had contact with. He did not have much to go on and hoped that whomever the Frenchman was meeting here would give him some kind of lead.

The previous evening at the rented house they had held a debriefing. Laszlo really hadn't found out much through his observations and neither had Jordi. Jordi's two friends, Sanchez and Pascual, had now arrived and they would continue to work with Jordi in staking out the Nice office. At least they had identified their two targets—the office and Gaubert—but neither had led to any substantial information.

Justin had looked ill this morning. That's what you get for sleeping too long in a hot tub. Laszlo started to smile, but the seriousness of the situation kept his mouth taut.

Everyone decided that Grady would continue to stay with Habib. It was too early to turn him over to the police who might inform the press, and then the kidnappers would know that they were in Nice, etc.

Things were going nowhere fast. And with the two women still held captive, they could not afford that.

Laszlo parked the motorcycle half a block away from the hotel. He walked back and waited outside for a few minutes. He was getting ready to go inside the hotel to keep Gaubert in his line of vision when he noticed Gaubert leaving the hotel with another man.

The man looked familiar. Laszlo thought for a moment and then remembered the face. It was one of the men who had visited Gaubert's home the night before, the same one who had arrived by taxi.

Something caught Laszlo's attention. A tall, thin man, who had been leaning against a building across the street, headed over to the hotel side. When Gaubert emerged from the hotel with the second man, the thin man began to follow them. Laszlo remained some distance behind them, keeping one eye on the thin man and one eye on Gaubert.

Here we go again, he thought.

⋆ ⋆ ⋆

"If you live in Nice you have to get used to this," said Jacques Gaubert, gesturing to the blue skies and mild, balmy air that Sam had just commented on. "We have good weather into November and sometimes even into December. It gets cold for a couple of months but warms up again in March. The Cote d'Azur has a very different climate from the rest of France."

"You're lucky. Southern California has a similar climate. I live in Santa Cruz, in the northern part of the state. We often have sunshine, but we also get a lot of rain and fog. At least it keeps the forests green," said Sam Oliver.

To enjoy the warm autumn, Gaubert had suggested they sit at an outside café for coffee and a croissant, though, he apologized, something had come up early this morning and he would only be able to chat for a quarter of an hour.

A block away, they came to a plaza with a couple of dozen outside tables, many of them empty. Some breakfasters looked up, recognizing

Gaubert as they chose a table.

Gaubert immediately ordered coffee for both of them. When the waiter left, Sam said, "I just want to thank you again for last night. It was an enjoyable evening and the food was mighty fine. I found your other guests to be very interesting, and I learned a lot about European business."

"It was my pleasure," said Gaubert, letting that pleasure fade a bit from his face as he lowered his voice. "I wanted to ask you something privately. "

"Fire away," Sam said, smiling.

The waiter returned with coffee and croissants. As he placed the cream on the table, a tall blond man sat down at a table nearby and opened a German newspaper.

"You don't have to answer it right now," Gaubert continued. "Again, I do apologize that I have a meeting in a few minutes on the other side of Nice. I hope I am not rude by running away too quickly."

"That's fine," said Sam. "I can just stay here and enjoy the sunshine. I'll go find an English newspaper and have a slow morning. We hardly have anything like this where I live—places where people can sit outside and watch people go by. I want to make the most of it."

"Just a moment," Gaubert said as he signaled the waiter.

The waiter came by, Gaubert said something to him in French, and the waiter went inside. A minute later he came back with a copy of the *Wall Street Journal*. Gaubert thanked him and then handed the newspaper to Sam.

"That was fast," Sam said.

"They usually have copies of newspapers in several languages. Now you can sit here and take your time like a true Frenchman."

Sam smiled and said, "Thank you. Now, I know you have to go, but what is your question?"

"As I said, it's something we can discuss at a later point, but now that EuroVinco and Unipac are merged, I am wondering how the European side of things will be represented within Unipac? As you know, business is quite different over here and if we are going to capitalize on the true synergies between the two companies, then we should make sure that the Europeans have some representation within management decision making. It's just something to think about."

"Yes, it is something we need to think through. Paul Kent will be here tomorrow and there's a management meeting on Thursday and Friday. Paul asked me to attend and present my impressions of

EuroVinco, which by the way, were quite positive."

"I am so glad you are thinking about this," said Gaubert. He scooted his chair backward, away from the table. "Again, I do apologize for being rude to you like this," he said, rising from the table.

"It's not a problem," Sam said. "I will enjoy myself here." He lifted the newspaper off the table with his left hand and extended his right to Gaubert.

They shook hands and Gaubert left. Sam unfolded the paper, looked around at the other customers, and took another sip of his coffee.

He was well into an article about management changes in a familiar U.S. electronics company when he heard a disturbance coming from within the restaurant. Seconds later, a medium sized thin man came running out of the restaurant with a stocking cap over his head, a brown paper bag in one hand and a gun in the other.

Sam's heart beat quickly. A robbery.

One of the waiters rushed to the door of the restaurant and yelled something at the robber, who turned around and shot his gun in response, hitting the window of the restaurant. It shattered to the ground in a spray of shards.

The couple at the next table ducked down. In an instant, Sam saw that the man turned to point the gun at him. Stunned, Sam instinctively dove beneath his own table. The gunman fired, and Sam could feel the impact of the bullet on the table. He glanced behind him to see the large blond man seated at the nearby table stand up, reach beneath his coat and pull out a pistol. Sam was between the blond man and the robber and assumed the worst—that the blond man's gun was also being pointed at him. The tablecloth blocked his view.

Another shot. Sam braced himself, but felt no bullet. He looked up in time to see the thief fall backward onto the concrete.

The blond man took a couple of steps toward Sam, grabbed him by the arm and said, "Get out of here. Now."

CHAPTER 24

They ran two blocks and Laszlo flagged down a taxi. The two of them jumped in and Laszlo directed the cab driver using the few words of French that he knew. "Go left, right, left, straight."

After about five kilometers, Laszlo finally said, "Stop." He paid the driver and they got out on the street of an upscale if faintly vacant neighborhood. Standing in front of a shuttered vacation house, Sam turned to Laszlo and asked, "Who are you? And why did you save my life?"

"First tell me who you are. That might give an indication of why they were trying to shoot you," Laszlo said.

"I am Sam Oliver, chairman of the board of Unipac, now who are you?"

The name rang a bell in Laszlo's memory, and he knew of Unipac because of Collins's audit. Ignoring Sam's repeated question, Laszlo said, "I think there is someone who would like to talk with you. You may have helpful information for each other. It's important."

"How do I know this isn't some trick? That those bullets back there were even real?"

"They were real," Laszlo said, his tone dispelling any doubt. "And that man was sent to kill you. He followed you from your hotel, I don't know why. But you may be able to help us find some people who have been abducted. Please come. We will do you no harm."

Sam was reluctant, but finally gave in. "I'll hear what you have to say."

They walked three blocks to the rented house and Laszlo knocked on the door.

Justin answered and saw Sam standing before him. "You're Sam Oliver," he said. He knew the face from pictures in the newspapers and on television, and he had once seen him give a speech to a large audience at a trade show in the San Francisco Bay Area.

"Yes, I am Sam Oliver. And who are you?"

"My name is Justin Collins." Sam remembered the name. The manager of the EuroVinco factory in Grenoble had mentioned it to him.

"Please come in," Justin said.

Justin led Sam into the kitchen where Dora was dunking a tea ball into a pot of boiled water. Sam recognized her immediately. "Dora. Dora Vine?"

At seeing Sam, Dora dropped the ball into the pot and brought her hand to her mouth. A second later, tears ran over her fingers.

"I can't believe it," said Sam. "What's going on?"

"That might be difficult to explain," replied Justin.

★ ★ ★

An hour later, Sam put down his cold tea and repeated, "This is all too much to believe. Do you have any evidence?" He had heard the full story—crash, kidnapping, conspiracy and all.

"Some," Justin said. He shifted uncomfortably in his chair. "We're not sure how sound it is. The most interesting piece of information we have is a report done by a," he paused to find the right words, "by a market research expert. It may even be of interest to you—EurcVinco is mentioned in the report."

Justin went to a cupboard, retrieved a few sheets of paper, and handed them to Sam. "Why don't you read through it and tell us if there is anything that jumps out at you?"

After several minutes, Sam laid the pages down and said, "I won't comment on the legality of his methodology, but the informazion is remarkable. The second page with all the accounting information may explain one of the questions I've been asking throughout this current business trip. In fact, I consider this report to be, for lack of a better word, explosive."

Sam got up from his chair and began pacing around the table, his hands behind his back. He explained that he had been making an introductory visit to Europe and how all of the EuroVinco entities were complaining about the high internal cost structures. Doby's report potentially provided an answer as to where the money was going.

Justin said, "That still doesn't tell us why Chantal and Gloria have been kidnapped, not to mention the fifteen months Dora, Chantal, and Sophie spent in captivity."

Dora whispered, "No, it doesn't."

Sam stopped pacing. "We need to take this to the police."

"I don't think so," replied Laszlo. "If the police are brought into this, then the word could get out to the kidnappers. We know for a fact that these are ruthless men. We need more time to explore this by ourselves, but we cannot just keep watching either. We need to take action soon."

Sam sat back down. For two hours they cross-referenced everything they could think of, looking for plausible alternatives. But in the end, the same questions remained. Why had someone tried to kill Sam? How was Jacques Gaubert implicated in this? What was the purpose of simulating the crash of the airplane and kidnapping the Vines? And most relevant for Justin, where were Chantal and Gloria being held and what did the kidnappers want from him?

Finally Justin said, "I think we need to get into that office in Nice. Someone there might have information about Chantal and Gloria."

Laszlo said, "I think you are right. That should be our starting point. Also, we need to continue to keep an eye on Gaubert. He seems to be playing a role in this, but we don't know what role." Laszlo rose from the table and went to the window. A few clouds had covered the sun and were rapidly moving eastward. "All we know is that someone was following Gaubert and Mr. Oliver from the hotel this morning, and it was the same person who tried to shoot Mr. Oliver." He turned to face them. "We need to be careful of Gaubert. He is a very powerful man in France. He probably has influence on the police here in Nice and he is known to have ties with the local Mafia."

"He sounds involved, doesn't he?" Justin stated, growing restless. He stood up to stretch his tired legs.

"Yes, so what should we do?" asked Laszlo.

"I suggest that Sam Oliver stays here for now. If they tried once, they will try again." Justin leaned forward, placing his hands firmly on the back of his chair. "We need to understand who they are and their intentions. Jordi and his team should continue to watch the office. Laszlo, can you continue to keep an eye on Gaubert?" Laszlo gave a small nod as Justin continued, "If the attempt to shoot Mr. Oliver was initiated by the office or by Jacques Gaubert, we should expect to see some unusual activity."

Laszlo turned to Sam Oliver and addressed him directly. "Mr. Oliver. You need to be extremely careful. The police will be investigating this morning's shooting at the café." He remembered his motorcycle. It was still in the vicinity of the hotel. "If the police are somehow connected to Jacques Gaubert, he will have inside information regarding you." His eyes made a quick sweep around the table. "In fact," he insisted, "we should all be careful."

"I'll gladly stay here," said Sam. "I would like to spend a bit of time with Dora."

A wiry man with a military style haircut came walking down the hall singing Willie Nelson's "No Place But Texas." It was Grady, and he was off-key.

"Who is he?" asked Sam.

"An insurance investigator," replied Laszlo and Justin at the same time.

CHAPTER 25

Justin grew tired of waiting. Managers were not taught to wait, they were taught to make decisions and then to act. If you waited you lost market share. But this was not business as he had known it.

He left the rented house to get some fresh air and decide what to do next. He walked through several streets, out toward the sea and down the promenade. He wondered if Jordi had found anything new.

Meeting Sam Oliver at the door had certainly been a new development.

He watched the palm tree shade shift with the breeze. It was highly likely that Gaubert was involved—but with the kidnapping of Chantal and Gloria too? A French politician, or any politician for that matter, would be ill-advised to get mixed up in something so illegal. Not that that had stopped "great" men of politics throughout history. And the report from Doby indicated a link.

What was that link?

They needed further proof. Laszlo was right—they could not go to the police. Especially since they were under Gaubert's thumb. He was a powerful man, and his reach extended beyond his reputation.

Then there was the thought he had not let himself focus on. Gloria and Chantal. His wives. Plural. Despite the recent emotional trauma involved, he found himself wondering…. He didn't have time to finish the thought. Something hard was rammed against his back and a voice said in French, "Don't turn around. This is a gun. Get in the van."

A white van came speeding up, a van that looked like thousands of others in France—a utility vehicle used by plumbers, carpenters, and every other kind of blue-collar business. The side door slid open and Justin stepped up into the bare space. The man with the gun said, "Lie, face down."

Justin immediately did what he was asked to do, the menacing gun now pressing against the back of his head. Quickly the man tied a blindfold across his eyes, tied his hands behind his back with a piece of rope, and put tape across his mouth. Justin tried to keep his hands apart, just enough to keep an operable space between his wrists. The man did his job with haste, and Justin could feel the slight slack.

★ ★ ★

After leaving the paved streets of the city and driving what felt like a kilometer on a gravel road, the van slowed to a stop. Justin could feel the pressure of the gun increasing along his spine.

"Get out," the gunman ordered. Justin tried to stand up, but with the blindfold and being bound, he banged his head on the brace above the van door, then tripped and fell on the rocks below. A sharp pain shot through his ankle.

"Get up," the man barked. Justin slowly pulled himself up. He felt the gun, solid in the middle of his back. "Move forward," the voice commanded. Justin started to walk forward, limping slightly.

The driver, or so Justin guessed, joined them and the two men led Justin across more gravel to a door. They held his head down as he entered. It must be old to have such a low lintel, Justin thought. A farmhouse? He had smelled the sour ripeness of vineyards outside, and inside the air was old and heavy.

The gunman pushed him down on a chair and said, "Don't move."

"Wait here," said one to the other. "I will go get the others."

* * *

A short time later, Justin heard a vehicle approaching. It came to a stop. At the sound of a door sliding open, the man with Justin went out. Justin now heard the footsteps of several people moving toward the building. "Walk straight ahead," the man instructed. "Move," he said firmly, several seconds later.

What sounded like a number of people entered the room. "Sit down," he heard the man say. It seemed the man was some distance away. "Sit down," he heard him repeat. Footsteps approached him.

Justin's blindfold was lifted off, and it took a moment for his eyes to adjust to the dim interior. He was in a dark room. Window frames, empty of glass panes, were shuttered against the light. He shook his head to clear it and noticed a dark stain on the hard-packed dirt floor at his feet.

Two men stood across the room, one with a gun in his hand. Next to the gunman sat two blindfolded women. Like him, their mouths were taped and their hands tied behind their backs.

While he could not clearly see their faces nor discern the color of their hair, he knew who they were. He tried to get up, but one of the men walked across the room and pushed him back in the chair while the other pointed the gun at him. Justin sat back down.

He knew that his only hope was to get his hands free. He began testing the strength of the rope. But his hands were big.

Justin's eyes gradually adjusted to the darkness, and he looked at Chantal and Gloria, every fiber in him aching to have the tape off his mouth and to speak to them, to tell them it would be all right.

But would it?

★ ★ ★

Justin was still twisting his wrists, attempting to loosen the rope when he heard yet another vehicle coming up the gravel road. The engine cut and a car door opened and shut. Footsteps stopped at the door, and a man entered the room. Justin had seen the round, glib face before. Many times before, in fact. It had been plastered on the front of Europe's newspapers regularly. Justin had seen it at prestigious business events. It even belonged to the same man who had donated his wine to the benefit jazz concert Justin and Chantal had attended in Paris.

The famous French businessman and politician Jacques Gaubert.

He was flashing his hollow, politician's smile. The smile of a salesman.

One of the men ripped the tape from Justin's mouth.

"What's going on?" Justin demanded. The two women stirred at the sound of his voice, trying to see through their blindfolds

"Silence," the gunman replied. *"C'est le Patron qui parle."*

"I have a right to know what's going on," Justin said with more force.

The gunman raised his gun and with a quick downward movement struck Justin on the side of the head. Justin saw a flash in his head like a lightning bolt and then he felt blood running down the side of his temple.

Gaubert laughed. "You are an impatient man, Mr. Collins, but I am so pleased to finally meet you."

Justin felt dizzy. "What do you want with us?"

"Ah, Mr. Collins, I so desire to discuss this topic with you, but let me first remark that you have been a problem for me, insignificant person though you are, you *have* been a thorn in my flesh. Today, we have an opportunity to take care of that thorn together. To turn it, shall we say, into a sword in my hand."

"Stop making speeches and get to the point," Justin growled.

"Pierre, teach Mr. Collins to address his superiors with respect," Gaubert said to the gunman.

The gunman stepped in front of Justin and punched him in the stomach. Justin doubled over, gasping for breath. One of the women made a muffled sound.

"Now, Mr. Collins. To answer your question, 'this,'" he gestured at everyone in the room and the circumstances they represented, "has to do with an important chain of events and the unfortunate fact that you kept looking into a certain airplane crash."

Justin interrupted, "You engineered that plane crash, didn't you? For some reason that has to do with Vine Industries, and Unipac and EuroTech. You murdered people, ruined lives."

"Well, Mr. Collins, I am amazed that you have discovered so much. You are a either a clever man or a lucky one." Gaubert paused, then added, "Of course, my assistants may be growing negligent—there are many pieces to the puzzle, and one has to constantly monitor the puzzle as one goes along, even change the shape of the puzzle as reality changes."

"Why did you kidnap my wife? The Vines? What use could you have had for them?" Justin shouted, shocked by Gaubert's casual indifference and weary of being the pawn in his game.

"Mr. Collins, use that business mind of yours." Gaubert came over and tapped his finger at Justin's temple.

Justin jerked away and said, "I will if you give me something to go on."

"Why do we do business?"

"I don't understand. You're asking stupid—"

"Why do we do business?" Gaubert asked, louder. "Money. Money is the only reason for business. This is nothing more than a business affair. One of my many business affairs."

"I still don't understand."

"I am here to make you a business proposal."

"What proposal?"

"You have an asset of mine that I want back."

"I don't have any asset of yours."

"Oh yes you do."

"What, then?"

"Dora Vine. I want her back."

CHAPTER 26

Dora Vine? The blow to Justin's head not only throbbed, it seemed to be affecting his hearing.

"There is a lot of money at play," Gaubert said to no one in particular, seeming to dream of what he could do with it were it in his hands. He returned to the present, looking Justin in the eye. "In this case, for instance, it makes sense for certain companies to come together. I, as a true professional, can see that. But leaders of such companies—leaders like Pete Vine, Sam Oliver—they are often not really thinking about the benefits available to the shareholders."

"What shareholders?" Justin asked, doubting now that any answer from this man would be an answer.

"That is a very simple question, Mr. Collins. Perhaps I have given you too much credit." Gaubert looked around the room as if he was addressing an audience and then said, "Even my friends Pierre and Serge know the answer to this. Don't you, my friends?"

The gunmen grunted an affirmation.

"That is right," Gaubert said. "I am a shareholder and like any shareholder I want the best return from the companies I own. For example, I am a majority shareholder in GauLux Holding. GauLux now owns six percent of Unipac, more in the future, and along with my partners we take the best strategy for the best return."

"And what is your strategy? Illegal takeovers?"

"Legal. Illegal." Gaubert smirked.

"So you do anything to remove the top managers, put in your own teams and then strip the assets of the company, don't you? That's what happened with EuroVinco, then Vine Industries and now Unipac."

"Sam Oliver and his team have had their time. Unipac needs new leadership, but that has nothing to do with you. We need to talk business."

"And that is?"

"I told you. I want my asset back and am willing to deal."

"What's the deal?" Justin demanded.

"You tell me where I can find Dora Vine and—"

Justin broke in, "Why Dora?"

"We talked about this already, Mr. Collins. Business. She is a valuable property, linked to a two-billion-dollar foundation. One way or another GauLux Holding will get a hold of that foundation."

"Not if I can help it," Justin said, his voice low.

"But you cut me off. You didn't hear the deal."

"Which is?"

"You tell me where I can find Dora Vine and I will only kill one of your wives."

★ ★ ★

Justin closed his eyes. He wanted to close his body, to not let anything worse enter his head or his being.

Gaubert paused, looked at Chantal and Gloria, and laughed a short bitter laugh. "Your wives. How funny. What an original dilemma."

He shook his laughter off and continued, "I have made a proposition to you. One or the other." He walked over and stood between the two women, running his finger down Gloria's jaw. "This Spanish one here has a graceful…" he let his finger trail down her neck to the opening of her blouse "…resistance. And the French one," he held his other hand to Chantal's shoulder, "has a fiery resolve."

Gaubert brought his hands together in a clasp of content, looking down at Chantal. "She actually turned out to be very useful to me, even though it was unfortunate for her that she stepped on that airplane. She provided companionship to Mrs. Vine after her husband's death. You see, I let her live because I am a humanitarian, even though she was an unfaithful woman to you and we had to abort the results. I can guess who it would have looked like." Gaubert made a look of refined disgust. "Yass is no beauty. The kid would have had a nose to here," he laughed, holding his hand half a foot from his face. "Still, she seemed to prefer him to you."

Justin saw Chantal furiously shaking her head and Justin yelled, "Chantal, I know what happened, I don't…" and then the butt of the gun hit him again.

"Mr. Collins, I have had enough of this. You are wasting my time. Now, as you cannot choose one of the women I will have to do it for you. After losing one, maybe you will come to your senses and try to save the life of the other. The deal is one wife in exchange for Mrs. Vine."

Justin cried out, "No!" still struggling with the rope that tied his hands, gaining some movement.

"Pierre, put the tape back on the mouth of Mr. Collins." Pierre ripped off a length of duct tape and slapped it over Justin's mouth, ending his shouting.

"Now here is the deal. Listen carefully. First, I will kill one of these fine women, perhaps by strangling; perhaps I will beat her to death myself. Of course, I may let Pierre and Serge have their way with her first. In front of you. After that, I give you exactly one minute to tell me where to find Mrs. Vine." Gaubert reflected. He walked around behind Chantal, stroking her hair, looking at Justin as if he were a game-show host waiting for a contestant's answer. Then he stroked Gloria's hair.

Justin tried to say something but only muffled sounds came through the tape.

"Take off the tape," Gaubert told Serge. "Maybe he has something to tell us now."

Serge ripped the tape from Justin's mouth.

Justin, his lips raw, asked, "How do I know you won't just kill us all?" He was attempting to buy time.

"You have my word. You will be free to go. If you tell your story to the police they will only laugh at your funny story, and in a well out back they will find a dead woman and a gun with your fingerprints on it. Anyway, the police work for me."

"I don't believe you will let us go."

"You have my word. Don't forget that Dora Vine will be my guest, and if any stories come out from you she will be killed. I don't believe you want that on your conscience." He paused and looked Justin in the eyes. "Give me Dora Vine and you can take one of these women."

Justin remained silent.

"I am being very generous with you, Mr. Collins, allowing one woman to live."

Justin looked over at Chantal, who struggled in her seat. He could hear her moaning through the tape over her mouth. He said to her, "Chantal, I know it was not your fault."

"Ah, how touching," Gaubert said, in mock sympathy. Then he returned to his business-like demeanor. "One minute. After that, Serge and Pierre will make their choice."

Justin sat frozen in horror. How to choose a life? Regardless of what he did, he knew that Gaubert would not let them all live.

Gaubert looked at his watch, the game-show host back and beaming. "Thirty seconds up. Thirty seconds left."

Justin struggled at the rope behind his back, did it just give?

"Time's up. Serge and Pierre, pick one and have your pleasure,"

Gaubert said, bowing from the waist.

Serge and Pierre began to move toward the women, big grins on their faces. Justin's heart closed. Gaubert had out-played him. He would have to agree to give up Dora to gain time. He might be able to devise a plan of escape in the mean time. He said, "Yes. I'll do it."

"I knew you'd see the sense of my plan," Gaubert said. "Where is she?"

As Gaubert finished speaking, Justin heard a sound, a faint sound on the gravel outside the building.

Suddenly, one of the window shutters burst open close to Pierre and Serge. A gun fired through it two times. Serge and Pierre fell one after the other. Gaubert ran toward the wall out of the window's aim. Justin saw him reach into his coat pocket and pull out a pistol, aiming at Chantal and Gloria.

Justin lunged forward between Gaubert and the women, his hands still tied behind him. He heard a shot. Almost immediately, a thud resounded from the other side of the room. Chantal slumped over and fell off her chair, and Justin moved toward Gloria to shield her.

He heard another shot and felt something burning in his shoulder. The impact sent him toward Gloria and he started to fall, hearing more shots as he continued falling forward, striking his head on the wall.

Everything spun to black.

CHAPTER 27

Justin woke up surrounded by white. White sheets, white curtains, white walls. Déjà vu? Or was he still in the Figueras hospital and everything since a dream? At this hope, he tried to sit up, but a deep pain moved through his left shoulder.

He looked up and saw someone moving toward him. *Laszlo Vartek,* said a voice in his head.

"Yes," the man answered. Justin must have spoken aloud. *Probably on some hefty pain killers,* he thought. But he finally made the connection. "You are the one who took me to the hospital in Figueras, aren't you?"

Laszlo looked at him with those cold blue eyes, just a hint of humor around the irises. "Maybe."

Laszlo had a large paper bag in his hand and said, "I brought you a change of clean clothing."

"Where am I?" asked Justin.

"This is a private hospital outside of Nice, mainly for cosmetic surgery. The doctors and nurses are highly qualified, and very discreet. For your information, the pretext for you being here has to do with the kidnapping of Chantal, at least that is what the doctors have been told, and they will abide by this story. We believe that no one on the outside associates you with Jacques Gaubert, with his death."

"With his death?"

Laszlo explained, "Yesterday it seems there was an incident outside of Nice in which Jacques Gaubert, the politician, was killed. Not much is known about it."

Justin looked at Laszlo and said, "Thank you. You saved my life. He was an evil man."

Laszlo nodded again and he said, "It's all finished. Gaubert is no longer in the picture."

"And Gloria. Is she alright?"

"Yes, she is alright. Quite a bit shaken though, and very worried about you. She is in a room down the hall. She was here by your side until three o'clock in the morning, but she could not last any longer and the nurses gave her a room—she kept falling asleep with her head on your bed."

"Thank God she is OK. I need to see her. I need to call her parents," Justin said.

"I already called them, just before I came to see you. They will wait for a telephone call from you. They are thinking to fly here from Barcelona, but would like to hear from you first," replied Laszlo.

"How are they taking it?"

"You can guess. They are extremely relieved to know that Gloria is safe and that you were not killed, but I did not tell them everything."

"What time is it now?"

"Eight o'clock in the morning. I came by to see how you were doing, and you were waking up." Laszlo sat in one of the visitor's chairs.

Justin could feel pain in his left shoulder and a throbbing in his head. "What happened to me?"

"Superficial wound," Laszlo said. "A bullet went through the left deltoid muscle, not hitting the bone. After being shot you fell and your head bounced off the wall, and you were out cold. The doctors thought that your concussion from a couple of months ago aggravated the blow and caused you to remain unconscious longer than you should have.

The butt of a gun did not help. They did a CT scan and found nothing serious. They stitched up the arm and gave you some pain medication, but you should be able to walk out of here today if you want to."

"Laszlo, tell me… Chantal?"

"After the shooting, I loaded you all inside the van and brought you here to this hospital. Chantal is here, but there is a problem. Gaubert shot her. The bullet hit a lung and there was considerable bleeding. It took quite some work to get it stopped, and she is in critical condition in intensive care. They think there was additional internal damage, perhaps to her heart or the arteries leading to it, but they need time to see if she can be stabilized. They are not sure she is going to make it."

"I have to see her," said Justin, and started to lift himself up, but the pain in his shoulder took over and the narcotics in his body made him dizzy. His head felt heavy, so he lay back on the bed. The severity of the situation sunk into Justin's mind, and he lay there trying to gather his thoughts. "Oh God please help her," he whispered, " I don't know how we all got into this situation, but please help her."

Justin turned to Laszlo and said, "Can you take me to see her?"

Laszlo made a disapproving face. "You don't look so well."

"Laszlo, you've got to help me. I need to see her before she dies."

"OK," Laszlo said, coming over to he bed. "First, slowly sit up for a minute. Don't move too fast. The blood needs to catch up with your head."

Laszlo put his hand behind Justin's back and helped him sit up. Justin's head was spinning, and his left shoulder was throbbing.

Laszlo saw that Justin's face was turning white and instructed, "Just wait a minute. If your head is dizzy, be still for a minute." They both waited while Justin took a few deep breaths. He started to feel slightly better.

"Just to let you know," Laszlo said, "Grady is still with Habib at the rented house. We don't know what to do with Habib. Though another day with Grady and he is likely to lose his mind. Jordi and his friends are still staking out the office in Nice."

Justin tried to get his head around something besides the pulsing. "We need to find out what's in that office. I think we should pay them a visit today."

"You're not in shape for that," Laszlo stated.

"Hey, it's a superficial wound, right?" He winced as he tested it. "I'm going to be there."

"Sam Oliver is particularly interested because of the links that office has with EuroVinco and Unipac. Doby is flying in today. We will need him in case there is any computer work to do."

"Whatever you do, wait for me. I want to be there when we start the questioning." Justin was glad *he* wasn't going to be questioned by Jordi and Laszlo.

Laszlo waited a moment then said, "Stefan flew down here last night. I had mentioned to Sam Oliver that he knew a lot about EuroVinco and could probably offer advice. Sam asked him to come. Paul Kent, the CEO of Unipac, also arrived late last night. He was in London when Sam called him. Kent was planning to fly here today anyway, so he took a flight last night instead. The four of them plan to meet this morning at eight fifteen to discuss what to do."

Justin had to think again who Laszlo meant by the four of them, and then placed the names: Stefan Von Portzer, Sam Oliver, Dora Vine and Paul Kent. He also had to think about what day of the week it was. He had no idea.

Laszlo continued, "They are all staying at the same hotel. I gave a briefing to Sam and Stefan last night, so they know what happened at the stone house. One concern they have is how the news media is going to treat the death of Gaubert, and of course Sam is concerned that this does not get mixed up with Unipac. It could have negative implications for the company. Stefan is trying to help. He knows a leading journalist in France and called him last night to find out how the press is treating the story. It's being positioned as a gang killing. We will see what the newspapers say this morning."

"Wait till the press hears about Mrs. Vine." Justin started to shake his head and then thought better of it.

"Mr. Oliver said the same thing. Stefan is working to figure out the best way to present all of this."

Justin was glad to know that others were helping to carry the load—one that was no longer his alone—and he could feel some strength coming back into his body. "And what about Sophie. Where is she?"

"We moved her to the hotel with Mrs. Vine. It does not make sense for her to stay at the rented house with Grady and Habib. Mrs. Vine may need to be with Sam, explaining things to the police and the press, so she is looking for a nanny."

The reality of his situation was beginning to come together in Justin's mind. Two women, each his wife. Two children, Sophie and a baby to be born. Justin looked up and said, "What would you do if you were in my shoes?"

"Don't know. Just glad I'm not in your shoes."

"Chantal and Gloria. I need to see them."

Laszlo lifted the paper bag and pulled out a clean shirt and clean pants. He handed them to Justin. "Get dressed."

CHAPTER 28

In a deluxe hotel conference room, the meeting was already under way—as was the aroma of warm croissants and coffee, mingled with scents of leather and polished mahogany furnishings.

Sam Oliver laid his hands on either side of the notebook in front of him and assumed his usual role as chairman. "The important thing is that we decide on a course of action, are we agreed?"

They all nodded and Sam continued, "Today, we have several things to consider. First, let me say a few general things about Unipac and EuroVinco to set the scene, and then say a few things about Dora."

Sam looked at her and said, "Dora, you have been through an extremely traumatic time and I greatly admire your strength. We want to protect you and do the right thing for you above all things."

Dora cleared her throat and said, "Thank you, Sam." Still tired, she looked noticeably less oppressed than when she arrived on the plane from Tunisia. Some of the stress was beginning to fade from her face, and a shadow of her former posture of confidence returned when Sam addressed her.

Sam went on, "Starting with the companies, Unipac and EuroVinco are now merged. That is a fact. In some ways we were duped, as careful as we are in Unipac. We know now that Jacques Gaubert had ulterior motives, evil motives. Had he had his way, he would have eventually taken over Unipac and the Vine Foundation and he would have used this as a platform for further illicit takeovers."

Paul Kent leaned forward and rested his elbows on the conference table, the arms of his suit pulling back from the wrists and displaying his cufflinks. "Sam, what is the impact for Unipac at this point?"

"That's the question. Whatever we do, we should try and avoid associating Jacques Gaubert with Unipac."

There was a knock on the door. As Stefan Von Portzer answered it, one of the hotel staff handed him several newspapers. Stefan shut the door, looked quickly through them, and promptly returned to his seat.

"What do they say?" asked Sam.

Stefan laid the papers on the table and read out the headlines. "It looks like Jacques Gaubert is across all the front pages. And so is his connection with the underworld." He lifted up *Le Matin*, one of the leading French newspapers and began to read from the front page, translating to English.

Gaubert Dead in a Hail of Bullets:

Today, Jacques Gaubert, the flamboyant businessman and politician, was found shot to death in what appears to be a gang-style shooting. Two other men known to be members of the French underworld with long police records were also found dead. Both were also known for associations with some of Mafia operating out of Nice and Marseilles. Gaubert has been under a number of government investigations for quite some time, and sources say personal or political enemies may be involved. The exact reason for the murders is not known, but police are continuing to investigate several leads.

"And so on," concluded Stefan.

"Does it say anything about Unipac or EuroVinco?" Paul asked.

"No, not that I can see," Stefan replied, skimming the page in front of him.

"So far, so good," said Sam.

Paul said, "Of course, if Unipac gets associated with this affair, we could lose customers and business. We don't want to lay off employees. Integrating EuroVinco is a delicate operation, and we need to keep our business momentum. We all know how the markets are reacting these days to anything that even whispers of scandal. Do you think Unipac and EuroVinco will get dragged into this?"

"It is unlikely," Stefan answered, "if you play it well on your side. GauLux Holding owned a large part of EuroVinco and now it has a six percent holding in Unipac after the merger. The legal owners of GauLux Holding are a number of offshore companies and trusts. Officially, Gaubert has a small share of GauLux Holding. All the offshore companies have nominal directors, and the ownership behind those companies is uncertain. I believe Gaubert had partners to minimize his taxes in France. While there is a link between Gaubert and GauLux and between GauLux and Unipac, I think it can be managed. You see, Gaubert had absolute control over his empire, but in all the legal structures it looked like he was a marginal player. We can leverage on this and minimize the damage to Unipac."

"Good, good," said Sam, adding celebratory sugar to the coffee in his cup.

"What about all the money he stole from EuroVinco over the years? Doesn't EuroVinco and now Unipac have a claim on that?" asked Paul. He was referring to the five hundred million dollars held in the various accounts listed in Doby's report.

Stefan took this question too. "Yes, Unipac could probably go after it, but that would open the entire affair to the outside world. You probably want to avoid that for the reasons you already discussed. The ultimate costs resulting from negative publicity, endless articles in the press, loss of business and reduction of share prices would undoubtedly be far greater than the five hundred million. At the same time my, ah, researcher, might be able to create a transfer from the Conquest Bank account, where most of the funds are held. Doby has some exceptional competencies."

Paul said, "That would be great if we could retrieve the money but for now we should probably focus on tossing the rotten apples out of Unipac—meaning anyone associated with Gaubert. We already know a couple of board members to be removed, and there are others."

"Agreed," Sam said. "And we must keep the Gaubert affair separated from Unipac." He looked at Dora. "Now the other and most important question concerns Dora. She has been greatly damaged through this… this fiasco. She endured a year of atrocious conditions in Tunisia. She lost Vine Industries, and now all the assets from this—and the sale of her home in California—are held in the Vine Foundation. These were criminal actions against her and, in a court of law, she would win in claiming damages against Gaubert and GauLux Holding. So my next question is how we break the news of her kidnapping to the press?"

Dora set down the last twist of her croissant. "That was the most difficult year of my life. I cried every day after losing Pete and vowed I would get revenge if I ever could. Having Chantal there with me was the greatest support. She gave me so much strength, morally and spiritually, and I came to love Sophie.

"Sam, you and I spoke, and the assets from the Vine Foundation are considerable. I know they are mine, and that is more than enough for me. I don't know if I could handle months and months of a court trial and all the pressure from the press that would bring, especially knowing that the villain behind this is dead. For me, that is already some justice."

"Dora, if that's the way you want it, I will respect your wishes. I do feel bad that you lost Vine Industries. Most of it is now absorbed into Unipac."

"It's really not that important, although there is one thing that is," she said. "Concerning Chantal. I also want her to be remunerated from the foundation if possible. Pete and I didn't have any children, and Chantal has become like a daughter to me. Sophie, a granddaughter. I want them taken care of by the foundation."

At the mention of Chantal, the room grew uncomfortably quiet. "What if she doesn't make it?" Sam asked gently. "The doctors are not hopeful. They say she has a very little chance."

"If we do lose her, I want Sophie looked after. And also Justin. He has also been deeply hurt through this affair. He was like a son to Pete. I want to be sure they get something substantial."

"I'll assist you in doing whatever you think is right. If you need lawyers to do the paperwork or to help in restructuring the foundation, we'll get them," Sam said, slapping his chair arm.

Stefan Von Portzer exhaled and said through the puff of smoke, "I can see that you are reluctant to take GauLux Holding to court, not wanting to associate their name with Unipac or Dora Vine." He turned sideways, looking out the window onto the Nice morning. "I think I have another idea how Dora might be remunerated. And how we can break news of her kidnapping to the press."

"What's your idea?" asked Sam.

"I don't think you want to be involved in this one, Sam."

CHAPTER 29

Leaving the elevator, Laszlo walked alongside Justin down the hall to the intensive care unit. Justin was now walking without assistance.

They came to a glass window and looked inside. Chantal was lying on a bed, a sheet spread across her in stiff perfection. From this distance, not even her shallow breathing disturbed the placid white fabric. A large tube led to her mouth and smaller tubes ran up to and disappeared below the sheet.

Justin and Laszlo were still standing there when a man walked down the hall wearing a white jacket with a stethoscope around his neck.

Laszlo said, "Justin, this is the doctor who is treating Chantal."

"Hello," Justin said, shaking his hand. "What is her condition?"

The doctor was straightforward. "She is stable, but weak. I think that the internal bleeding has stopped, but she should still be considered critical. She is getting the best of attention. We are monitoring her very carefully. Someone in this condition can turn very quickly, but for the moment, all I can say is that she is stable."

Justin kept quiet, hating that there was nothing he could do. He looked into the room again and then back at the doctor. "Can I go inside?"

"Yes, but don't stay long."

Justin headed for the door to the room and Laszlo said, "Look. I don't think you need me anymore around here. I need to go check in with Stefan. This afternoon I will come back and see how you are doing and give you an update."

"Thanks Laszlo, for all you are doing," Justin said.

Laszlo headed down the hall and Justin went into the room. Chantal was breathing, her eyes shut and her face so pale he could see veins beneath her freckles. The freckles he had known so well. There were few now. So much time inside had kept the sun from touching her much. He leaned over and kissed the top of each cheek, trying to ignore the foreign tube leaving her lips.

Justin moved over and held her hand. An intravenous tube was also taped to a vein in her wrist. He spread his fingers against her smaller ones, feeling the jagged tips of her fingernails and the dry knuckles. She had loved to keep her hands soft, especially after a day with harsh paint removers in the studio. Their bathroom counter top in Paris had always been littered with pots of citrus creams and bottles of rich moisturizers.

It felt so strange to touch her. It had been over a year. With her skin so deathly pale, he half feared he held the hand of a corpse. Had he ever thought to see her again, that is what he would have expected. Instead, a slight warmth still ran through those veins. He said a silent prayer, pressing her fingers one by one as if saying one of Gloria's rosaries.

Gloria. Dear God. What on earth was he going to do?

★ ★ ★

The telephone rang in the office and after nine rings a voice answered, "Who is it?"

"Are you sleeping on the job?"

"What do you want?" Ziginiglou asked. It was Yass. He regretted answering the phone.

"What do you mean, what do I want? I am just following instructions. I am supposed to call in to you twice a day. Why did it take you nine rings to answer the telephone?"

Ziginiglou did not know if he should tell Yass. Maybe he should leave him down there in Spain and let him find out later.

"What have you found out?" asked Ziginiglou.

"Turk and I are still sitting here waiting, waiting for nothing. Collins has not shown up yet. I think we are wasting our time. Maybe we should get back to Nice," Yass said, his mind fixed on the young woman they had snatched in Barcelona, hoping he would get the assignment of guarding her.

Ziginiglou came to a decision. "You no needed down there anymore," he said.

"Why not?"

"There has been a change of plans." He took a deep breath. "*Le Patron* no longer in charge."

"What do you mean?"

"He got shot. Killed. He and Serge and Pierre. You know he was always involve with Mafia gangs from Marseille. The newspapers say they shot him. But I think Collins involve."

"Shot? Killed?" Yass could not believe what he heard.

"Late yesterday afternoon. It's in all the newspapers today, and television." Ziginiglou felt he had the upper hand for once, and he found himself enjoying it. He debated whether or not to say more, but could not resist the urge to present himself one step ahead of Yass. "The two women also missing. I receive additional information this morning. One of our computer men has a girl friend, a nurse at that expensive private hospital outside Nice. Last night, several people come—an American guy, and two women. One Spanish, one French. I have been on the phone for an hour this morning trying to find out more."

"*Le Patron* dead?" Yass wasn't bothered by death. He was, on the other hand, bothered about losing his source of income. "He owes me my salary. I want to be paid," he demanded.

"I'm running the show." Ziginiglou had made that up, knowing it was now or never. Yass was dangerous. "If you want to have work, then get back to Nice. If you want to work for someone else, then that is up to you. Your employment with *Le Patron* has come to an end."

"Get screwed. I'm not working for you."

"Have it your way."

"Just get my money ready. And a bonus."

Ziginiglou understood this was an opportunity to get rid of Yass, although Turk might be useful. He had access to one of the accounts of GauLux Holding and he could pay Yass from that. "OK, I will transfer the money into your account."

"You mentioned two women," Yass said. "I know about the Spanish one. We snatched her in Barcelona. Who is the other one?"

Ziginiglou realized that Yass did not know about getting the Collins woman from Tunisia, and he flaunted his inside knowledge again. "*Le Patron* had people in Tunisia. One of them was French woman. When he send you to Barcelona, he also send instructions to bring French woman to Nice. Strange story, but she made sex with someone while locked in Tunisia. She got pregnant. They abort the baby. *Le Patron* was holding both of the women here in Nice. Really strange part is, both of these women are wives of Collins." He laughed.

Yass was perplexed. He knew about the French woman in Tunisia. He was the one who had done the setup about a year ago, no, more than a year ago. She was often in his dreams. In Tunisia he had only known her as Chantal, but he never thought to learn her family name. So she was married to Collins. His concubine was married to the infidel he had been ordered to kill. But wait, Ziginiglou mentioned something else.

"Ziginiglou, I know about Tunisia. I was the one who set everything up for *Le Patron*. You said something I don't understand. You said that the French woman got pregnant. Something about aborting a baby."

"Yes. As I said, very strange. I only been in Nice couple of months, so I do not know all the background from Tunisia. When we give orders to bring the French woman to Nice, I find out about her pregnancy."

"What pregnancy?"

"*Le Patron* saying the woman was… promising? No," Ziginiglou racked his brain for the right English word. "No, *promiscuous* when she down there. She gets pregnant. They no want to have baby around compound. So they kill it."

"She got pregnant?"

"It no take her long to leave Collins in Paris and find a man in

Tunisia. You know what French women are like," he said, chuckling.

Yass made the calculation in his head. He knew, too, that he had left instructions to the other guards not to touch the woman. They would be fools to do so.

"Where did you say the woman is?"

"We think in private clinic. The one that is at edge of Nice, up on the hill on the main road to Monaco," Ziginiglou explained.

Yass knew it. He said, partly under his breath, "She was wrong to allow them to kill that child."

"Why do you say that?"

"We're leaving for Nice and will be there in three or four hours." He hung up the telephone. They killed his child—*she* let them kill his child. He spit on the floor. He walked into the bar where Turk was drinking a beer. It was nine o'clock in the morning.

"Let's go," said Yass.

"Where are we going?" asked Turk.

"To Marseille. I want to see my uncle. He knows about blood for blood, life for life. Then she will repay me for taking my son."

Turk gaped at this incoherence but put a some euros on the table to pay his bill. He stood up, downed half a bottle of beer in one long gulp and followed Yass out the door.

Yass was running. Turk had never seen him move so fast.

CHAPTER 30

Justin went down to the reception desk and asked for the number of Gloria's room. He took the elevator to the second floor, found the number and knocked lightly. When no one answered, he went inside.

She was asleep, exquisitely and perfectly asleep. Too perfectly? She resembled a painting he had seen of Ophelia, elegantly rendered and drowned in flower-strewn waters. After those disturbing corpse thoughts by Chantal's side, he needed to reassure himself that Gloria was breathing.

He crossed the room and touched her cheek. She opened her eyes. She smiled and sat up. "Justin. I was so worried about you."

"I was so worried about you too," he said.

He sat next to her, kissed her and held her tight for a long time, running his hands through the red hair that fell long down her back.

She pressed her hand against his back as well. A sharp pain shot through his shoulder, and she felt him wince.

"Oh love, I'm sorry," she said, wincing with him and breaking the embrace to look at the injured spot.

"It's just a small wound. But it still hurts."

"My pain has not been physical, but it too has hurt."

Justin looked deep into her eyes. "We need to talk."

She nodded. "Let me shower and dress."

Justin stood looking out the window until Gloria came back from the bathroom, a towel wrapped around her. As she went over to a cupboard where her clothing was hanging, the towel dropped as it had on the first morning of their honeymoon. He saw her body, beautiful and familiar. He longed to hold her and took a step in her direction.

But how could he with Chantal in a room on the next floor? Instead, he watched Gloria get dressed.

She asked, "Did you have anything to eat?"

"No," he said. "I could use a coffee."

"There is a small cafeteria on the main floor. Why don't we order something?" she said.

A young woman brought in a tray less than ten minutes after Justin called. She set it on a table in the room, and the sight of fruit, croissant and coffee made him hungry. They sat down in two chairs at the table, Justin pouring coffee and Gloria pulling grapes from vines.

After half a cup of coffee, Justin said, "Gloria, you must be overwhelmed with all of this. Whatever happens, I want you to know that I love you very much. I know this is a stupid question, but how do you feel?"

"Shaken up," she replied, setting down the jam. "I had a physical exam last night. The good news is that I have not lost our baby."

"Thank God," he said. "I was worried about you, how they would treat you. Do you want to tell me what happened?"

Her eyelashes grew wet with tears and she said, "It has been so terrible, so frightening."

"What happened?" he said, reaching for her hand across her plate, stopping it from picking crumbs off the table's surface.

"On Sunday I was walking from my parents' house to the local grocery store. A man came up behind me and grabbed me. He held his hand over my mouth, and the next thing I knew I was being dragged into a utility van. The man kept holding me from behind with his hand over my mouth. He kept touching my breasts, my thighs. I was so scared. Somewhere outside of Barcelona they tied me up and blindfolded me. Initially there were four men, but at a certain point I think that two of them got out. We drove for hours. After a couple of hours we stopped in a small forest where I was allowed a break, but the men watched me. And then we drove some more.

"Finally we came to a building and they put me in a room. They locked the door and brought me food. I was alone. Several times they came to let me go to the bathroom down the hall, but they always watched me. It was very humiliating."

Justin's face said it for him, but he spoke aloud, "Gloria, I am so sorry. For you. For us."

Gloria heard him, but she was still lost in her narrative. She kept speaking, "Yesterday afternoon two of the men who had taken me in Barcelona came to get me. They tied me up—blindfold, tape, all again—and led me into the utility van. They made me sit down. I waited for a few minutes and then I sensed that someone else was being brought into the van. It started and we drove for some distance. Finally they brought us to that place where we were yesterday."

Justin was filled with anger and with relief at the same time, anger at the men who had done this to Gloria and relief that she had not been more harmed and was now safe.

He looked up at Gloria and said, "The other person in the van was Chantal."

She held his look with her green eyes, once so sparkling in the Llanca sunlight, now so sad. She said, "I know. I realized it in the farmhouse when that evil man spoke."

"I don't know what to say."

"Nor do I," she responded. "But when you went off to Tunisia, I thought about…" She waved a hand in the air to indicate the situation. He was oddly reminded of Chantal's arm gestures. "And I wondered what would happen if Chantal were still alive."

"I never thought about it," he said, shaking his head. "I always thought she was killed in the air crash and that is the reality that I lived with, that I believed. To find out that she is alive." He stopped, at a loss how to finish his sentence, conscious of the true fragment he was facing, no phrase to complete it.

He remained silent for a moment, holding his head down in his hands, and then Gloria asked, "How is she doing?"

He raised his head slightly, bringing his nose to the level of his coffee cup. He saw his reflection in its cylindrical surface, stretched out of proportion. No foreign feeling, that. "I went up there, to intensive care," he said, partly to Gloria, partly to his reflected self. "She's not doing well. The doctor said she is stable, but they need time to see what direction she will take."

"She has been through so much."

Justin nodded.

Gloria looked at him and said, "I feel bad for her. Justin, what are we going to do?"

"I don't know, Gloria. I just don't know."

She looked at him and said, "Justin, I have always had confidence that you will do the right thing, that you will make the right choices, however hard they might be."

She moved her chair close to his and leaned her head on his shoulder. Señora Pascual had said to do the good and honorable thing. Gloria had said that he would do the right thing, but what *was* the right thing?

Finally he said, "It sounds callous, but we will have to wait and see what happens with Chantal."

"I know." She paused. Gloria pulled the silver cross from where it hung beneath her collar, brought it to her lips, and kissed it. She asked, "This Dora. Where is she now?"

"At a hotel. Why?"

"Justin, do you think I could spend some time with Dora Vine? I would like to ask her some questions, alone."

CHAPTER 31

Laszlo arrived at the rented house and went into the living room where Sam Oliver was talking to Grady and Habib. Grady and Habib were sitting together on a couch, Habib no longer in handcuffs. Paul Kent was present, as was Jordi.

When Laszlo entered, Sam asked, "How are they doing?"

Laszlo replied, "Justin is up and around. Gloria was still sleeping when I left, but I suspect she is up by now. The problem is Chantal. She is stable, but the doctors do not want to commit themselves. I'm not sure." Laszlo turned the conversation. "What have you decided?"

"Two things," said Sam. "First we are going to schedule a small press conference today to announce the release of Dora Vine from her kidnappers. It will be a short event and we just want to let out some news. Grady and Habib will be the stars of this show, and we need to work out their story line. Stefan is bringing in an international lawyer from Geneva who has experience in dealing with the press. This lawyer will take the lead in handling press releases over the coming weeks. We need to make sure that the story is well managed."

"What's the second thing?" asked Laszlo.

Jordi responded, "Stefan feels it's time to investigate the small office in Nice. We need to question the people in it and see what they know, especially concerning EuroVinco. They can also explain the link to Jacques Gaubert. Laszlo, we need you for this one."

"Justin wants to be there when we go in," said Laszlo. Jordi looked at him and nodded. Though wounded, Justin's presence would be a matter of honor.

★ ★ ★

Ziginiglou was a bundle of bottled-up energy. All morning he had been working with the team in the office, trying to make a strategic decision, a business decision.

The problem was that Ziginiglou was not used to thinking strategically. He was an accountant. Most recently he was working as an implementer. Someone else made the decisions and he implemented them. Now that person was gone.

He sat in his office wondering what to do.

On the positive side, a network of accountants worked consistently at transferring money out of EuroVinco into special accounts. It was a cash machine and one that could provide him with extraordinary future income. There was also the money in all of Gaubert's accounts. He knew how much that came to, right to the last red cent. His small team in Nice kept all the records. The problem was that he did not have direct access to those accounts. They were electronic bank accounts and Gaubert had been the one with the codes. Gaubert's financial advisors, the international lawyers Féret and Jaccoud, also had records of the codes. They were the nominal directors of all the offshore companies behind GauLux Holding.

Ziginiglou wondered if there was any way to gain access to the bank account codes. He needed to discuss this with the accounting team and the two computer engineers.

But there was also a negative side: that the office in Nice could be connected with Jacques Gaubert. The police would be very active these days with the death of Gaubert. It would be bad news if they investigated this office. Should he vacate and move the operation somewhere else?

And there was another negative. Yass was headed back to Nice. If there was anyone Ziginiglou was afraid of, it was Yass. Yass was more than just a paid thug. He was a fanatic. He was violent and would not hesitate to use any kind of force that suited him. Ziginiglou knew that he would have to face Yass, and he did not look forward to it.

After weighing these positives and the negatives, Ziginiglou was no closer to making a decision.

If only they could access Gaubert's accounts. Then they could close up the office forever. Five hundred million dollars, some split between five accountants, two computer technicians, with most of it going to himself. It would be more than enough to give him an excellent life until the end of his days.

With this pleasant retirement in mind, a strategy started to form itself after all.

★ ★ ★

Gloria knocked on the door of the hotel room. Standing before her was a woman in her early sixties. Her hair was nicely done back in a twist. She wore a simple blue dress and a tired expression.

The woman smiled and some of the tiredness faded. "Hello, Gloria. I am Dora Vine. Call me Dora. Please, come in."

Gloria shook her hand and entered the room. She found herself in a well appointed suite formed by a large living room and a bedroom on either side of it. In one of the bedrooms a woman was reading to a small girl.

"Please sit down," Dora said. "If you don't mind, I have ordered a small lunch to be brought to the room. Justin may have told you, but we scheduled a press conference this afternoon, and I really don't want to go down to the restaurant in the hotel for fear of running into reporters."

"Thank you for the lunch invitation," said Gloria, adding, "You look very composed and ready to face the press."

"I had a hair dresser come to the room to give me a cut and color. It was the first time in over a year. Felt like heaven to have someone shampooing my scalp." She laughed. "Simple pleasures. This afternoon a local women's clothing shop is sending some dresses by for me to try. You don't know how all of this makes me feel, the hair, the new clothing—or even clean clothing."

"I can only imagine," said Gloria, leaning back in the plush chair in a relaxed sympathy. "It must have been so hard for you."

"More than you can know," said Dora.

Gloria looked into the bedroom, then asked, "The child in there, is that Sophie?"

"Yes," Dora said. "I just hope and pray that this experience will not scar her too much in life. She's a bright little girl. We hired a nurse to help take care of her for a few days, or longer if needed." She paused and angled her head to meet Gloria's gaze. "We need to wait, don't we?" she said. Chantal's presence hovered there in the suite air that carried Sophie's voice.

They heard a knock at the door. Dora rose to answer it, and a waiter wheeled in a trolley loaded with food. He opened its side flaps and locked them in place, creating a round table. A selection of small dainty sandwiches, a plate of warm chicken, several kinds of salads and small French pastries spread before them as the waiter removed lids and then departed.

Dora called into the next room and said, "Sophie, the food is here. Joseline, can you come too?" Then Dora turned to Gloria and said, "Please serve yourself."

Sophie came running into the room, looked at the table and said, "Good food." She was a striking child with blond hair and blue eyes that seemed to see more than a toddler's world.

Dora said to her, "Sophie, I would like to introduce you to Gloria. Can you shake hands?"

Sophie held out her small hand and Gloria took it. The hand was fragile, but it squeezed hers in abbreviated strength.

"Let's eat," Sophie said. Gloria smiled, her hand inadvertently resting on her stomach.

Dora served Sophie sandwiches. "Joseline, I wonder if you might take Sophie back into the bedroom to eat once you've chosen what you like," Dora requested. "Maybe there is a children's program on the television. Gloria and I need to spend some time together." Joseline nodded and helped Sophie keep a pickle from rolling down her frilled dress in its mustard.

The nurse and child returned to the bedroom, and soon Gloria heard the unmistakable sounds of animated characters crashing into each other.

Dora and Gloria brought two chairs around the edge of the trolley table and both sat down. "Did you sleep OK last night?" Dora asked. "You've had a rough couple of days."

"Yes, but nothing compared to what you have been through. Justin told me about Mr. Vine's death and your dreadful captivity."

"At least you have some understanding," said Dora.

Gloria nodded her head and then took a bite of a sandwich.

Dora changed the subject and said, "Justin told me that you are a banker."

Gloria smiled and said, "A junior banker. My father is an economist, and I guess it rubbed off."

"Justin said that you called your parents. Are they coming up here?"

"I asked them not to. I would like to see them, but I told them there was no need to come. Having them here might complicate things even more. The important thing for me is to support Justin. This is not an easy time for him, for any of us."

"I know," said Dora. "How did your parents handle the news?"

"Justin talked with my father and told him everything about the kidnapping. Well, just about everything. My father took some time to understand, but he is Scottish and a very practical man. He said he would talk with the policeman who is working on the case and tell him my absence was a mistake. The story is that I told my sister that I needed to go back to our house in the Costa Brava, but she spent a couple of nights with some friends and forgot to tell my parents. We hope it will work. The police are so busy, it can be put aside as another false-alarm missing person."

"Do they know about the rest, not just the kidnapping?" Dora asked.

"No." Gloria squeezed a corner of her sandwich, squishing the bread and its tomato insides together. "I want to talk with them face to face."

"Dora, may I ask your advice on something?"

"Of course." Dora waited, though she was fairly sure what was on Gloria's mind.

"You know that we are in a difficult situation," Gloria said, trying to swallow away a crumb that had stuck in her throat. "And we haven't had a lot of time to think about it. It was so sudden that you, Chantal and Sophie reappeared. Before we were married, Justin was very open and honest with me about his feelings for Chantal, and I saw how much he grieved over her death. You have to accept the history of the person you love.

"I saw that Justin was a good man, a kind man. We fell in love so fast and got married. I knew I loved him and didn't want to waste a lot of time with a long engagement. That was my fault. I wanted him so badly. Now all of this has happened and I wonder.... Chantal and Sophie are here. Chantal was Justin's wife. She *is* Justin's wife. Sophie is his child. The problem is that I am pregnant, and I too am his wife. Have I done the right thing?"

CHAPTER 32

Yass broke every speed limit between Llanca and Nice. He had yelled out the window at a car when it passed him doing 220.

Turk repeatedly begged him, "Slow down, I don't want to die today," but Yass' answer was to accelerate.

Throughout the trip Yass ranted, "She allowed them to kill my child, my son. Someone must pay blood for blood, life for life. Her girl will be mine."

At first Turk did not know what he was talking about. After asking Yass some questions when he could get a word in—and a response—he gathered that Yass had fathered a child by a French woman in Tunisia, but the child was never born.

Turk advised, "Just let the woman keep her child. It will only complicate your life."

Yass struck the steering wheel with his fists, and Turk resisted the urge to grab the wheel as Yass emphasized his words with thumpings. "Blood for blood. This is now my child." He stopped pounding the wheel and held it. He started to speak with exaggerated clarity as if Turk was a child too, incapable of understanding what was so twistedly clear to Yass. "An infidel will not raise it. It is a girl, yes," as if this were Turk's sole bone to pick with the situation, "but even a girl can be raised as a true believer. This daughter will be the mother of twelve freedom fighters. She will marry the right man and raise her children to be warriors, martyrs if necessary."

Turk rolled his eyes out the passenger window and repeated, "Like I say, you are just complicating your life."

Yass' face hardened again. "You claim to be a believer, but you are nothing. My uncle said that false believers are worse than the infidels. You are worse than a dog. I should throw you out of the car."

Turk tried to reason with him. "What are you going to do with it?

You don't know anything about raising children."

"If necessary I will take the French concubine with me to keep the child alive. If that does not work, then I will find another means."

"But where will you take it?"

"To Marseille. My uncle will take me in. Women in his community will watch out for my child. The child will be raised in my ways and the ways of my uncle. If they come looking for me, I will take the child away."

Turk had met the uncle several times when Yass had insisted on it. Being raised by Yass' uncle would be one of the worst things imaginable. The uncle seemed even crazier than Yass. In fact, an entire community of crazy fanatics lived around the uncle. All their talk about holy wars and infidels scared Turk, and they had even tried to recruit him. There were a bunch of them, armed to the teeth. They were looking to send freedom fighters out into the world, and he knew for a fact that they directly sponsored terrorist activity.

Turk did not share their religious zeal. Of course, he had nodded his head and agreed with them. Afterwards, he had vowed never to go there again. It was the shortest conversion in history.

Yass was still speaking. "...so we go speak with my uncle in Marseille and discuss my plan."

"No. First take me to Nice," Turk demanded.

"Impossible. We speak with my uncle. Then you help me find the child and take her to Marseille. You can join my uncle's community in Marseille. The concubine should not have let them take my son from her womb."

Turk could not contain himself any longer. "Yass, you're crazy. I will not help you this time. Take me back to the office in Nice. I want to work with Ziginiglou."

At that Yass turned toward Turk and spat at him, leaving a moist spot on the side of Turk's shirt. Yass said, "You are worse than an infidel dog. I should kill you."

Turk did not say a word the rest of the trip. When they got to Nice, Yass drove him up to the office and said, "Get out."

Turk got out of the car, shut the door, and Yass sped away in the direction of Marseille. Turk breathed a sign of relief and went through the office door to find Ziginiglou.

★ ★ ★

"How could you have done the wrong thing?" Dora set down her wine glass and leaned toward Gloria, placing a hand on her shoulder. "How could you have guessed what would happen?"

"I don't know. I don't know what to think, what to feel."

"You made the right decision for what you knew. How were you to know that Chantal was not dead? All the evidence said otherwise."

"I know, but now Justin must make a decision," Gloria said, wiping at the tears that she could not keep back.

"It's not only Justin. You all must choose. You must choose what you want, although there is no guarantee of getting it."

Gloria asked, "Can you tell me about Chantal? About, well, how the rape affected her?"

Dora turned and looked at the bottle of mineral water, watching its bubbles shooting to the surface behind its label. "She was devastated, but even more so when she realized she was pregnant. Then they... they aborted the child. Eventually, though, she began to find some strength. She found solace and strength in prayer."

"How does Chantal feel about Justin?" Gloria asked.

Dora looked at Gloria and knew she had to be honest. "Gloria, Chantal loves Justin just like you, with all her heart. It was the thought of him that helped her to make it through each day. But I think you know about that kind of love."

Gloria said, "I should be jealous, but how can I be jealous of someone who has been through so much? If I were in her place I don't know what I would do. She has been kidnapped, threatened, raped, and impregnated. Undergone a forced abortion. She has also found out that her husband, the man she loves, has married another woman. And she has been shot." Gloria threw up her hands as if the cosmos could not possible throw any further horror Chantal's way. "How can I be jealous of someone who has suffered so much? At the same time, Justin is my husband. What would you do if you were me?"

"That is a loaded question," Dora said. "The thing is, Chantal isn't doing well and the doctors don't know about her state. If she doesn't make it, it will be so hard on me. I don't have any children and Chantal has become a daughter to me. I lost a husband, and now I may lose a daughter. It sounds harsh, but I suppose you don't have to make any decisions until we know if she survives."

Gloria looked at Dora and said, "I know that you have suffered pain and her death would add to the pain. For you, I will pray that she lives." For the second time that day, she reached for her silver cross and raised it to her lips.

Dora watched this in silence, then took Gloria's hand and said, "Now I understand why Justin married you. You are a woman of compassion."

They sat there in unspoken prayer, a cross and their own hands between them.

CHAPTER 33

The Geneva flight arrived at half past one. Stefan and Laszlo stood at the gate watching the passengers as they left the plane. One of them, a man in his late twenties, walked toward them in dark denim jeans, a light blue windbreaker, and retro running shoes. He carried a medium-sized backpack about half full. Doby pushed his glasses in place and smiled when he saw Stefan.

Laszlo approached him, smiled and held out a hand. "How is the computer person?"

Doby shook hands and laughed. "You mean the geek? Glad to see you, big man. It wasn't easy to get a flight down here. You'd think all the planes would be empty in October, but every holidaying Swiss student is headed south to the beaches."

Stefan extended his hand and Doby pumped it cheerily. "Hi boss."

Stefan lifted a dark eyebrow. "Please refrain from calling me 'boss.' Let us keep it as 'paid consultant.'"

Doby said, "I like 'paid consultant,' although poorly paid consultant would be more appropriate." He grinned as Stefan drew his brows together as if to counter this. "So, I had to break a lot of work just to get down here. What's the assignment?"

"Let's get in the car," Stefan said. "I'll explain on the way."

While Laszlo drove, Stefan explained that the computers in the small office in Nice contained critical information that Doby needed to obtain. If there were people entering data on those computers or acting as technicians, Doby would be the best person to interrogate them.

They finally arrived at a large house facing the sea in a residential section of Nice. Laszlo explained that it was a vacation house Justin Collins had rented for the week.

Justin met them at the door, made introductions, and led everyone to the living room to discuss strategy. The sounds of showering and the lyrics of "The Yellow Rose of Texas" followed them down the hall.

Doby looked at Laszlo and back in the direction of the atonal crooning.

"Someone getting ready for a press conference," said Laszlo. "I will explain later."

⋆ ⋆ ⋆

Sam Oliver had the feeling that the press conference was going to be off to a late start.

News media organizations kept asking for delays. They needed to get their people and infrastructure in place. All the major U.S. news organizations were there, which made things worse. The press conference was being broadcast live on Fox News, CNBC, CNN, Sky and the BBC.

They had all mobilized faster than Sam expected. Many of the organizations had representatives in Nice, and all the U.S. and British news organizations based in Paris had made it down to Nice as well. As the French media organizations were already in town to cover the Jacques Gaubert affair, this story was an additional godsend for them. They could get more bang for their buck.

Nice was crawling with journalists from every sort of political orientation—right, center, left—and every journalistic style, from mainstream to scandal. The kidnapping of Dora Vine was major headline material. The supposedly dead wife of a famous American industrialist had been found alive. The media had to be there, and the conference had to be broadcast worldwide, live.

This was not exactly Sam's idea of starting small and carefully releasing information over the following weeks. The story was just too unusual.

⋆ ⋆ ⋆

Justin, Laszlo and Jordi walked straight into the office, followed by Sanchez and Pascual. Earlier in the day Sanchez had entered pretending to seek directions, and those few moments in the office had given him time to sketch out its layout for the others.

In one spacious room to the left, five men worked behind their cluttered desks. Two men occupied another, fairly large room full of computers and electronic equipment. And in a smaller office to the right, just one man worked, probably the supervisor.

Earlier that afternoon, a car had driven up and its passenger, a broad man with a black mustache, had left it and entered the office.

The main door was unlocked. Justin and Laszlo turned right and Jordi turned left, guns raised, covering each other.

Each man or team simultaneously found their designated room. Jordi burst into his, gun in hand, and told the five men, "Don't move." They just raised their hands. Sanchez and Pascual entered the computer room where two men were lost in numbers on their monitors. In a combination of broken English and French, Sanchez said, "Stop. *Attention.*" Justin and Laszlo took the small office were two men sat across a desk from each other. Laszlo pointed his gun at them. "Raise your hands."

The taller of the two started to reach into his coat, but Laszlo pointed the gun at his head. "Do not even try," he warned.

The man raised his hands and Laszlo went over and pulled a revolver from the man's coat.

"Move over to the wall," Laszlo said.

Arms still raised, the two men did as directed. One was large, broad shouldered with a dark mustache. The other man was smaller with a big nose.

"Face the wall and put your hands up against it," Laszlo directed. The two men obeyed.

"Justin, cover me," Laszlo called.

Justin stood back and pointed his gun at the two men.

Laszlo moved his hands swiftly across their bodies. The smaller one was clean, but the larger man carried a switchblade in his pocket. Justin took their wallets and thoroughly emptied the contents of their pockets.

All were led into the largest room, hands tied behind their backs with nylon cords. When the office inhabitants were all seated on the floor as if ready for a game of 'Duck, Duck, Goose,' Laszlo said, "Now, we wish to question each one of you individually. Who wants to be first?"

The supervisor said, "You are not police. We have nothing to tell you."

"There is plenty to tell, and you just volunteered to tell it first," Justin said.

Jordi grabbed the man, jerking him off the floor.

"I have nothing to tell you," he insisted as Jordi hustled him out of the room. Sanchez and Pascual stayed behind, their guns pointed at the eight men on the floor.

The other men took the supervisor to another room. "Sit down, on the floor," Justin ordered.

Stefan and Doby were waiting for them. The man did as told, but repeated, "I have nothing to tell you. You are mistaken."

Laszlo did not listen, but looked at the man with his cold blue eyes and said, "There are eight other men out there that will see your still, lifeless body as an example of what will happen to them. If you don't talk, they will. What do you want? To answer questions, or be an example?"

Ziginiglou, with a precedented fear in his eyes, looked at Laszlo. "Answer questions."

Laszlo picked up the man's wallet and pulled out an identity card. "This says your name is Gingiz Ziginiglou and that you are Turkish. Is that correct, Mr. Ziginiglou?"

Ziginiglou nodded his head.

Laszlo said, "Answer me, Mr. Ziginiglou."

"Yes."

"Good. Now we are on the right track. I need information. You will tell me all about yourself, what you are doing here, what you were doing before you got here, and what this office is all about."

Ziginiglou nodded, glad he was sitting, because his knees were shaking.

CHAPTER 34

Sam Oliver and Paul Kent did not attend the news conference. They had thought it better to show no presence and were watching live from Sam's hotel television.

Justin had left the Nice office after several rounds of questioning to join them. He and Gloria needed to hear what was said. This was the smallest of steps toward some sort of resolution. Some way of making sense of their unsolvable circumstances.

The four of them sat in front of the television switching from one news station to the other. The press conference was being broadcast live on all of them. Four o'clock in the afternoon in France meant that it was mid-morning on the east coast of the United States. Millions of people would be watching this.

Dr. Gilbert Chevrolet, the international lawyer friend of Stefan Von Portzer, had flown down from Geneva, and it was planned that he would open and lead the news conference. He was a man of sixty years, impeccably dressed with a dark suit, white shirt, and classical solid red silk tie. He looked distinguished with his silver gray hair, and his manners showed him to be completely at ease in a courtroom, classroom, political rally, concert, formal dinner, or news conference. An excellent choice, Sam thought.

There were approximately fifty chairs in the room, all of them occupied. Many people lined the walls and stood in the back of the room where the television cameras were positioned. About a dozen photographers sat on the floor at the front of the room and had already started to click away.

On a slightly raised stage in the front of the room, Dora Vine stood next to Dr. Chevrolet. She had chosen an understated but elegant light blue dress with yellow flowers from the selection brought to her room earlier. It was from a boutique exclusive and upscale enough to send armloads of apparel to her hotel room. With her new haircut, she looked at least ten years younger than two days before, thought Justin.

Next to her stood Curley Grady and Habib Benhabib, both wearing brand-new business suits, Grady's dark blue and Habib's dark gray. Grady almost looked handsome, standing tall like a soldier, tan and composed. He looked confident, ready to face the crowd.

Habib, on the other hand, held his head slightly down, shoulders hunched, occasionally darting a glance at the crowd and then back down at the floor, shifting his weight from one foot to the other. He was out of his element. Sam, Paul and Justin knew that this was Habib's opportunity to redeem himself in some small way and hoped he would follow through.

Dr. Chevrolet raised his hand, quieting the crowd almost immediately. "Ladies and gentlemen, my name is Gilbert Chevrolet. I am a partner at the law firm of Chevrolet and Fischer in Geneva, Switzerland, and I represent Mrs. Vine who is here today to make a statement. You all received a one-page document when you entered the room and our purpose this afternoon is to provide you with further details. We are here to present the facts of this case, a case in which Mrs. Vine and her husband Mr. Pete Vine were kidnapped by a group of terrorists."

He looked down at the notes in front of him. Nothing in the room moved.

"Dora Vine was held fifteen months at a location in North Africa. The purpose of the kidnapping, according to the information we have, was to obtain a ransom privately. A plane crash was fabricated in order to make it appear to the public that the passengers had been killed. This was also to minimize the possibility of anyone seeking the hostages' whereabouts. But an insurance company in the United States, Baltimore Life, had an investigator working on the case who managed to ascertain the precise location of Mrs. Vine and free her. He had the help of a pilot who provided critical information and assisted in the rescue of the victims. Both of these gentlemen stand behind me."

He continued to gaze across the crowd of reporters. "The investigator from Baltimore Life is Mr. Curley Grady," he gracefully gestured toward Grady, "and next to him is Mr. Benhabib, the pilot.

"We are sorry to confirm that great tragedy occurred during those months. Mr. Pete Vine died during his captivity. This has been attributed to a heart attack. His captors were evil men and while they did not apply direct violent physical means to Mr. Vine, we maintain that the conditions under which he was held, combined with the lack of medical help, served as major factors contributing to his death.

"Now, for this press conference, Mrs. Vine will read a statement and then Mr. Grady will read one concerning his role and the rescue. Then, Mr. Grady and Mr. Benhabib will take any questions. I hope you understand that Mrs. Vine has been through an extremely traumatic experience and she does not need any further stress."

Before continuing, he paused for a moment to look seriously out at the crowd of reporters and then said, "I would ask the press to respect her condition. At some point in the near future when Mrs. Vine feels she has recuperated adequately, then she will be available for interviews with the press. Today she will give a statement only. Now, I invite Mrs. Vine."

So far so good, Sam thought as he watched the conference. The lawyer was in control.

Dora Vine made her way to the podium and read from a piece of paper that had been previously placed there.

As you can understand, this has been a very difficult experience for me. Kidnapping is a horrendous event for anyone, and I now personally know what it means. What was particularly difficult was losing my husband Pete

Dora stopped reading the text, looked at the crowd for a brief moment and then stepped back from the podium. The crowd of journalists remained miraculously silent except for the flashing and clicking of photographers. The conference was under control.

Next Grady came up to read his prepared statement. His face was serious as he looked out at the crowd, yet simultaneously slightly theatrical. He looked down at his written statement and then at the crowd and he waited a moment.

He proceeded, "I will read a statement, as the good doctor lawyer said, and then Habib and I will answer any questions."

Grady paused, looked down at his prepared statement, and then looked up at the crowd and said, "You know, the good doctor lawyer's name is Chevrolet. Now I always thought that was an American name, because our most popular American car is named Chevrolet, but I learned from the good doctor lawyer that it's a Swiss name. In fact, a guy whose name was Louis Chevrolet first built our Chevrolet cars, and he came from Switzerland. He was a car racer and built cars and he went to America and built Chevys and at some point General Motors bought the Chevrolet car company and the rest is history. In fact, you know the little symbol on the front of Chevrolet cars? That is straight off the Swiss flag, the cross, you know, except it has been stretched a bit."

Grady looked at the crowd, contented with himself that he had explained that bit of information. Then he looked at Dr. Chevrolet for affirmation. Dr. Chevrolet shifted on his feet, his composure rattled. Grady looked back at his paper and then at the crowd again and said, "Now I will read the statement and then we can have some questions."

Three months ago the Baltimore Life Insurance Company assigned me to the case of the Vines, who were clients of theirs. Baltimore Life suspected that there were certain open issues with the case concerning the crash of the airplane upon which the Vines were passengers. One such discrepancy was the fact that the airplane had never really been found on the bottom of the Mediterranean Sea, so I began my investigation. After following a trail of evidence to Tunisia, and with the help of Mr. Benhabib, we found the place where they were held. In finding the location, and in interrogating the captors, we were put in a situation where we had to defend ourselves, and a gunfight broke out and all the captors were killed. The police in Tunisia have been informed and they are now investigating the case. We are thankful that Mrs. Vine has been rescued and is safe, but saddened to learn about the death of Mr. Vine. To conclude, I am grateful that I could be of assistance in this case. Thank you.

"And now we will take any questions," Grady said.

The room broke out in a loud cacophony as dozens of news reporters started to ask questions all at the same time. Dr. Chevrolet came forward and raised his hand and the crowd calmed. He then pointed at one of the news reporters who asked, "Mr. Grady. How did you know how to find the kidnappers in Tunisia?"

Grady stepped forward again and said, "I have got a lot of experience in these things. You see I was a cop, a first-class detective on the police force in Los Angeles, California, I might add. Now, I saw all kinds of cases, like robberies, beatings, murders, domestic fights and stuff like that, and I have used all that experience since I set up my private practice and started to work for Baltimore Life and other insurance companies. These insurance companies like what I do, and they like how I get to the bottom of any case they give me, like this one. The people at Baltimore Life want to treat their customers well, but if they think there are any shenanigans going on they take great displeasure in them, and then they assign someone like me who knows the ropes. So, it took some doing and a lot of asking questions of a lot of people, but I found the trail and found the place, along with the help of my good friend Habib here."

Justin and Gloria, Sam Oliver and Paul Kent watched the television in Sam's hotel room, all of them cringing in their chairs. Sam had a sudden realization. "I don't know how he did it, but he completely sidestepped the question."

A reporter made herself heard above the others. "We know that there were other passengers on that plane, a Mrs. Collins and her daughter Sophie."

Grady didn't bother to wait for the question. "That's right. We rescued both of them too, except Mrs. Collins was hit by a bullet, and we had to get her up here quick to a hospital. Habib flew the plane here, he's a real hero. I think you should write something about him in your newspapers."

"Where is Mrs. Collins?" the reporter asked.

"Well, if you got a bullet in you, where would you go?" Grady rolled his eyes like it was a dumb question, and to make it sound dumber, he said, "Where do you think she is, lying around on some beach drinking French wine?" He looked at the reporter in the manner of a stern professor sharing serious information with a slow student. "She is in a hospital."

"Which one?"

"Like we're going to tell you all," Grady said, sniffing.

Before Dr. Chevrolet could do the honors, Grady pointed to another reporter who asked, "May we ask Mr. Benhabib a question? Mr. Benhabib, what was your role in the rescue?"

Habib walked sheepishly up to the podium, looked at Grady, then looked at the crowd, and slowly said, "I help."

"What do you mean you helped?" yelled the reporter.

"I help Mr. Grady," answered Habib.

Grady jumped in and said, "That's right, and he flew the airplane. That was another big help. This man is a hero. That is all I can say."

Sam and Paul didn't know if they should cry tears of happiness or of sorrow. Sam could see Dora Vine in the background standing behind Dr. Chevrolet. She had her head down and looked like she was crying, but when he looked closer, he was certain she was trying to keep from giggling.

The interview went on for another fifteen minutes and Dr. Chevrolet attempted to regain his position as lawyer in charge, but the reporters directed their questions toward Grady who gave them no real information beyond his opinions. But they did not seem to mind. They were used to these kinds of content-less press conferences and interviews. At least this one was entertaining.

Finally, Dr. Chevrolet brought the news conference to a close with a suave finish. "We hope that you now have sufficient information regarding this case. We will be releasing further written statements for you in the days to come, and we will inform you when Mrs. Vine will be available for interviews. Thank you for your sensitivity in this regard. You may reach me at my offices in Geneva. My telephone number can be found on the printout that was handed to you when you entered. Thank you."

The news conference ended, but a hoard of reporters came up to Grady, gathering around him and sticking microphones in front of his face, while Dr. Chevrolet led Dora out a side door. Habib stuck carefully to the side of Grady, while Grady kept talking about what a hero Habib was. Several news reporters from the major networks gave their cards to Grady and asked for individual interviews.

In his hotel room, Sam Oliver turned to the other three and said, "Well, the lawyer put up a good smokescreen to protect Dora."

Justin started nodding then changed to shaking his head. "And Grady. Grady missed his calling. He should have been a stand-up comedian or a politician."

CHAPTER 35

Justin and Gloria left Sam's room and took the elevator two floors down to theirs, the room next to Dora Vine. As Justin opened the door he heard the telephone ringing and walked over to answer it.

"Hello. This is Justin Collins."

"Mr. Collins, this is the clinic. We just wanted to inform you that Mrs. Collins is now conscious. She asked for you."

"Thank you. Can you tell her that I'm coming immediately?"

Justin put down the receiver and said to Gloria, "She's awake. I have to go see her."

Gloria looked at him. "I want to go with you."

"Are you sure?" he said, aware that this was a difficult step. He was both overjoyed that Chantal was awake and daunted by the implications of her survival.

"Yes," she replied. "This is our life, our problem. I want to be there, not necessarily there in the room with you both, but at least to be with you." She had tilted her head back as she did when listening or refusing to back down.

She wasn't listening.

He bit his lip. "OK, let's go to the hospital."

The taxi ride to the hospital took fifteen minutes. They headed past the reception desk and up the elevator to Intensive Care.

They looked through the glass and saw Chantal lying in the same bed, but no longer flat. Her back and head were slightly raised. The tube in her mouth was gone and her eyes were shut.

He looked at Gloria, for once unable to read her face. She gave him an impenetrable look and said, "I know this is hard. Take courage."

He entered the room and walked slowly toward Chantal, not wanting to wake her, yet wanting to see her awake. As he approached she opened her eyes, those clear blue eyes, and she weakly smiled. "Justin." His name was barely audible.

"Chantal," he said as softly as she had spoken. He bent down and kissed her on the forehead. She closed her eyes.

She opened them again and searched his face. "You don't know how long I have wanted that," she whispered. "I have missed you more than freedom."

"I've missed you too, Chantal." His 'missing' had been different than hers. He had had to deal with her death.

"How are you feeling?" he asked.

"Not myself," she said, her weak voice reinforcing this.

She was groggy, but he could tell her mind was there. He reached for her hand and held it, the intravenous tube getting in the way.

"They told me I was in poor shape."

"I was here this morning and spoke with the doctor. He didn't tell me too much, other than we would have to wait to see if—how you would recover." He paused. The drone of a nearby machine hummed low. "You don't know how I have grieved over you," Justin whispered, stroking her hair back from her forehead.

"And me for you." Her lips and mouth felt dry.

He reached across to the bed stand and poured a glass of water. He gently lifted her head with one hand and held the glass to her lips.

"I left Vine Industries about six months after the airplane crash, or I should say after you went missing." He put her head back on the bed and she blinked her eyes as a nod. "I went to Spain. I was so grieved. That is where I live now."

"Justin," she whispered. "The other woman." She swallowed. She struggled to find the energy to speak. "In the *Mas*. She is your wife?"

At this point he could only manage a nod that pulled his head forward until it rested on her heart.

She lay still for a long moment then said, "They gave us newspapers. We read about the crash. I know you. I thought about it, in Tunisia. I knew you would find someone to love. You are that kind of man. You need to love and be loved. You could not wait for a dead woman." The words came slowly.

"It happened fast. Gloria reminded me of you—similar but different. All I can say is that I am so sorry."

"Don't be sorry. What is her name?" Her eyes flickered a bit, then her train of thought shifted and she said, "He made me pregnant…so awful. I didn't want to share my body with anyone but you."

She shut her eyes and fell into sleep.

Justin held her hand for a while, thinking about what she said. 'Don't be sorry.' She understood that he would move on with his life. She understood that he had made certain choices and had remarried.

He had not chosen this dilemma. Other people had forced this situation on him. Unlike many men, he had not chosen to have a woman on the side. He had always been faithful to Chantal, and his intention was to be faithful to Gloria. This situation was beyond his control. It just happened. The problem had no solution as he could see it.

Chantal or Gloria?

Should he just leave, just get on a boat and go somewhere? That might be best for everyone. But, no, he had a responsibility to both of them, and to his children.

The words of Señora Pascual flashed through his mind—"will or want." What did he want? Things were happening so fast he didn't have time to think. He felt that grief and anger and indecision had been blended together and poured liberally down his body, into his core.

Finally, he put down Chantal's hand and walked out into the hall. Gloria was seated in a chair, waiting for him.

"How is she doing?" she asked.

"Tired, but we talked."

"What did she say?"

"Several things. She knows about you. She remembered what was said in the farmhouse and wants to meet you."

"I would like to meet her too," said Gloria.

The doctor he had seen in the morning was walking down the hall. He approached Justin and asked, "Did you talk with her?"

"Yes. Is she going to make it?"

"As you can see, she is doing better. At least she is conscious. It appears that the internal bleeding has stopped, and my feeling is that she will recover. She has a long way to go, but the signs are positive."

"Thank God," Justin said. "Is it OK to spend time with her?"

"Yes, for short periods and with no emotional shocks. When she falls asleep she should not be awakened. In the next few days she should be able to take more stimulus, but not today."

The doctor left. Justin stood next to Gloria in the hall. They looked in through the glass window watching Chantal sleep. Justin reached for Gloria's hand. "Thank you for being here with me."

A nurse came running down the hall, her rubber-heeled shoes squeaking. She was carrying a cordless telephone. "Monsieur Collins?" she panted.

"Yes?"

"You have a telephone call. The man said it was extremely urgent."

"Thank you." He took the telephone to his ear and said, "Hello."

"Hello, Justin. This is Stefan. Something has come up."

"What is it?"

"We finally got to questioning the big guy, the one with the black moustache. They call him Turk."

"What did he say?"

"He and a guy called Yass were staking out your place in Spain. They were the ones who kidnapped Gloria in Barcelona, but Gaubert told them to stay behind in Llanca to look for you. The little guy with the big nose, Ziginiglou, spoke with them on the phone this morning. After that, this Yass has gone crazy, so he says."

Yass and anger were becoming synonyms in Justin's mind. "Where is he? What does he want?"

"Turk isn't completely positive. It seems Yass had been ranting, but he kept talking about a French concubine allowing his son to be killed. He wants payment in return. Turk thinks he wants to take a little girl in exchange. I think he means Sophie."

"Where is he now?"

"His uncle runs a religious training center in Marseille. Turk said he planned to go there and talk with the uncle. He said they are a bunch of fanatics, so we don't know what we are getting into."

"Does Yass know the hotel where we are staying?"

"Turk doesn't think so, but Yass is a professional at tracking people around. He may have followed one of us. Who knows?"

"I better get back to the hotel to be with Sophie."

"Justin, do you have your gun?"

"Yes."

Stefan hung up.

Gloria placed her hand on his arm. "Go. I will stay with Chantal." Then she gently pushed him toward the doors.

CHAPTER 36

For two hours, Gloria sat next to Chantal who did not move except for her steady breathing. Then, slowly, she opened her eyes and focused on the ceiling. "I am alive."

Gloria looked at her and smiled. "Yes."

Chantal waited for a moment and then said, "I thought I was dying. I kept dreaming I was dying. When I woke up and saw you there I thought you were an angel, a beautiful angel."

"I am not an angel."

"Are you a nurse?" Chantal asked.

"No, not a nurse," Gloria said. She was uncertain what to say. The doctor said that Chantal should not receive an emotional shock.

Chantal lay there for a moment and then said, "Could you move my head up a bit? The bed has a button on the side."

Gloria found it and pushed the one with a plus sign, and Chantal's back began to rise.

"There. That is good. Thank you."

Gloria adjusted Chantal's pillow and asked her, "Would you like some water?"

"Yes."

As Gloria handed it to her, Chantal said, "I feel terrible, but better, if that makes sense."

"It does. The doctors say you are improving, although you need to stay calm. If you keep improving, they may even get you on your feet for a short walk in a couple of days."

Chantal took a breath. "I almost died, didn't I?"

"They were reluctant to make any predictions," replied Gloria.

"Typical doctors," said Chantal.

Chantal sat there for a minute as Gloria remained silent and Chantal asked, "Where is Sophie?"

"Sophie is with Mrs. Vine. They are staying at a hotel in Nice. Sophie is being pampered."

Chantal smiled. "That makes me happy. Where is Justin?"

"In Nice. He had to meet with Stefan Von Portzer and some other men who have been helping him."

"Stefan? Stefan is here?" Chantal looked toward the door as if he would appear there.

"Yes, with all that has been happening, Justin asked for his help."

"Stefan is a good man," Chantal said.

They sat for a minute or two, not saying anything until Chantal looked straight at Gloria. "You are Gloria, aren't you?"

"Yes, I am."

Chantal's eyes rimmed with tears and she shut them, sending two rivulets down along her jaw. Gloria brushed a tissue against the tears.

"It's the drugs," Chantal said. "It's hard to control emotions. Words are difficult," she said, speaking slowly. "It's hard for me to accept."

"I understand. For me too," Gloria replied.

There was more silence. Gloria asked, "It's not our fault—yours or mine, is it?"

Chantal replied, "No. Neither Justin's."

Gloria nodded. She knew she had to be careful.

They were quiet, and Chantal shut her eyes and kept them closed so long that Gloria assumed she had gone to sleep. Then she heard a faint, almost inaudible whisper, "Do you love him?"

"Yes," Gloria breathed. "And you?" she asked, clenching her eyes closed against the answer she knew.

"With all my heart."

"This is painful for all of us."

"No, no more pain," Chantal whispered. She closed her eyes for a moment, opened them and then said, "I am getting tired. Can you lower the bed?"

Gloria pushed the button with the minus sign and the bed went back to a flat position. Gloria asked, "Can I do anything for you?"

"Yes, read me a Psalm."

"Is there a Bible here?"

"Yes. There is one in the drawer over there. A hospital chaplain came by today, and I saw him take a Bible from the drawer."

Gloria retrieved the Bible, came back to the bedside, and asked, "Which Psalm?"

"Any."

Gloria turned to Psalm 25, skimmed it, and started reading at the fourth verse.

Show me the path where I should go, O Lord; point out the right road for me to walk. Lead me..."

When Gloria finished, Chantal was asleep.

★ ★ ★

A maid came out of one of the hotel rooms with an armload of towels just as Justin ran down the hall. She jerked back into the doorframe, losing the top of her pile as Justin left a 'sorry' in the air over his shoulder.

He knocked on Dora's suite where Sophie was supposed to be with her nanny. Joseline opened the door and first looked at his heaving chest, her eyes on a level with it. She then raised her wide eyes to Justin's panting face.

"Bonjour Monsieur Collins," she finally said, stepping aside to let him in.

He was already halfway to the bedroom door when he asked, "Sophie is here? She is all right?"

"Oui, oui. She is sleeping. Finally." Joseline rolled her eyes to indicate that the little girl's energy was in indirect proportion to her own.

Justin pushed open the bedroom door and saw his daughter in a tangle of blankets and curls. He took a deep breath and crept over to her. He leaned over and kissed her fat, warm cheek where a strand of hair stuck to a spot of jam.

He had lamented his lack of choice. Here was a child who only had to choose whether she would go to bed without a fuss, whether she wanted jam or honey. What he chose would affect her and set her life in a direction she had no control over. The responsibility of this made him ill.

He left the room, closing the door behind him, and went over to Joseline, who was picking up books and large crumbs from the floor.

He picked up a pink plastic necklace and held it toward her. "I'm sorry for rushing in like this. But I have reason to believe that Sophie may be in danger."

Joseline's face went pale and she gripped the necklace and books tight. Justin continued, "I don't want to alarm you, but I do want to forewarn you. A man—a crazy man—may try to take Sophie."

Justin moved toward the phone. "I'll have someone come over and stay with you." He dialed a number and waited, wiping sweat from his temples.

After two rings, Justin spoke into the phone, "Hey Stefan. Can you put Sanchez on the line?"

★ ★ ★

At eight thirty on Thursday morning, Sam Oliver entered the conference room.

Earlier at eight o'clock Stefan had stopped by his hotel room and shown him a sheet of paper with a list of names and a number next to each name.

Nothing had been signed. Stefan had not wanted Sam to be implicated in any way. They shook hands. A gentleman's agreement. But not a gentleman-like plan.

Now, Sam was one of the last ones to arrive. There were close to thirty people in the room, mostly men, few women. He had a cup of coffee in his hand and found an empty chair in the back and looked around. Many of the faces he knew. After four weeks of European travel, he had visited most of the EuroVinco offices and had gotten to know a lot of people.

It was to be a two-day conference. These were the top managers of EuroVinco, and it was the first large management meeting since the company had merged with Unipac. People would be worried about their jobs. Sam was glad that Paul Kent was running the meeting. He felt tired. It was not only a result of all the visiting. What drained him most was the Jacques Gaubert situation.

Still, he felt optimistic. This affair had uncovered the source of the corporate overhead problem. Now it could be fixed. Sam was confident of it.

And Doby's report had been extremely helpful. Sam knew that Doby would be working with the two computer engineers in that office to uncover further information. They now knew the names of the accountants who had been working for Gaubert in the EuroVinco headquarter offices in London, Frankfurt and Nice. Sam had not been sure what to do about this. He discussed the situation with Stefan Von Portzer and Dr. Chevrolet. Together they formulated a plan whereby these accountants would be charged for their crimes but in such a way that nothing was linked to Jacques Gaubert. Dr. Chevrolet knew what to do, and Sam trusted him to do it well.

The biggest issue now was this office in San Jose. Somehow those two new directors were implicated—Randolph Sutter and Karl Schubach. Jacques Gaubert must have planted them. And then Sam's own phone had been tapped. He valued privacy, and such an invasion of it disturbed him.

According to Stefan, people in the Nice office had uncovered transcripts of all the telephone calls made to and from Sam's home. They had also planted listening devices in Paul Kent's home. Apparently, someone by the name of Ziginiglou, an accountant working for Gaubert, had confessed this information. It was uncertain if they would be able to bring charges against Ziginiglou without revealing the entire affair between Gaubert and EuroTech. They had no desire to do that.

Questioning would just have to continue.

CHAPTER 37

Paul Kent's brother, George, was a detective on the San Jose police department. He was currently on assignment in Brussels liaising with a task force of law officers trying to bust an international drug smuggling ring.

Sam had finally gotten through to him the previous night and discussed their alternatives. Wire-tapping was a federal offense. They agreed to talk about it when Sam was in Brussels on the weekend.

Sam looked around at all the people in the room—top managers of EuroVinco, the hope of the company. People were still taking their seats, and someone slipped in next to him. It was Jean-Claude Dubois, the manager of the EuroVinco factory in Grenoble.

"Hello," Sam said. "How are you doing?"

Dubois replied, "Well, thank you. I am looking forward to the meeting and especially your report."

"Ah, don't expect too much," Sam said, making a small swipe at the air with his hand. "I'll just waste your time."

"I doubt that," Dubois said, smiling. "Somehow I feel things are going to change now that we are a part of Unipac."

"And hopefully for the better," Sam said. He remembered his time in Grenoble and the lady supporting her four children. "How is that employee... Adelle Leclerc?" Sam asked.

"You have a good memory for names."

"Have you talked with her lately?"

"I talked with her yesterday. She said to say hello, if I saw you here."

"I am glad she remembers me," Sam smiled.

"Oh, yes. She felt confident after your visit. A lot of people felt confident."

"I did too," Sam admitted. "You have great people working there. If we do the right things as a company, your employees should have a good future. But it's not so much up to me any more. It's up to Paul Kent and the others in this room."

Sam paused for a moment and said, "By the way, when I was in Grenoble, you mentioned someone named Justin Collins. Do you remember?"

"Yes, I do."

"For your information, I ran into him. He is doing better."

"I heard about it on the news. Such tragic circumstances." Dubois shook his head and ran his fingers along the edge of the table. "Do you know if he has joined another company?"

"No idea," Sam said. "I just met him briefly."

"He was one of the best managers in Vine Industries."

Sam watched as Paul Kent walked to the front of the room. Paul looked out at the people, smiled, and began, "I just want to welcome you to this meeting—the first joint management meeting of EuroVinco since the merger with Unipac. This meeting was called together quickly. We felt it would be helpful to talk about some of our ideas and to engage you into the process of drawing up strategies and plans for the future. I would also like to invite you all to come to California for a week next month for the Unipac annual management meeting." Managers around the room murmured their approval.

"I would also like to take this opportunity to introduce to you Sam Oliver, the chairman of our board. Many of you have already met Sam during his visit to your operations during the past few weeks. Now he has a chance to give us some feedback concerning his trip."

Sam walked to the front of the quiet room and looked out at the faces in front of him.

"My thanks to Paul for inviting me to this meeting, but I don't know about thanking him for asking me to sleep in so many hotel rooms over the past four weeks. I am looking forward to getting back to my own bed." Pockets of laughter broke out across the room.

"Seriously, thanks to Paul for giving me the opportunity to meet so many of you. I want also to thank all of you for your kind hospitality, for the information you shared, and for allowing me to meet so many of your people. My purpose today is to give you some feedback of what I have observed, what I learned."

Sam made eye contact with his audience, sweeping his gaze around the room. "Let me start with the first part, the quality of the people in EuroVinco."

★ ★ ★

Laszlo walked into the office in Monaco and blinked. Obviously Féret and Jaccoud were doing very well.

Monaco was not far from Nice, and Féret and Jaccoud's offices were based here. They were '*Fiduciaires*'—lawyers handling the fiduciary affairs of their clients, advising in such things as corporate setup, tax planning, accounting and other financial matters. An impressive list of clients represented all continents, wealthy individuals, and corporations who relied on their services. The list was internal information, never shown to anyone outside their office. All the services at Féret and Jaccoud were provided on a confidential basis.

Laszlo had come with Stefan Von Portzer and Dr. Gilbert Chevrolet. He was wearing a business suit for the first time in months. It had been quite squashed up in the bottom of his travel bag, but the hotel had cleaned and pressed it and he looked as if it were his daily costume. In here, he felt like he needed a tux. He looked up at the enormous crystal chandelier suspended directly above him. He took several steps to the side.

Dr. Chevrolet walked over to the receptionist, with his elegant press smile and said, "I am Dr. Chevrolet and these are my associates. We have an appointment to see Mr. Féret and Mr. Jaccoud."

The receptionist/fashion model stretched her glossy lips into a returning smile and said, "Could you take a chair? I will inform them that you are here."

Stefan and Dr. Chevrolet found two chairs, but Laszlo wandered around the room, looking at the lithographs and paintings on the walls. He stopped in front an original painting by El Greco. *Must be worth a fortune,* he thought.

The receptionist kept looking over at Laszlo. She was used to controlling people, especially men, and it was her role to make sure that anyone entering into the offices of Féret and Jaccoud were kept under control. The large blond man had not followed her instructions.

She said, "Sir, you are welcome to take a seat."

Laszlo merely glanced her and continued to stand in front of the painting.

For some reason this was making her uneasy, and she started sorting papers and opening drawers in an attempt to look occupied. Laszlo guessed that her main duties were answering the occasional telephone call and directing traffic coming into the office. Her irritation did not bother him.

A buzzer sounded. She picked up the telephone in relief, listened and returned it to its cradle, rising. "Would you follow me?"

She led them down a small hall into a conference room. She walked the hall carpet like it was a catwalk, her hips shifting. Laszlo looked at her unimpressed, as though his steel-blue eyes saw through her futile attempt at seduction. This bothered her even more.

She said, "Please take a seat. Mr. Féret and Mr. Jaccoud will be with you shortly. May I bring you anything to drink?"

Stefan and Dr. Chevrolet both said, "Coffee, please."

Laszlo declined. "No, thank you."

A few minutes later she came back carrying a tray with two coffees, cream and sugar and placed them at the table where Stefan and Dr. Chevrolet were seated. Laszlo was still standing and when she looked at him, he returned the look. She spilled the cream.

"I am so sorry," she said, and she left the room. She immediately returned with a cloth and wiped up the cream, leaving in a hurry.

Stefan enjoyed this and liked that Laszlo was already having an impact on this office before Féret and Jaccoud even arrived.

A few minutes later Mr. Féret and Mr. Jaccoud entered the room. Everyone shook hands, and they all sat down, Laszlo last. He had a way of unsettling people.

Mr. Féret spoke first. "How can we help you gentlemen?"

"Thank you for meeting with us on such short notice," Chevrolet began. "This meeting is rather urgent. We would like to explain our situation to you and then determine how you might assist us. That is, if you agree."

Laszlo saw that Féret and Jaccoud were cautious, but Féret nodded his head for Dr. Chevrolet to continue.

"First, I would like to introduce ourselves. I am Dr. Gilbert Chevrolet from the law firm of Chevrolet and Fischer in Geneva. This is Mr. Stefan Von Portzer, an international businessman and financial advisor, also based in Geneva. His associate is Mr. Laszlo Vartek."

Féret and Jaccoud looked across the table at Stefan and Laszlo. Stefan smiled. Laszlo did not.

Chevrolet continued, "There are a number of issues we would like to discuss with you that will impact GauLux Holding, of which you gentlemen are directors. I should preface that by saying that the Unipac corporation has given my law firm a mandate to represent them in their legal affairs in Europe, particularly pertaining to legal structures." Chevrolet let them absorb this and then continued, "Unipac is also concerned about certain irregularities concerning GauLux Holding. Mr. Von Portzer will describe these irregularities in detail, and we will be asking you gentlemen to take corrective actions."

Dr. Chevrolet's mention of the word 'irregularities' caught the two men's attention. "We are the directors of GauLux Holding," said Féret, "and we can assure you that there are no irregularities concerning this company."

"Gentlemen, we would like you to see the information and evidence we have collected, and then you can make your judgment. We will then make a proposal you can consider," said Stefan.

"What information do you have?" asked Jaccoud.

"I think it is best to first lay out some alternatives for you to keep in mind. Very simply the first alternative is litigation. The second is remuneration."

CHAPTER 38

"Litigation?" asked Féret.

"Yes, we will get to that," Stefan said. "Now we have three elements to consider. First, we know that the ownership structure behind GauLux Holding consists of ten different companies, some registered in European countries and some registered offshore—Monaco, for instance. Interestingly, the directors of all those companies, as well as of GauLux Holding, are the executive members of the fiduciary firm of Féret and Jaccoud. We also know that the main shareholder of those ten companies appears to have been Jacques Gaubert. We assume there are other shareholders, but we will ignore them."

Féret leaned forward, his face pinched in disapproval. "This is all confidential information."

"Gentlemen," Stefan said, "we are not here today to engage in complex iterations. We want to keep this simple. I am only laying out the facts. Then we will discuss the two alternatives I mentioned. Another fact is that each of those companies has bank accounts in various legal jurisdictions around the world. There is nothing illegal about that. So that is the first element that we want to consider.

"The second element is this: we have records that show that money has been illegally skimmed out of EuroVinco. The amounts are considerable. I have all the evidence in this report."

Stefan reached into his leather attaché case, pulled out a thick, bound stack of papers, and said, "These are all accounting records and can be independently audited. We also have witnesses who know about these transactions, and in some cases these witnesses were involved in this fraudulent activity. They are willing to testify."

Féret and Jaccoud looked blankly at Stefan, and then at each other. Jaccoud said, "We know nothing about these transactions. Is this a setup?"

It was Stefan's turn to look stern. "Mr. Féret, you know this is not a setup, and you had better start thinking very seriously. So here is the third and last element: the firm of Féret and Jaccoud acts as directors for these ten companies that are performing these illegal transactions. May I remind you again that the amounts are not negligible. This has serious ramifications for you. We know that this firm does considerable business around the world. GauLux Holding was a notable client, but there are others. It would be a pity if the reputation of Féret and Jaccoud were damaged in any way. Your many important clients would not be pleased to know that their fiduciary firm was implicated in an unsavory affair. And to remind you who those clients are, I would like to present you with a list."

Stefan again reached into his leather case and pulled out several pieces of paper. The complete client list of Féret and Jaccoud. Doby had been successful. The list contained recognized names of politicians, entertainers and people in the business world.

Féret took the list. His face turned white. He handed it to Jaccoud who looked at it in turn. "How did you get this?" Jaccoud asked.

"It doesn't matter. It's a reminder to you that this firm has a lot to lose," said Stefan.

"What do you want?" Jaccoud asked.

"Two simple things. The first is that you give us the codes to all the bank account numbers for the ten companies that own GauLux Holding. You have those codes in a safe here in this office. In fact, while we are here you will initiate transfer of all the money from those accounts into one account number that Dr. Chevrolet will give you. We will wait here until that is done, as will my associate Mr. Vartek. You will not leave these offices. That is the first thing. By the way, we know how much is in those accounts down to the last digit."

Féret turned even whiter and said, "That's a lot of money."

"As I said, I know," Stefan replied.

"And the second thing?" Jaccoud asked, not really wanting to know the answer.

"Also simple. On paper, Mr. Jacques Gaubert is the primary shareholder of all the ten companies. Now that Mr. Gaubert is deceased there is no reason to continue with the current ownership structure, nor for those companies to continue to exist. Therefore, what we want is for you to close those companies. There will also be a change of ownership of GauLux Holding, a registration of new shareholders. It will only take you a few minutes to do that. There will be two new shareholders of GauLux Holding, fifty-fifty. Mrs. Dora Vine will own half and Mr. Justin Collins the other half. In addition, the fiduciary responsibility over GauLux Holding will also be transferred from Féret and Jaccoud to the firm of Chevrolet and Fischer in Geneva, Switzerland."

"That is complex and will take time," Jaccoud said. "There are other shareholders."

"Does Unipac know about this?" Féret asked.

Dr. Chevrolet intervened. "Gentlemen, Unipac does know. As their European lawyer, I can confirm that they have agreed to this. Secondly, I know that it will take less than an hour for you to arrange the paperwork for the transfer of ownership and the transfer of fiduciary responsibility. As I mentioned before, we are not concerned with the other shareholders, and we would advise them to forget this affair."

"So, that brings us back to our two alternatives," Stefan said. The first is litigation. If you do not do as we ask, Unipac will immediately file for damages against the firm of Féret and Jaccoud. Unipac is a large corporation with deep pockets. Personally I would not want to face them in a court trial, especially seeing the evidence we have."

"What is the second alternative you mentioned, something about remuneration?" Féret asked.

Stefan explained, "If you immediately do what we say, then we will not take you to court, and the remuneration is that you get to keep all your current customers, the ones on the list before you."

"You are asking a lot," Jaccoud said.

"Not so much," Stefan said. "And there is one consideration that we did not explore. Currently there is a considerable amount of money in the accounts of those ten companies. Because that money is tempting, there is a theory that Féret and Jaccoud were involved in a conspiracy to kill Jacques Gaubert, in order to have the money. Interesting theory, don't you think so? What do you think the judges in France would do with that one?"

"We had nothing to do with that," Féret said.

"Can you prove it?" Stefan asked, making his first real threat. "I'll tell you right now that we will do everything possible to produce that evidence in a court of law."

Not wanting to waste any more time, Dr. Chevrolet decided this was an excellent place to conclude and said, "We have no further information to present to you. Now it's up to both of you to make a decision. We'll give you fifteen seconds."

* * *

Over the next two hours they monitored Féret and Jaccoud—Laszlo hovering as only he could—until all the required actions were completed. Instructions were sent to banks to transfer all funds to one Swiss account, registered under the name of the law firm Chevrolet and Fischer. They would distribute it from there.

The record of shareholders of GauLux Holding was changed from the ten shell companies to two new owners, each with fifty percent. And the fiduciary management of GauLux Holding was transferred from Féret and Jaccoud to the law firm of Chevrolet and Fischer in Geneva. The next step in Geneva would be to consult Dora Vine and Justin Collins and rename the holding company. GauLux Holding would cease to exist.

In addition, Féret and Jaccoud signed various certified statements, indicating that all actions taken that day were definitive and legal.

When all the transactions had finally been completed, Dr. Chevrolet shook the hands of Mr. Féret and Mr. Jaccoud and said, "It has been a pleasure to do business with you gentlemen. I wish both of you a prosperous future. But may I offer you one word of advice? Be very careful whom you choose as clients. When you chose Mr. Gaubert as a business associate, you came uncomfortably close to receiving very long prison sentences. If we ever hear from you again, that option will be reconsidered. Thank you and goodbye."

Mr. Féret and Mr. Jaccoud said nothing. They stood side by side and looked as if they needed to lean on each other or the wall for support.

Laszlo walked out into the reception area to leave the office. He looked over at the receptionist and smiled. She slammed a drawer shut and turned back to her monitor.

They went to the parking lot where the minivan was parked, got inside and drove away. When they reached the *autoroute* between Monaco and Marseille, Stefan asked Laszlo to pull over at a rest stop. Laszlo parked the minivan and turned off the key. Dr. Chevrolet remained quiet in the back seat.

Stefan said, "Laszlo, I would like you to look at this." Stefan handed him a single sheet of paper. A list of names paralleled a list of amounts.

Jordi Pujols	*$5M*
Doby	*$5M*
Curley Grady	*$5M*
Laszlo Vartek	*$5M*
J. Sanchez	*$1M*
P. Pascual	*$1M*
Habib Benhabib	*$1M*
Chevrolet & Fischer	*$5M (5-year mandate)*
Total	*$28M*
Approx. remaining	*$472M (split 50/50% between Vine & Collins)*

"That's incredible," Laszlo said. "Does Sam Oliver know about this?"

"I showed it to him this morning. We shook hands on it and that was it. Dora Vine also agrees to it."

"The five million each for Jordi, Doby, Grady and myself. Would you mind explaining that?"

"You did a great service for Unipac. Legally, Unipac could ask for all the money back from Gaubert's companies, since the money was stolen from EuroVinco. That would only open up a can of worms and raise accounting questions and investigations. It would hurt the image of the company. Sam is confident that Unipac will be able to 'stop the bleeding,' as he put it. He says that the payment to the four of you, as well as to Sanchez and Pascual, is well worth it. As for the five million for Doby, his research enabled us to identify the office in Nice and the connections to Gaubert. By the way, Doby likes some of the equipment they have in the office here in Nice, very high tech, you know. He is going to have it all shipped to his farmhouse in Switzerland."

"There is nothing for you," Laszlo remarked.

Stefan looked at the dashboard. "I prefer to stay neutral. I wanted to help a friend." He looked back at Laszlo. "Anyway, Sam made another proposal to me, and if I received any of this money it would be questionable."

"That is admirable of you. The amounts going to Dora and Justin are considerable. They have suffered immensely," Laszlo said.

"Sam feels that way. Concerning the payment to Justin, Sam and I know that Justin will take care of Gloria and Chantal. Justin will make sure everything is equitable in case they decide on a separation option."

Laszlo reflected and then said, "That would be hard on all of them. What a choice." But thoughts of Collins's dilemma receded a bit. "That is quite a bit of money for me, five million. I didn't do this for money." He turned the key in the ignition. "But I'll take it," he said, smiling for the second time that day. Perhaps a record.

CHAPTER 39

Justin felt like a clock pendulum swinging between Chantal and Gloria. And gravity seemed to hold him longest when he hung between them, a heavy weight preventing time from moving forward.

He spent the morning at the office in Nice with a splitting headache that no amount of coffee or aspirin seemed to help. Sanchez was staying with Sophie and Dora.

They were running out of questions for the nine men, now held in one room. Everyone was getting testy. The room smelled foul. The questionees were all untied, except for Turk. The big question was what to do with them?

Justin sat in a chair in an empty room sipping a cup of coffee. He was worried about Yass and hoped he would have the sense to stay in Marseille. Hatred was too mild a word for what he felt for that man, for what he had done to his family.

His family.

Who was more his wife now? Or, who would his wife be? Chantal had had his child. Gloria was carrying his child. What was right and what did he really want?

He looked into the outer office and saw Jordi standing over Ziginiglou, asking him something. Ziginiglou looked like a broken man—large patches of sweat stained his shirt. He seemed to be telling them everything he knew.

The telephone in the large office rang and Justin picked up the extension. "This is Justin Collins."

"Hello, Mr. Collins. I'm calling from the hospital reception with a message from Mrs. Collins. She would like you to come here."

"What did she say? Is something wrong?" Justin asked.

"That is all the note said."

"I'll be there right away."

After he hung up, he realized he did not even know *which* Mrs. Collins had left the message.

★ ★ ★

The hospital elevator seemed to be delayed on the third floor, so Justin charged up the stairs. By the time he reached Chantal's room, he was out of breath and nervous. He walked in and saw that her bed was empty.

He backed out of the room and stood frozen in the hall. Like too many dreams in one night, a thousand thoughts flew through his head and heart. And the one he least wanted to recall was that if Chantal died, the agony of decision would no longer be in his hands. But the second this thought congealed, he felt a heavy regret for it.

He was still staring at the empty bed when the doctor he had seen the previous day came out of a nearby room. He saw Justin's distraught expression and asked, "Is there something wrong?"

"Why isn't my wife in her room? Is she in surgery?" Justin looked back at the vacant room, "Or..."

"She's making some progress, Mr. Collins. We moved her this morning to a better room that came open, the last room on the right, over there." He pointed toward the end of the hall.

"Thank you," Justin said. He felt relieved and somewhat foolish. The doctor smiled and left to continue his rounds.

Justin looked after him. His head hurt, his shoulder hurt, and his emotions were stretched to their limit. He wanted to sleep. But he went to the last door on the right, knocked gently, and pushed it open.

Chantal was in bed, propped up with her back against some pillows. She looked up at him with a weak smile. Gloria's smile was just as weak, though not from physical frailty.

Justin wanted to kiss them both, but felt that would just make things more awkward. He took a chair on the other side of Chantal's bed, facing Gloria.

He said to Chantal, "I thought something had gone wrong when I got the phone call from the hospital. I am so glad to see you are better. How do you feel?"

Chantal's cheeks were no longer pale, and her large blue eyes seemed brighter. Someone had helped her gather up her hair into a soft twist. "I am better," she said, without further elaboration.

Gloria gave it. "The doctors say that she should be able to walk by the end of next week. But we might be able to bring her home earlier, perhaps in a wheel-chair."

Home? Justin was not sure what Gloria meant. He looked at Chantal to see her reaction, but she lay there without expression.

What have you two talked about? he asked himself, and then realized he wouldn't get an answer to an internal conversation. "What have you two talked about?"

Gloria looked Justin square in the eyes, but was circling her bracelet around and around her wrist. "Yes, we have been talking about the next step."

He steeled himself, then asked, "And what have you been saying about the next step?"

Gloria continued, "We talked for some time and realized we need more. Time, that is. Time to get over the shock and pain. We need time to heal—all of us. And Dora is a precious friend and a mother to Chantal and needs to be close to her."

Justin felt that they were playing back his own thoughts, but he wanted to reiterate how he felt about them both before this went further. "You know I would have never chosen to hurt either of you. I never meant to put either of you in a situation like this."

Gloria let go of her bracelet and folded her hands. "Justin, we know that. Call it fate, but now we find ourselves here."

"Well then," he said, not wanting to plead with them, but at a loss for ideas, for words.

Chantal spoke from her pillow. "Fate may have brought us to this point. But we are not fate's slaves. We can make new choices." She turned to Justin. "But we are too weak and exhausted at this point."

Gloria nodded her head.

What was going on? Justin felt like they were delaying informing him of some heavy decision. Perhaps they had both decided to leave him. He had been bombarded by one shock after another. That would send him over the edge. "Please," he began, but could get no further.

"Justin," Gloria began, "Chantal and I agree that we cannot hate each other. When we were in the farmhouse, we both thought we would die. We felt fear, but also sorrow. Sorrow for each other. I saw that Chantal's life had recently been so full of suffering, and I dreaded that it should be cut short without her having any more joy. Chantal saw me, tormented by the same men who had tormented her. We cannot make any more pain."

She stood up, turned as if to pace, then sat down again on the edge of her chair. "Maybe we are afraid of a future without you, the man we both committed to, the man we both love. Maybe we are only delaying what is sure to come. But both of us need the friendship of one who can understand our suffering. We feel we should support each other, as well as Dora."

Justin felt like the hangman school kids draw to guess a word, adding a body part to the gallows with every wrong letter. One more and he would be complete. And dead. "Fine. Good. But *please* tell me where that puts us?"

Chantal moved her hand across the sheet and pointed at him. "We want to ask you two questions. And we want honest answers."

"What do you want to know?"

"*Mon Cheri*, do you still love me?" Chantal asked, speaking slowly.

He did not let himself think. "Yes."

"And do you love Gloria?" Chantal continued.

"Yes, I do."

"Then you must tell us what to do with those answers."

★ ★ ★

Jordi smiled to see Laszlo walking through the office doors.

Laszlo joined him at the coffee machine saying, "I think this assignment is coming to an end. Stefan asked me to do something back in Geneva. I will be flying back with Dr. Chevrolet." He held out his hand. "It has been good to work with you."

Jordi extended the hand without his coffee and agreed, "We had fine teamwork."

"Maybe we will have an opportunity to work together again some time."

Jordi laughed. "*Hombre*, I hope not. Once in a lifetime with something like this is enough for me." He looked into the other room at the nine men in the small room. "What do we do with them?"

Laszlo said, "Stefan and Sam said Unipac will not file charges. Sam feels we should let them go, that is, under certain conditions. Dr. Chevrolet drafted some documents."

"What are the conditions?" asked Jordi.

"Follow me," Laszlo said.

Laszlo summoned the five accountants and two computer engineers into the larger room. He told them to sit down. "Five of you are not citizens of countries within the European Union. We never want to see you back in the EU. You will now sign a prepared confession and you have twenty-four hours to get out of the EU. In twenty-four hours your confession will be given to the police. If anyone from my own extensive organization ever finds you in the European Union, you will be shot. Do you understand?"

They nodded at him, sheepish, tired, and ready to agree to anything.

Laszlo looked at the two computer engineers, who sat anxiously awaiting their sentence. "You are French citizens. You have committed crimes. You dwell in local residences. We know your families—your mothers, sisters, brothers. You will now sign a confession of your crimes, which will only be given to the police if you fail to follow my instructions."

He held out a paper. "Now sign."

One pen was passed from man to man. They all left their signatures at the bottom of the confessions without reading them.

"Gentlemen, I give you thirty seconds to get out of here. Go."

The seven men did not hesitate but hurried for the door, colliding with one another. The man in front, shoved from behind by an equally harried colleague, fell forward. After a tangled pile up, they struggled upright and rushed out of the building in single file, shoeless, beltless, and without their identity papers. Laszlo knew that five of them would have a miserable time getting out of the country in twenty-four hours, but he was confident that not one of them would be left behind.

Finally Laszlo ordered Ziginiglou and Turk into the room. Turk still had his hands bound. They looked swollen.

"Stand still," Laszlo commanded.

Jordi stood next to a desk, polishing the handle of a gun.

Laszlo took out a disposable camera and snapped mug-style facial shots of Ziginiglou and Turk.

"Sit down by the desk there," said Laszlo, sounding as if he would far rather be out enjoying the sunshine than in here messing with crooks. The crooks took the hint and did exactly as told.

Laszlo cut the cords on Turk's hands. He then pulled out an ink pad from his coat pocket. Finding clean white paper on a shelf, he took several sheets over to the desk, grabbed Turk's right hand and carefully rolled each finger across the pad and pressed in onto the paper. Ziginiglou was next.

When he was finished taking fingerprints, Laszlo placed before them two printouts. "These are your confessions. Sign them. If you choose not to sign them, you will be shot here and now."

The barrel of Jordi's newly shined gun was pointed directly at Turk.

They picked up their pens. Turk read nothing. Ziginiglou glanced over the form, swallowed, and reached for the pen—dropping it before getting a writing hold on it.

"In twenty-four hours," said Laszlo, his ice blue eyes fixed upon them, "we are going to pass on this information and your identity papers to the French police, who will pass it on to their counterparts in other countries. You are not welcome in any country in Europe and never will be. Now go."

In seconds, the only two people left in the room were Jordi and Laszlo. Jordi holstered his gun. "That was impressive. Are you going to turn all those confessions over to the police?"

"Only Ziginiglou's and Turk's," Laszlo replied. "In twenty-four hours, the French police will receive an anonymous envelope with some incriminating contents. We need that time to get everything cleared out of this office. A moving company will be arriving in an hour."

"Do you think they read the confessions?" Jordi asked.

Laszlo said, "Ziginiglou caught some details. He is an accountant and should have an eye for them. I think there was one detail on that confession that will keep them running for a long time."

Jordi too had seen it. He just laughed and turned to pick up a box.

Laszlo picked up one as well and said, "There is one last small thing."

"What is that?" They faced each other with cardboard boxes between them.

"Dr. Chevrolet would like to talk about bank accounts with you. With Sanchez and Pascual too."

CHAPTER 40

Justin put his head in his hands. He looked down at the placid cream tile on the floor of the room. Square, square, square—their diagonal pattern made sense. What his wives said did not.

He looked up. "You are suggesting we go to Spain? *All* of us?"

"And Dora too," added Chantal. "We need a person around who is not… directly involved, but knows what has happened. It seems the best choice for now. Before we can decide what to do next."

Justin stood up, placing each foot firmly within a single square tile.

He raised his gaze to Gloria. "Do you remember what Señora Pascual told us on our wedding day, about the history of Llanca's name?" Gloria nodded and Justin turned to Chantal, explaining the town's coat of arms—three lances rising from the sea, pointing toward a crown suspended above them.

He glanced back at Gloria. "Later that day, you asked me why I thought there were three spears. And I asked you why they pointed at the crown." He looked down at his feet on their tiles. "Maybe I am the sort of person who has to interpret things personally, to filter them through my own experiences and understanding. And so it may or may not be relevant, but I now see those three spears as you," he looked at Chantal, "and you," at Gloria, "and me. So *your* question, at least, is answered." He gave a short, bitter laugh that Gloria did not return.

"But my question," Justin went on, "why the crown?" He shook his head. "Whoever is wearing it must have a clearer picture of this from above. I will trust that—it's all I can do."

He stepped out of his tiles and went past Gloria to the window. "Yes. I will come with you all to Spain. It will be a place to rest and think. And a good place for Sophie."

Gloria rose and stood between Justin and Chantal. She took Chantal's hand in one of her own and reached for Justin's with the other.

Justin took it, still looking out at the Mediterranean, distant from this hill, but visible. He turned to face the two women he loved, smiling. "And for a while, I think we should stay away from the sea."

★ ★ ★

Eight hours later Ziginiglou and Turk walked through the massive marble arches of the Milan train station. It was dark outside as they crossed a small park and made their way through dark narrow streets until they came to a gloomy building.

"I don't like this," Turk said in his mother tongue.

"Me neither," Ziginiglou replied, "but we have no choice."

"Are you sure?" Turk asked.

"Without identity papers we can't get out of Italy. They," he nodded at the building, "can arrange something, maybe give us some work."

"I don't like working for them. For hundreds of years we were the masters; the Albanians were servants to the Turks. Now it's the other way around."

They entered, took a flight of stairs and knocked on a wooden door. It opened to reveal two guards with guns.

"Come in." A voice in English came from across the room.

"Hold it," one of the guards said. "Turn around."

They patted them down and the guard said, "Clean."

"Hello Ziginiglou, Turk," the voice from across the room said.

"Hello Mustafi," Ziginiglou replied.

"Sit down."

They moved toward a desk piled high with papers and sat down. Mustafi sat behind the desk, his large middle brushing against its edge, his thick, folded fingers catching light from the squarish gold rings around them. The two men with guns remained standing behind Ziginiglou and Turk.

"I heard *Le Patron* had some problems," Mustafi said. "Why didn't you protect him?"

"I was working, and he," Ziginiglou nodded at Turk, "was in Spain when it happen."

"*Le Patron* owed us money," Mustafi said. "He did not pay up on the last shipment."

"I don't know anything about that," Ziginiglou said.

"His other partners in GauLux Holding will also want their share of the settlement," Mustafi stated. "Where's the money?"

"We don't know," Ziginiglou replied. "We only came here because we need identity papers. And work."

"We'll see what we can do, but tell me anything you can about *Le Patron's* money."

"We don't know much," Ziginiglou answered, hoping that Mustafi would not discover that he and his team had handled *Le Patron's* accounting.

Turk scanned the papers on Mustafi's desk. His face changed from his usual tough-guy stare to one of surprise. On top of a stack lay a grainy black-and-white photo of two men. They were standing in front of a desk, one dark with broad shoulders, the other tall and blond. A large knife was stuck upright in the table. Shivers went down his spine.

Mustafi saw Turk looking at the photo and leaned forward. "Do you know these men?"

Turk looked at Ziginiglou. Ziginiglou nodded.

"I think so," Turk said.

Mustafi spoke. "One of our intermediaries in Paris took that photo when those two men were in his office. Other people recognized them as being in Le Magreb restaurant the night Shafi Khanoum was killed. Who are they?"

Ziginiglou said, "They are involved with the disappearance of *Le Patron's* money. We think they are thugs working for Justin Collins."

"Who is Justin Collins?"

"We are not sure."

"I think we should talk with him. How can we find him?"

Turk broke in, "I know where he lives, at least the town where he lives. I can take you there."

"No you can't, Turk," Ziginiglou said with emphasis. "You can tell how to get there, but you no can go back to Spain."

"What do you mean?" Turk exclaimed. "We never went to his house, but I know the town where he lives. If we ask around, someone can find him."

"So you think this Justin Collins can lead us to *Le Patron's* money?" Mustafi asked. Ziginiglou had scooted to the edge of his chair and was busy folding and unfolding his hands.

"Yes," Turk replied. "He lives in a town called Llanca in Northern Spain."

"Zog," Mustafi said to one of the bouncers, "get some men together and have Turk here take you to that town. I want to ask this Collins some questions."

Ziginiglou kept quiet but was blinking rapidly, trying to think what to do. He turned to Mustafi and said, "May I speak to Turk in private for a minute?"

"Why?" Mustafi asked. "We want to talk with Collins."

"Please. Just give us a minute."

Mustafi nodded and they went into an adjoining room.

"What's wrong?" Turk asked, annoyed. "I can take them to Collins."

"No you can't. Tell him where Collins lives. They find him on their own. And then we go to Kosovo if they give us work. If no, back to Turkey. We no can stay in Western Europe."

"Why not?" Turk asked.

"Did you see the confessions we signed?"

"No. Why?" Turk asked.

"We confessed to killing Jacques Gaubert."

CHAPTER 41

Justin sighed, letting the shower's hot water all but scald his tired skin. If only he could wash away problems like he could wash away dirt and sweat.

When the bathroom was swirling with steam, he turned off the tap and dried off. He turned to the mirror to check how his shoulder was healing, but its glass was clouded to opacity. Other than a dull ache now and then, the wound did not really disturb him.

He pulled on his pants, belted them, and took the towel again to his wet hair to keep his t-shirt from getting soaked.

Head still partially wrapped in terry cloth, he heard a scream from the room next door. He threw the towel to the floor and ran out of the bathroom. On his way out of his room, he grabbed his gun from the bed and bolted into the hall. Dora was climbing up from the carpet outside her door, still yelling, "He took Sophie!"

Justin ran to help her up, demanding, "Where?"

"A man! A man took Sophie!"

"Which way?" He asked as he stuck the gun in his belt.

She pointed, and Justin was down the hall, barefoot and shirtless, the steel of the gun cold on his shower-hot flesh.

At the end of the hall he saw the service elevator closing. A digital display on the wall showed it was going down. Justin ran for the emergency stairs next to the elevator and took them two and three at a time, jumping down the landings.

He reached the ground level and pushed open the stair door. No one in sight. He looked at the digital display next to the elevator shaft. It read minus one. He rushed back to the emergency stairs, went down one more level, and carefully opened the door. In front of him stretched a long hall. At the end of it he saw a man carrying Sophie. She was screaming.

The man pushed on a long metal bar that opened a service door. He started to step out into a parking lot behind the hotel.

Justin sprinted silently on the pads of his feet toward them.

The man turned and Justin recognized his face. It was the same scarred face that he had seen in his hospital room in Figueras, the face of the man who said he was a doctor. The man who had raped Chantal.

"Yass." Justin's voice was laden with hate.

"Justin Collins," Yass said, with a forced calmness that bordered on the casual. "Stay away from my French concubine." He stepped back into the hallway toward Justin and the exit door closed behind him.

"You're crazy," Justin exclaimed.

Yass smiled and said, "The woman let them kill my child. So I will take yours." Sophie continued to scream.

Adrenalin mixed with the hate and pulsed through Justin's body. If he ever wanted revenge, it was now.

Yass moved a sharp knife toward Sophie's neck. Her wailing changed to a whimper.

Sophie. Justin tried to control himself. "Would you kill her?"

"What difference does it make?" Yass said. "It's only a girl. A boy would be different. Besides, I would rather have her in paradise than in the hands of infidels. More important—she is mine. Blood for blood."

Justin lifted the gun but saw that his hand was shaking. He was afraid that if he pulled the trigger he would hit Sophie.

"Shoot and I will kill the girl," Yass threatened. "I am taking her with me. Don't move."

But Yass did not walk away. He moved toward Justin, the knife still held to Sophie's throat.

With a disturbing smile on his face, Yass said, "The French concubine is not yours either. She too is mine. You do not imagine the pleasure she gave me when she screamed when I took her. And I will take her again." He paused to enjoy this fantasy for a second then went on, "And I look forward to the satisfaction from the Spanish one." Yass laughed.

Anger burned in Justin. He raised the gun toward Yass' face, but Yass raised Sophie between himself and the gun, and then in one quick movement he threw Sophie toward Justin. "Catch her."

From reflex, Justin dropped the gun and caught Sophie. At the same moment, Yass lunged for Justin. Justin lifted his leg and kicked. Yass fell backward, but not before slicing across the skin of Justin's shinbone.

Justin set Sophie down but had no time to grab the gun. Yass regained his balance and lunged again with the knife. Justin used Yass' own momentum to throw him off balance. As Yass moved forward again wielding his knife, Justin grabbed Yass' wrist and rolled his left shoulder into him. Yass fell to the ground with Justin on top of him. Justin felt pain shoot through his left shoulder.

Yass was on his back but fighting like a wild animal. He struggled to raise the knife, spit at Justin's face and hissed, "Burn in Hell, infidel!"

Those words gave Justin a shot of strength. He grasped Yass' hand, forcing the knife toward his throat. "You dared to touch my wife."

Yass pushed back to keep the blade from penetrating, and they remained locked in tension, in a momentary impasse of strength against strength.

But Justin had greater rage. When Yass saw this, his eyes betrayed his fear.

"This is for Chantal!" shouted Justin. He forced the blade downward, but with one last mighty effort, Yass managed to redirect the knife. It missed his jugular and plunged into the muscle at the base of his neck. Justin lost his balance and rolled to the side while Yass lunged to his feet and pulled the knife out of his neck.

Knife still in hand and blood pouring from his neck, he lunged again toward Justin, who was still on his hands and his knees. Justin saw him coming, rolled in the direction of the gun, grabbed it in his right hand and pulled the trigger. The gun jumped in his hand. Had it hit? Yass staggered backwards, putting his left hand over his chest. Red ran through his fingers. Justin saw darkness staring back at him with a smile.

Justin raised the gun again. "You've brought enough evil to this world," he charged. "Enough evil. Blood for blood, you bastard." He pulled the trigger again, aiming at Yass' stomach, and Yass fell backward onto the door's metal bar. The weight of his body pushed open the door as Yass fell to the ground. His upper torso and arms flayed back, landing between the door and its jamb in an awkward position. He lay still.

Through the crack in the door Justin saw that two men were climbing out of a car and running toward the open door, guns in their hands. Sophie was weeping.

Justin grabbed her with his left arm, pain running through his shoulder as he ran back down the hall and turned right into another hallway. He heard noise behind him and ducked back for a glance in the direction of the exit door. It was closed.

And Yass was gone.

He squeezed Sophie tight, thumped the elevator button, entered and pushed the button for the fourth floor. As the doors shut he took one last look at the metal exit door where a smear of red stained the ground. The elevator sealed closed and began to rise.

Sophie sobbed low, holding her small hands tightly around his neck. She pressed her tear-stained cheeks against his bare chest. He laid his head to rest on hers, leaning against the elevator wall and stroking her hair.

"It's OK *ma petite*. You were so brave. I'll never let that man near you again. Never."

EPILOGUE

"So, is Unipac set on a positive trajectory?" Justin asked Sam Oliver.

Justin, Sam and Stefan had just been seated at a balcony table at La Terasse du Colonial Café—the tenth floor showcase restaurant in their Nice hotel. The waiter poured a rich smelling Arabica coffee from a silver coffee pot into three cups.

Sam lifted his cup to take a sip, then said, "I think so, now that we have an opportunity to stop all the corporate theft taking place in EuroVinco. We've made a couple of decisions you might be interested in." He smiled. "First, we made a proposal to Stefan here to be our lead advisor for Europe. He will help us with the merger. And," he paused for effect, "we have asked him to help identify and remove any EuroVinco accountants and managers whose hands are dirty."

Justin looked at Von Portzer who was lighting up his pipe and smiled. "He'll be excellent. I guess you also have some board members to take care of?"

"Sure do," Sam replied. "Sutter and Schubach, those two Gaubert surrogates. Paul Kent's brother has agreed to deal with that. He has a prominent position in the San Jose Police Department. By chance, he is in Brussels right now as part of an international police task force. Paul and I will join up with him tomorrow when we go to see my granddaughter."

"Your granddaughter?"

"Yes, Anne. She's doing graduate work at Cambridge University in the U.K.: a Ph.D in Economics. I'm really proud of her. Maybe she'll run Unipac some day." Sam smiled.

"In that case, I'll buy some shares in the company," Justin laughed, then reflected, "although my net worth just took a big hit."

Sam asked, "What about your net worth?"

The waiter returned with a porcelain platter of croissants, fresh jam and butter and placed them in the center of the table.

"Yesterday Grady knocked on my door and told me that Baltimore Life wanted the insurance money back, saying 'they don't like any shenanigans.' I understand. The money is not mine. Even so, it hurts to think I am one-and-a-half million dollars poorer, just like that." He snapped his fingers, realizing belatedly that they were still slightly raw from his tousle with Yass.

"I guess Grady's just doing his job," Sam said.

Justin smiled. "At first I thought he was some sort of scam artist. And while I don't exactly endorse his attitudes, I have to admit he is effective. I think it was fortunate he came along."

"Did he mention his plans to you at all?" Stefan asked, adding several sugar cubes to his coffee cup.

"Grady told me he was getting homesick. He wants to get back to his riverfront home in Idaho to do some fishing. But I suspect that he scored a lot of points with the insurance company, and they'll be offering him enough to keep him busy for a while. He's not the type of man to retire," Justin said.

"Those journalists seemed to like him," Sam commented, "I heard one of them offering him a talk show appearance. He would be billed as an anti-terrorist hero. I don't know how he did it. I'm sure he'll be plastered all over the American papers when I get home. And Habib. Grady somehow managed to make Habib out to be a superman."

"I haven't seen Habib around since yesterday morning," Justin said. "I took Sophie out for a walk along the promenade." He gestured toward the long walkway, ten stories below their terrace, where people were strolling in their finery, enjoying the October sun. "After we returned, he was gone. Where did he disappear to?"

Stefan answered, "Home to Morocco. He is moved by a commitment to family as well."

"I heard that after Grady and the French journalists finished with him, the whole of Morocco considered him their champion," Sam put in. "When his plane landed in Casablanca, he was greeted by high ranking politicians, and a pack from the local media wanted to feature him in their papers and programs."

Justin replied, "That explains a lot. Grady told me last night that Habib had thanked him—saying that he owed him his life." He shook his head. "I must admit that I owe my life to him too in a way. If he hadn't come to my door, who knows if any of this would have happened. I might never have found Chantal and Sophie."

"I was so pleased to see Chantal," Stefan said, quietly. "I hope that she will be able to continue her art. She had a remarkable style." He took another croissant from the platter.

"And then Laszlo and Jordi," Justin said. "I would not have made it without them. I regret that I never had a chance to say goodbye to Laszlo." He looked out over the balcony toward the *Baie des Anges*. The blue sea spread before them like a wide road, sparkling beneath the sun.

Sam waited a moment and said, "I mentioned that we made a couple of decisions and told you about the first one."

"Is there another?" Justin asked.

"Yes. Dora made a decision. You should know that she is looking out for you. A considerable amount of cash was stolen from EuroVinco. Unipac will not press charges or ask for the money. We can't afford the negative publicity and all the time wasted in court. But we do feel that Dora needs remuneration. She didn't want it all and distributed portions of it to others. She gave you something."

"I'm not asking for anything. I can't take anything from her."

"Your share is slightly over two hundred million dollars," Sam stated. "That is, to you Chantal and Gloria."

"Two hundred *million*?" he asked, dropping the knife. The butter on it skidded across his plate with a cushioned clatter.

"Yes," Sam answered. "It was her decision."

"Unbelievable," Justin said, the enormity of it just beginning to settle on him. "There's something more," Sam said.

"What do you mean, more?"

"Due to the merger of EuroVinco and Unipac, GauLux Holding owns six percent of Unipac. We felt that should go to Dora. She only took half. The other three percent goes to you."

Justin's face went white. "Those shares must be worth hundreds of millions."

"Something like that," Sam smiled. "Maybe closer to billions."

"She is quite an admirable woman," Stefan said. "Many people would not be willing to part with one gram of their wealth, no matter how great their resources." He took a long puff from his pipe.

"Yes, we have seen too many examples of that kind of greed in the last few weeks," Sam said. "But I feel for Dora. She has all of that money but she is alone."

Justin gave up on the rest of his breakfast and pushed his plate away. He wasn't alone, or was he? He had two women he loved. And they loved him. But he could not be with one without losing the other. Time to think and heal, they had said. Yes, they were right. And Dora would be with them. An unorthodox family, to be sure.

Sam looked at his watch and set his napkin next to his plate. "Well boys, I'll have to be going soon. Got to catch my flight to Brussels." He looked around for the waiter and then at the sky. "This was the perfect weather for an outdoor breakfast. Before I leave, I propose a champagne toast. Care to join me?"

"Sure," Justin said.

"It would be a pleasure," Stefan agreed.

Sam finally saw the waiter return his glance, and he immediately approached their table. He returned within minutes carrying three flutes filled with champagne. He placed a glass before each man.

Sam lifted his glass, the bubbles rising to the surface, and announced, "I want to toast the good people who helped us and the future they will make possible."

"*Santé*," Stefan said.

"To the people and the future," Justin repeated.

They drank from their flutes and then Sam said, "Justin, we've talked about Unipac and Stefan's future with us. But what about you? What will you be doing in the next few months?"

"Before I plunge into anything new I want to make sure that my… family is OK." He did not know what else to say.

After another sip of his champagne, Sam asked, "Will you stay here in Nice for a while—until Chantal's health improves?"

"No," Justin said. "The doctors think that she can be moved by Monday. We will take her to Spain. Gloria, Dora and Sophie too." He supposed this arrangement sounded strange, but it was starting to seem the right choice. At least until they could make better sense out of their situation.

"I don't know your plans once you get there, but if I can help in any way please let me know," Stefan offered.

"Thank you Stefan. I have always appreciated your wisdom."

Since Stefan was being very Swiss and not inquiring about Justin's plans, Sam decided to try to satisfy his curiosity. "If I might ask, what will you do once you get there?" Sam asked.

"Gloria and Chantal have been talking between themselves. They want to support each other during this time of healing and transition. We are going to need a lot of time to talk and to be alone. Our little house in Llanca is too small for that. Jordi has found us a place in the mountains outside of Figueres. It's an old monastery that has been converted into a small conference center. It is well equipped and will be ideal until we get… organized. We can have the entire place to ourselves."

"Is there a way we can get in touch with you?" Sam asked.

"You can always send me an e-mail," Justin replied.

"Okay," Sam said, but it was obvious his mind had wondered. He gazed into the distance and then his eyes moved back to Justin. "This is so strange, so different, I just can't seem to grasp it… a very different destiny. It makes me wonder how many people think about their lives as having a destiny. Most people try to survive by following the rules of the culture they live in. I don't know many who ask the bigger questions."

"Well, I must admit that I didn't," Justin said. "Until the plane crash, I just moved through life following the rules of my business culture. And then a cold blue fate hit me. My life just spun out of control and I couldn't do anything to stop it. I feel, to a certain extent, like it's still spinning. Now I continually have to think about my destiny, about the choices I must make, about what matters in life, and about what life means. I feel that I've been thrown into a situation that forces me to go against the culture around me. And to question who or what drives our destinies."

"I have always believed in a God," Sam said. "I find it helps."

"Well, I'd be fascinated to know what he was thinking about me," Justin said, no trace of sarcasm in his voice.

"You would be surprised," Sam responded.

Stefan, the humanist–agnostic, said nothing.

"I believe clarity will come," Sam stated.

Justin thought about his choices, relieved to find he did have them. He could make them—even within this fated framework that had become his life.

The waiter quietly approached and placed the bill on the table. Sam signed it and set it aside. "I suppose the time has come to move on," Sam said, pushing back his chair and standing up. Justin and Stefan stood as well, and after one last look at the sea, they made their way toward the elevator.

Sam paused, watching Stefan straighten his tie and hat in a mirrored panel near the exit and said to Justin, "Call me when you get to Spain."

"I will," Justin said.

Stefan and Sam entered the elevator. As the door closed Stefan tipped his hat.

Justin turned around and walked back to the restaurant terrace and stared out toward the deep blue sea. His heart was heavy knowing what these two women had faced, especially Chantal. He was glad they were now safe. He wanted the absolute best for both of them, yet something in his inner soul felt squeezed.

By the beach there was a snack bar with some old wooden tables and chairs, originally painted red, but now faded by the sun.

Someone had moved one of the round tables and two of the chairs close to the water. He looked at the chairs and imagined one for Chantal and one for Gloria and he wondered where he belonged.

AUTHOR'S NOTE

During my travels around the world I've made a simple observation. For the most part, people are bound by their cultures. From this I've wondered how much control we have on what we become. And, to what extent do we chose our destiny?

William Ernest Henley in the poem *Invictus* said, "I am the master of my fate: I am the captain of my soul." Alfred Lord Tennyson in *Idylls of the King* said, "For man is man and master of his fate." Is this true? While humans have the ability to make choices that produce certain outcomes, either for good or bad, to what extent are we absolute masters of our own fate?

In reality external dynamics can influence our destiny. Unforeseen events or even a chance meeting with someone can set us on a new trajectory. The choices of others can put us into predicaments we never expected. How much control do we have on our destiny, and how much of it is it in the hands of others, or even a higher being?

So, is fate something of our own choosing or is it something external?

In *Squeeze*, Justin Collins finds himself with an unusual dilemma. It was caused by sinister men that took over Vine Industries, and they didn't stop there. Within this, fate has dealt Justin an unexpected hand. Now he is in an extraordinary situation that he didn't directly choose. How does he reconcile this?

In the next novel, *Pursuit* (Blue Fate 5), the story continues as three people must deal with a new reality. Their situation is further complicated when adversaries believe Justin holds a fortune that belongs to them.

Cass Tell
Costa Brava, Spain

Your opinion is important to me!

I hope you enjoyed my book and I'd love to receive your feedback. As the book is still fresh in your mind, please leave some comments or a review on any of the following websites:

Amazon — www.amazon.com
Barnes & Noble — www.barnesandnoble.com
Goodreads — www.goodreads.com

And I invite you to visit my website www.casstell.com to find out more details about all books in the Blue Fate series and my other books.

Thank you!